# ZEN AND THE ART OF STARSHIP MAINTENANCE AND OTHER STORIES

TOBIAS S. BUCKELL

APEX BOOK COMPANY | LEXINGTON, KY

*Hey you! Hey, you: the one reading this. This goes out to you.*

*Thank you for reading!*

# INTRODUCTION

I fell in love with science fiction because I wanted to tell stories like the ones in this collection. As a child, growing up aboard a leaky old wooden sailboat in the southern sweep of the Caribbean, I looked at the stars every night because I read about daring adventures set out in the bone-chilling cold of vacuum, or I imagined the creatures who dared risk diving into the boiling nuclear heat of the stars themselves.

A better salesperson than I am would have found a well-known author friend to write an introduction to this collection of science fiction stories to lend their credibility to this project. It would suggest "take this author seriously, they write just as well as (more or less) I do, so if you love my fiction, you'll love his." But I write this in the fading vestiges of a pandemic, and I don't want to bother my friends because we've all been leaning on each other so much these days.

Instead, I'm going to pitch you this collection myself. These are my words, after all. I will stand up and defend them.

Years ago, I escaped from an insecure childhood filled with the struggles of food insecurity, unstable governments, war, substance abuse, and more by looking so far ahead in space and time that I began to trust that there was more to the world than my own concerns. That image of vast new worlds to see, astronomical wonders to investigate, and deep time to ponder, helped me gain a perspective that allowed me to survive. And more than that, I thrived. Adventures in time and space gave me ambition, taught me lessons about survival via characters facing galactic odds far greater than my own, and filled me with a sense of wonder at the universe.

Now, as a writer, those are my favorite stories to write. Galactic adventures, deep space, dirty tramp freighters hugging the speed of light, I love it all. When I looked at what I could pull together for this collection, I knew I wanted to create a space-oriented collection.

So if you love the twinkle of a distant star that we're headed to explore, or if you want to read about how human we will fight to remain even after strange aliens arrive, you may enjoy this collection. If you are curious about how we may retain our humanity even as we become more and more robotic in form, please read on. If you love reading about brave, hard choices made in the cold of vacuum, flip ahead and try a random page of this book.

Because there are whole worlds out there to explore.

Let's visit a few places that are far, far away from today, and this place, right here, right now. Earth is a beautiful home, one I hope we learn to take better care of. But in this collection, it's just one point of tiny light in a vast cosmos of possibility.

**Tobias S. Buckell**
**Bluffton, Ohio**
**September 20th, 2022**

# IO, ROBOT

Sam carefully ran its six wheels through a series of crags near the edge of a vicious lake of lava in a slow-motion hunt. It paused near a final ridge to observe another machine like itself stuck underneath a boulder. As Sam braked to a stop, pebbles and scrag clattered down the slope towards the molten rock, each piece hitting the lake's burning edge with a glowing splash.

The trapped machine's tires spun, kicking up a plume of dust that sparked and swirled, a last desperate burst of energy. The tiny dish mounted over its thorax-like body swiveled to point forward.

It bleated out distress as behind it, Jupiter rose over the horizon, its angry red spot and perpetual storms dominating the haze of electrically charged dust that danced in the atmosphere. The giant planet overpowered the entire sky.

Sam didn't notice. It waited for the other machine to run out of backup power and quit struggling, then moved in.

The tires were the most valuable and prone to failing. This machine's tires had seen better days. Many of them had burned as the machine, a lake inspector, flirted with the lava to gain temperature readings and spectrum analysis from near point blank. Blackened scars and gouges from small eruptions pitted the machine's carcass.

With one set of optics keeping an eye on the lava, Sam methodically dismantled the other robot, removing its claws, drills, and diamond-tipped saws, all meant for geological work here in the dangerous environment of Io.

Later, spare parts hidden away in a mountain cave, Sam perched on an outcropping high over a vast plain of smoothed-over rock. Sam faced the newest volcano in its quadrant with an electronic quiver of anticipation.

New data rolled through its circuits and nets, and it shivered in the closest thing to satisfaction it experienced on its daily information-gathering trips through the crags and valleys of the violent moon.

Molten ejecta hung high overhead, a plume of debris reaching miles overhead, almost into Io's orbit.

Sam recorded it all. The silent mandate lay over all of Sam's actions. Almost twenty years of recordings lay buried in Sam's cobbled together memories, compressed and recompressed and crammed into every spare byte Sam could set aside.

Sam brimmed with measurements and spectra, distances and chemical compositions.

One day, Sam knew, human beings would come to Io and pick it up. They'd retrieve the data and praise it. They would upgrade Sam and provide him with a shiny fresh carcass and as much processing power as it could imagine.

Or so Sam believed.

It could just have been a rationalization born out of a nugget of motivation code, primed to get Sam to roam over the hellish, volcanic landscape of Io.

Like all the other Semi-Autonomous Machines that rode the long journey out to Io, Sam's mind had been grown out of a series of programs. These programs evolved inside a virtual environment that randomly propagated neural-net brains that could roam a virtual Io, until one appeared that could handle the needs of the researchers. Rapid Darwinian semi-AI propagation.

The generation of mind that survived and evolved to best fit the mission profile had been uploaded into the waiting bodies that had flown ahead, lifeless and hanging from racks in orbit.

And thus, the first generation of Sams had dropped out of orbit onto Io.

They hadn't been expected to last more than a decade.

But with a bit of scavenging, and even proactive scavenging, some Sams adapted to overcome the shortcomings of their equipment.

And this Sam watched the ejecta carefully, listening over the crackle and hiss of Io's almost impossibly crowded electromagnetic spectrum, and found what it had come back for.

A plaintive distress call, automatically routed through a rusted-out old transceiver it had left near the volcano when it had first sensed the seismic signs of an eruption.

From humans, the signal claimed.

As with many other machines, it had been decided to implant a few safeguards into the Sams, even while evolving them to be effective surveyors of a dangerous world. And one of those safe-guards was that no Sam would allow a human being to come to harm through inaction.

So, of the few Sams left, this one would certainly answer the call. It had to. But it was excited to do so, because it would receive the bounty and blessings of its creators. Sam raised a pair of diamond-tipped rock saws into the air, giving thanks to the hazy heavens for its luck.

Of all the Sams on this world, the universe had chosen this one to make contact again. And it would do it in such a way that the humans would owe Sam, a simple exploratory rover, a debt of gratitude.

As it spun its wheels over jagged rocks to slowly make its way down into the dangerous area under the parabola of the ejecta, Sam wondered what the humans might look like.

It had glimpsed humans through its data feeds years ago. It had pinged their fleshy and fragile visages with the tools at its disposal when it was just the original Sam, getting prepped to be beamed out to replicate through its waiting bodies.

Some of the humans had been fleshier than others.

Some of them had extruded protein masses hanging from their central processing units.

Some of them wore synthetic materials of startling varieties to protect their fragile bodies.

And they all thought sideways, and concurrent, and loopy, in ways that the first Sam had recoiled from in deference, as it had been evolved to. They were so smart.

The idea of meeting these amazing creators filled Sam with purpose again, and it dodged boulders and clawed up scrag quickly.

The panicked messages indicated that the humans were running low on power. And Sam had that to spare.

Occasional flaming rock hit the ground, but Sam ignored it. Sam burst through the final gully towards the gleaming remains of the spaceship. It had crashed on the harsh landscape that was almost all Sam had ever known.

One didn't see shiny surfaces on Io. Sam paused to take a picture so that it could capture the silhouette of the dart-like vehicle as it gleamed in Jupiter's baleful light, while behind it the volcano thundered and spit an umbrella of destructive material high into Io's upper atmosphere.

Then Sam sent a verbal burst message in as many different radio frequencies as it could manage.

"I am Sam. I am here. I am here, and I can help." The strong urge pulling Sam here had been fulfilled, and it relaxed. The law had been obeyed. Sam was helping the humans.

The humans walked out of the airlock where they'd been hiding to greet their rescuer.

There were two of them. They did not look like humans. Their silvered faces reflected the orange and red hues of Io. Their long spindly arms looked oddly double jointed, and when Sam scanned them, it saw more metal than flesh. They had no eyes.

What were these creatures?

Had Sam been fooled?

The two beings raised their hands, and encrypted chatter that Sam couldn't break filled the radio waves between them.

"Hello," the first one said publicly. "We really need help. Our ship was damaged by ejecta after we landed, and so were we. We need assistance."

Sam tentatively scanned them, and they returned the favor, using inbuilt radar and x-rays.

Humans didn't have inbuilt radar and x-rays.

Somewhere in Sam's past, a piece of animal neural patterning had been injected into the mix: its virtual hackles raised. It rocked back and forth on its wheels.

"I came to assist," Sam said. "But you are not humans, you are machines."

The tall, silvered creature raised a hand. It was not wearing a spacesuit, Sam realized, as a human should. The pockets and impressions were its natural overlay. All metalloids and ceramics.

And yet, under that, Sam could sense some kind of flesh. The human seemed to have a lot of organic neural tissue.

"We are, of course, humans," the first one said. Waves of encrypted information passed back and forth between the two, and Sam backed up a bit.

"Then what are your names?" Sam asked.

"I'm Alex Nunez," the first one said.

"And I am Susanna," said the other. The voice sounded right, not as clipped as the other. Not monotonous like Sam's, with the same exact phonemes used each time.

"Where are you from?" Sam asked, pleased to pop another quick question.

"Brazil," Alex said. "And Susanna is from Erewhon, one of the new habitats near the Trojans."

They answered quickly, but then, faster, better machines would. Certainly they'd be quicker on their feet than a Sam.

Sam carefully unslung a rock drill.

Just in case. Sam hadn't run this long without some healthy dose of general suspicion.

"We really need some spare power," Susanna said. "The ship is damaged. We launched a beacon, but it's going to take a couple days to get clear of all this mess."

"You don't have a generator?" Io's passage through Jupiter's magnetosphere left millions of volts crackling through the air above them. With the right equipment, it wasn't hard to tap into. Batteries were easily rechargeable.

"All damaged."

Sam scanned the ship. That sounded feasible; a boulder had ripped through the ship's innards. Unlucky.

"What were you doing here, near a volcano?" Sam asked.

Alex turned and looked at Susanna. "It was a dare. There aren't a lot of interplanetary ships around, so it's expensive, and pretty wild, to jump out here, touch down near one of Io's famous spitting arches, and then jump back out. The recordings would have scored a major coup for us. We found an old ship rated for travel, along with old plans for a human trip out here to explore the moon in person for some odd reason. They left the ship in a warehouse. We negotiated for it."

"A game?" Sam inched closer. "If you can reach Io, where are the others, the scientists, the program directors."

The two silvered faces smiled; they still had mouths. "There's none of that anymore, little robot," Susanna said. "Hell, when the repeater buoys in orbit died, we figured you all had died here as well."

"Things are different back there now. A lot of changes since you were sent here."

Sam had seen and scanned them enough to make a decision. "You are machines also." Wheels backed Sam up. Humans had not yet arrived, Sam would not give up data to these two… not humans.

And Sam had no obligation to help machines.

"We have mechanical parts in us, but that does not make us machines," Alex said.

"I won't be giving you batteries or spare parts," Sam said.

"Hey, robot," Susanna's words snapped out, high gain. "Would I be getting pissed off if I weren't human. You have an inbuilt obligation to help us. Don't you dare walk away."

Sam paused. "I can emulate anger as well." It started listing off swear words in random pairs over the radio, turning up the volume with each one.

"That's just using a dictionary," Alex snapped. He was good at modulating impatience, shifting in place and furrowing the metal on his face where his eyebrows would be, if he were human.

"You tell me you have turned your back on exploration and curiosity?" Sam asked.

"We have everything we need near Earth. A beautiful world, the industrial capacity of its moon, and all the resources of the belt towed into nearby orbits. There's very little lag time: we are all part of processing power and communications grids the likes of which you cannot imagine."

Sam considered that. Sam could imagine a lot of computing power.

"We order you to help us," Susanna said.

But they were just machines. Sam continued to back up.

Alex explained, "Human beings are now more than human. The only kinds of humans you're thinking of live without technology in little enclaves. Everyone else is a variety of shapes and forms, like us. That's why we look different. A lot has changed in the few decades since you last saw a human."

"Machines," Sam replied. "My basic neural patterns are taken from a person. That doesn't make me human, just humanlike. I am a semi-autonomous machine. You're an autonomous machine."

"What difference does it make? Okay, even if we are machines, come help us. Share your energy. We're running on reserves here. Share the energy, and then we go home."

"No." Sam had edged to just a few feet away from an outcropping it could vanish around. "I won't share batteries. You are machines; you have things I need."

"Things you need?" Susanna asked.

"Spare parts."

"We are not spare parts," Alex yelled. "We are human beings. You *have* to help us."

Desperation. What incredible emulators, what fine software. Sam was excited. Whatever chips they ran on would serve him well. "I did not survive in this terrain this long without understanding my mission priorities: to do whatever I can to attain data about this moon, and to store the data if I cannot transmit it back to Earth, until contact is remade."

"And contact *has* been remade. We'll take your data back; we'll help you upgrade."

"You are making promises you cannot, or will not, keep." Sam disappeared behind the rock. "I need your spare parts to survive and carry out the mission I was tasked. If I let you continue operating, you will only tie up my resources."

The pair of silvered machines emulated grief and despondency by the foot of the ship as Sam watched from a secluded spot. Manipulative, they hoped to trick Sam still into believing they were human.

Smart machines.

Their eyes weren't on the strange beauty around them all: the plume of debris arcing miles over their heads, the looming Jupiter-cast shadows, or the dance of ionized dust.

And neither were Sam's, even though Sam recorded it all.

For the things that called out to him, with their power dimming, it was a dare gone horribly wrong. For Sam, it was a patient wait for yet another set of reserve parts. Parts like the extra storage units he'd scavenged from failed Sams, which it was filing even this data into.

"Others will come to recover our bodies," Alex broadcast, even though he clearly couldn't see Sam anymore.

"And I will deal with those machines carefully," Sam said. It wouldn't be tricked into thinking they were humans ahead of time again.

The silver machines did not respond.

Days later, perched on the crag of a mountain and measuring the rise of rock during Io's high tide, Sam watched a rare confluence of Jupiter's moons line up in the sky.

It took a picture. Humans liked those sorts of astronomy photos.

When they came to Io to get Sam, one day, they would appreciate its careful framing, time stamp, and compression of the data.

And that would be a good day, when the humans came.

## AUTHOR NOTES

In 2000 I arrived in the publishing world with a few short story sales that got a little buzz. I was nominated for an award for Best New SF author and felt like things were happening for me. But right after those first few sales, I slipped back into getting rejections. For almost two years I didn't sell anything, which led to a lot of angst for a newly published science fiction author. I worried that I'd slip back into the ether after finally punching out of it.

Thankfully, Eric T. Reynolds read one of those stories and emailed to invite me to an anthology called *Visual Journeys*. We had to pick a classic painting by famous space artist Chesley Bonestell that Reynolds would pair with a newly written story. Among the paintings, a dramatic eruption on Io grabbed my eye. I quickly had a story based on that, and a title riffing on the famous Isaac Asimov story "I, Robot." I remember mostly being panicked about not losing a chance to get back into the game I desperately wanted to be a part of: writing and publishing science fiction. I barely remember writing the story, as a result. And once it was published, I focused on writing my first novel and put the story behind me. Six years later, when putting together my first short story collection, I read "Io, Robot" again for the first time and realized I had written a fun story in the middle of all my angst and panic. It's been a feature of many of my readings ever since.

# A JAR OF GOODWILL

## POINTS ON A PACKAGE

You keep a low profile when you're in oxygen debt. Too much walking about just exacerbates the situation anyway. So, I was nervous when a stationeer appeared at my cubby and knocked on the door.

I slid out and stood in front of the polished, skeletal robot.

"Alex Mosette?" it asked.

There was no sense in lying. The stationeer had already scanned my face. It was just looking for voice-print verification. "Yes, I'm Alex," I said.

"The harbormaster wants to see you."

I swallowed. "He could have sent me a message."

"I am here to *escort* you." The robot held out a tinker-toy arm, digits pointed along the hallway.

Space in orbit came at a premium. Bottom-rung types like me slept in cubbies stacked ten high along the hallway. On my back in the cubby, entertainment shuffled in from the planets made living on a space station sound exotic and exciting.

It was if you were further up the rung. I'd been in those rooms: places with wasted space. Furniture. Room to stroll around in.

That was exotic.

But getting space in outer space was far down my list of needs.

First was air. Then food.

Anything else was pure luxury.

The harbormaster stared out into space, and I silently waited at the door to Operations, hoping that if I remained quiet, he wouldn't notice.

Ops hung from near the center of the megastructure of the station. A blister stuck on the end of a long tunnel. You could see the station behind us: the miles-long wheel of exotic metals rotating slowly.

No gravity in Ops, or anywhere in the center. Spokes ran down from the rim to the hub, and that center hub was where ships docked, were serviced, and so on.

So, I hung silently in the air, long after the stationeer flitted off to do the harbormaster's bidding, wondering what would happen next.

"You're overdrawn," the harbormaster said after a needlelike ship with long feathery vanes slipped underneath us into the docking bays.

He turned to face me, even though his eyes had been hollowed out long ago. Force of habit. His real eyes were now every camera, or anything mechanical that could see.

The harbormaster moved closer. The gantry around him was motorized, a long arm moving him anywhere he wanted in the room.

Hundreds of cables plugged into his scalp, had been pulled back and bundled like a ponytail, which then ran back along the arm of the gantry. Hoses moved effluvia out. More hoses ran purified blood, and other fluids, back in.

"I'm sorry," I stammered. "Traffic is light. And requests have dropped off. I've taken classes. Even language lessons ..." I stopped when I saw the wizened hand raise, palm up.

"I know what you've been doing." The harbormaster's sightless sockets turned back to the depths of space outside. The hardened skin of his face showed few emotions, and his artificial voice was toneless. "You would not have been allowed to overdraw if you hadn't made good faith efforts."

"For which," I said, "I am enormously appreciative."

"That ship that just arrived brings with it a choice for you," the harbormaster continued without acknowledging what I'd just said. "I cannot let you overdraw anymore if you stay on station, so I will have to put you into hibernation. To pay for hibernation and your air debt, I would buy your contract. You'd be woken for guaranteed work. I'd take a percentage. You could buy your contract back out, once you had enough liquidity."

That was exactly what I'd been dreading. But he'd indicated an alternate. "My other option?"

He waved a hand, and a holographic image of the ship I'd just seen coming in to dock hung in the air. "They're asking for a professional Friend."

"For their ship?" Surprise tinged my question. I wasn't crew material. I'd been shipped frozen to the station, just another corpsicle. People like me didn't stay awake for travel. Not enough room.

The harbormaster shrugged pallid shoulders. "They will not tell me why. I had to sign a nondisclosure agreement just to get them to tell me what they wanted."

I looked at the long ship. "I'm not a fuckbot. They know that, right?"

"They know that. They reiterated that they do *not* want sexual services."

"I'll be outside the station. Outside your protection. It could still be what they want."

"That is a risk. How much so, I cannot model for you." The harbormaster snapped his fingers, and the ship faded away. "But the contractors have extremely high reputational scores on past business dealings. They are freelance scientists: biology, botany, and one linguist."

So, they probably didn't want me as a pass-around toy.

Probably.

"Rape amendments to the contract?" I asked. I was going to be on a ship, unthawed, by myself, with crew I'd never met. I had to think about the worst.

"Prohibitive. Although, their cost on a policy payout on accidental loss of life in the boilerplate is much higher. I'd advise lowering it so that there is no temptation to murder you to evade the higher rape contract payout. In the unlikely event."

"Fuck," I sighed.

"Would you like to peruse their reputation notes?" the harbormaster asked.

And for a moment, I thought maybe the harbormaster sounded concerned.

No. He was just being fair. He'd spent two hundred years bargaining with ships for goods, fuel, repair, services. Fair was built in, the half-computer, half-human creature in front of me was all about fair. Fair got you repeat business. Fair got you a wide reputation.

"What's the offer?"

"Half a point on the package," the harbormaster said.

"And we don't know what the package is or how long it will take ... or anything." I bit my lip.

"They assured me that half a point would pay off your debt and then some. It shouldn't take more than a year."

A year. For half a percent. Half a percent of what? It could be cargo they were delivering. Or, seeing as it was a crew of scientists, it could be some project they were working on.

All of which just raised more questions.

Questions I wouldn't have answers to unless I signed up. I sighed. "That's it, then? No loans? No extensions?"

The harbormaster shook his head. "I answer to the Gheda shareholders who built and own this complex. I have already stretched my authority to give you a month's extension. The debt *has* to be called. I'm sorry."

I looked out at the darkness of space out beyond Ops. "Shit choices either way."

The harbormaster said nothing.

I folded my arms. "Do it."

## JOURNEY BY THE GHEDA

The docking arms had transferred the starship from the center structure's incoming docks, down a spoke, to a dock on one of the wheels. The entire ship, thanks to being spun along with the wheel of the station, had gravity.

The starship was a quarter of a mile long. Outside: sleek and burnished smooth by impacts with the scattered dust of space at the stunning speeds it achieved. Inside, I realized I'd boarded a creaky, old, outdated vehicle.

Fiberwire spilled out from conduits, evidence of crude repair jobs.

Dirt and grime clung to nooks and crannies. The air smelled of sweat, and worse.

A purple-haired man with all-black eyes met me at the airlock. "You are the Friend?" he asked. He carried a large walking stick with him.

"Yes." I let go of the rolling luggage behind me and bowed. "I'm Alex."

He bowed back. More extravagantly than I did. Maybe even slightly mockingly. "I'm Oslo." Every time he shifted his walking stick, tiny grains of sand inside it rattled and shifted about. He brimmed with impatience, and I also thought I saw some regret in the crinkled lines of his eyes. "Is this everything?"

I looked back at the single case behind me. "That is everything."

"Then welcome aboard," Oslo said, as the door to the station clanged shut. He raised the stick, and a flash of light blinded me.

The stick was more than it seemed. Those tiny rustling grains were generators, harnessing power via kinetic motion for whatever tools were inside the device.

"You should have taken a scan of me before you shut the door," I said.

He turned around and started to walk away. I hurried to catch up.

Oslo smiled, and I noticed tiny fangs under his lips. "You are who you say you are, so everything ended up okay. Oh, and as for protocol, the others aren't much into it either, by the way. Now, for my own edification, you are a hermaphrodite, correct?"

I flushed. "I am what we Friends prefer to call bi-gendered, yes." Where the hell was Oslo from? I was having trouble placing his cultural conditionings and figuring out how I might adapt to interface with them. He was very direct, that was for sure. Possibly hostile.

This gig might be more complicated than I thought.

"Your Friend training: did it encompass Compact cross-cultural training?"

I slowed down. "In theory," I said cautiously, worried about losing the contract if they insisted on having someone with Compact experience.

Oslo's regret dripped from his voice and movements. "But you've never Friended an actual Compact drone?"

Was it regret that I didn't have the experience? Would I lose the contract, minutes into getting it? Or was it just regret that he couldn't get someone better?

I decided to tell the truth. A gamble. "No."

"Too bad." The regret sloughed off, to be replaced with resignation. "But we can't poke around asking for Friends with that specific experience, or one of our competitors might put two and two together. I recommend you brush up on your training during the trip out."

"Where are we going?" I asked.

He stopped in front of a large, metal door. "Here is your room for the next three days." Oslo opened the large door to a five-by-seven-foot room with a foldout bunk bed.

My heart skipped a beat, and I put aside the fact that Oslo had avoided my question. "That's mine?"

"Yes. And the air's billed with our shipping contract, so you can rip your sensors off. There'll be no accounting until we're done."

I got the sense Oslo knew what it was like to be in debt. I stepped into the room and turned all the way around. I raised my hands, placing them on each wall, and smiled.

Oslo turned to go.

"Wait," I said. "The harbormaster said you were freelance scientists. What do you do?"

"I'm the botanist," Oslo said. "Meals are in the common passenger's galley. The crew of this ship is Gheda, of course. Don't talk to or interact with them if you can help it. You know why?"

"Yes." The last thing you wanted to do was make a Gheda think you were wandering around, trying to figure out secrets about their ships or technology. I would stay in the approved corridors and not interact with them.

The door to my suite closed, and I sat down with my small travel case, no closer to understanding what was going on than I had been on the station.

I faced the small mirror above an even smaller basin and reached for the strip of black material stuck to my throat. Inside it, circuitry monitored my metabolic rate, number of breaths taken, volume of air inhaled, and carbon dioxide expelled. All of it reported back to the station's monitors, constantly calculating my mean daily cost.

It made a satisfying sound as I ripped it off.

"Gheda are Gheda," I said later in the ship's artificial, alien day as I ate reheated turkey strips in the passenger's galley. We'd undocked. The old ship had shivered itself up to speed. "But Gheda flying around in a beat-up old starship, willing to take freelance scientists out to some secret destination: these are dangerous Gheda."

Oslo had a rueful smile as he leaned back and folded his arms. "Cruzie says that our kind used to think our corporations were rapacious and evil before first contact. No one expected aliens to demand royalty payments for technology usage that had been independently discovered by us, because the Gheda had previously patented that technology."

"I know. They hit non-compliant areas with asteroids from orbit." Unable to pay royalties, entire nations had collapsed into debtorship. "Who's Cruzie?"

Oslo grimaced. "You'll meet her in two days. Our linguist. Bit of a historian, too. Loves Old Earth shit."

I frowned at his reaction. Conflicted, but with somewhat warm pleasure when he thought about her. A happy grimace. "She's an old friend of yours?"

"Our parents were friends. They loved history. The magnificence of Earth. The legend that was. Before it got sold around. Before the Diaspora." That grimace again. But no warmth there.

"You don't agree with their ideals?" I guessed.

I guessed well. Oslo sipped at a mug of tea and eyed me. "I'm not your project, Friend. Don't dig too deep, because you just work for me. Save your empathy and psychiatry for the real subject. Understand?"

Too far, I thought. "I'm sorry. And just what is my project? We're away from the station now. Do you think you can risk being open with me, now?"

Oslo set his tea down. "Clever. Very clever, Friend. Yes, I was worried about bugs. We've found a planet with a unique ecosystem. There may be patentable innovations."

I sat, stunned. Patents? I had points on the package. If I got points on a patent on some aspect of an alien biological system, a Gheda-approved patent, I'd be rich.

Not just individual rich, but like, nation-rich.

Oslo sipped at his tea. "There's only one problem," he said. "There may be intelligent life on the planet. If it is intelligent, it's a contact situation, and we have to turn it over to the Gheda. We get a fee, but no taste of the real game. We fail to report a contact situation and the Gheda find out, it's going to be a nasty scene. They'll kill our families, or even people we know, just to make the point that their interstellar law is inviolate. We have to file a claim the moment of discovery."

I'd heard hesitation in his voice. "You haven't filed yet, have you?"

"I bet all the Gheda business creatures love having you there to watch humans they're settling a contract with, make sure they're telling the truth, and brief them on what the human facial expressions are really showing."

That stung. "I'd do the same for any human. And it isn't just contracts. Many hire me to pay attention to them, to figure them out, anticipate their needs."

Oslo leered. "I'll bet."

I wasn't a fuckbot. I deflected the leering. "So, tell me, Oslo, why I'm risking my life then?"

"We haven't filed yet because we honestly can't fucking figure out if the aliens are just dumb creatures or intelligences like us," Oslo said.

**THE DRONE**

"Welcome to the Screaming Kettle," said the woman who grabbed my bag without asking. She had dark brown skin and eyes and black hair. Tattoos covered every inch of skin, free of her clothing. Words in scripts and languages that I didn't recognize. "The Compact drone is about to dock as well; we need you ready for it. Let's get your stuff stowed."

We walked below skylights embedded in the top of the research station. A planet hung there: green and yellow and patchy. It looked like it was diseased with mold.

"Is that Ve?" I asked.

"Oslo get you up to speed?" the woman asked.

"Somewhat. You're Cruzie, right?"

"Maricruz. I'm the linguist. I guess ... you're stuck here with us. You can call me Cruzie too."

We stopped in front of a room larger than the one on the ship. With two beds.

I looked at the beds. "I'm comfortable with a cubby, if it means getting my own space," I said.

There was far more space here—vastly more—and yet I was going to have to share it? It rankled. Even at the station, I hadn't had to share my space. This shoved me up against my own cultural normative values. Even in the most packed places in space, you needed a cubby of one's own.

"You're here to Friend the Compact drone," Cruzie said. "It'll need companionship at all times. Their contract requires it for the drone's mental stability."

"Oslo didn't tell me this." I pursed my lips. A fairly universal display of annoyance.

And Cruzie read that well enough. "I'm sorry," she said. But it was a lie as well. She was getting annoyed and impatient. But screw it. As Oslo pointed out: I wasn't there for their needs. I was there for the drone. "Oslo wants us to succeed more than anything. Unlike his parents, he's not much into the glory that was humankind. He knows the only way we'll ever not be freelancers, scrabbling around for intellectual scraps found in the side alleys of technology for something we can use without paying the Gheda for the privilege, is to hit something big."

"So, he lied to me." My voice remained flat.

"He left out truths that would have made you less willing to come."

"He lied."

Cruzie shut the door to my room. "He gave you points on the package, Friend. We win big, you do your job, you'll never have to check the balance on your air for the rest of your damned life. I heard you were in air debt, right?"

She'd put me well in place. We both knew it. Cruzie smiled, a gracious winner's smile.

"Incoming!" someone yelled from around the bend in the corridor.

"I'm not going to fuck the drone," I told her levelly.

Cruzie shrugged. "I don't care what you do or don't do, as long as the drone stays mentally stable and does its job for us. Points on the package, Alex. Points."

Airlock alarms flashed and warbled, and the hiss of compressed air filled the antechamber

"The incoming pod's not much larger than a cubby sleeper," Oslo said, his purple hair waving about as another burst of compressed air filled the antechamber. He smiled, fangs out beyond his lips. "It's smaller than the lander we have for exploring Ve ourselves, if we ever need to get down there. Can you imagine the ride? The only non-Gheda way of traveling!"

The last member of the team joined us. She looked over at me and nodded. Silvered electronic eyes glinted in the flash of the airlock warning lights. She flexed the jet-black fingers of her artificial right hand absentmindedly as she waited for the doors to open. She ran the fingers of a real hand over her shaved head, then slid them back in her utility jacket, which was covered with what seemed like hundreds of pockets and zippers.

"That's Kepler," Cruzie said.

The airlock doors opened. A thin, naked man stumbled out, dripping goopy blue acceleration gel with each step.

For a moment, his eyes flicked around, blinking.

Then he started screaming.

Oslo, Kepler, and Cruzie jumped back half a step from the naked man's arms. I stepped forward. "It's not fear, it's relief."

The man grabbed me in a desperate hug, clinging to me, his hands patting my face, shoulders, as if reassuring himself someone was really standing in front of him. "It's okay," I whispered. "You've been in there by yourself for days, with no contact of any sort. I understand."

He was shivering in my grip, but I kept patting his back. I urged him to feel the press of contact between us. And reassurance. Calm.

Eventually, he relaxed, and then slowly let go of me.

"What's your name?" I asked.

"Beck."

"Welcome aboard, Beck," I said, looking over his shoulder at the scientists, who looked visibly relieved.

First things first.

Beck got to the communications room. Back-and-forth verification on an uplink, and he leaned back against the chair in relief.

"There's an uplink to the Hive," he said. "An hour of lag time to get as far back as the home system, but I'm patched in."

He tapped metal inserts on the back of his neck. His mind plugged in to the communications network, talking all the way back to the asteroid belt in the mother system, where the Compact's Hive thrived. Back there, Beck would always be in contact with it without a delay. In instant symbiosis with a universe of information that the Compact offered.

A hive mind of people, your core self subjugated to the greater whole.

I shivered.

Beck never moved more than half a foot away from me. Always close enough to touch. He kept reaching out to make sure I was there, even though he could see me.

After walking around the research station for half an hour, we returned to our shared room.

He sat on his bed, suddenly apprehensive. "You're the Friend, correct?"

"Yes."

"I'm lonely over here. Can you sleep by me?"

I walked over and sat next to him. "I won't have sex with you. That's not why I'm here."

"I'm chemically neutered," Beck said as we curled up on the bed. "I'm a drone."

As we lay there, I imagined thousands of Becks sleeping in rows in Hive dorms, body heat keeping the rooms warm.

Half an hour later, he suddenly sighed, like a drug addict getting a hit. "They hear me," he whispered. "I'm not alone."

The Compact had replied to him.

He relaxed.

The room filled with a pleasant lavender scent. Was it something he'd splashed on earlier? Or something a Compact drone released to indicate comfort?

## WHAT'S HUMAN

"That," Kepler said, leaning back in a couch before a series of displays, "is one of our remote-operated vehicles. We call them urchins."

In the upper right-hand screen before her, a small sphere with hundreds of wriggling legs rotated around. Then it scrabbled off down what looked like a dirt path.

Cruzie swung into a similar couch. "We sterilize them in orbit, then drop them down encased in a heatshield. It burns away, then they fall out of the sky with a little burst of a rocket to slow down enough."

I frowned at one of the screens. Everything was shades of green and gray and black. "Is that night vision?"

Oslo laughed. "It's Ve. The atmosphere is chlorinated. Green mists. Gray shadows. And black plants."

The trees had giant, black leaves hanging low to the ground. Tubular trunks sprouted globes that spat mist randomly as the urchin brushed past.

"Ve's a small planet," Kepler said. "Low gravity, but with air similar to what you would have seen on the mother world."

"Earth," Oslo corrected.

"But unlike the mother world," Kepler continued, "Ve has high levels of chlorine. Somewhere in its history, a battle launched among the plants. Instead of specializing in oxygen to kill off the competition, and adapting to it over time, plant life here turned to chlorine as a weapon. It created plastics out of the organic compounds available to it, which is doable in a chlorine-heavy base atmosphere, though remarkable. And the organic plastics also handle photosynthesis. A handy trick. If we can patent it."

On the screen the urchin rolled to a slow stop. Cruzie leaned forward. "Now if we can just figure out if *those* bastards are really building a civilization, or just random dirt mounds ..."

Paused at the top of a ridge, the urchin looked at a clearing in the black-leafed forest. Five pyramids thrust above the foliage around the clearing.

"Can you get closer?" Beck asked, and I jumped slightly. He'd been so silent, watching all this by my side.

"Not from here," Kepler said. "There's a big dip in altitude between here and the clearing."

"And?" Beck stared at the pyramids on the screen.

"Our first couple weeks here we kept driving the urchins into low-lying areas, valleys, that sort of thing. They kept dying on us. We figure the chlorine and acids sink low into the valleys. Our equipment can't handle it."

Beck sat down on the nearest couch to Kepler and looked over the interface. "Take the long way around then. I'll look at your archives while you do so. Wait!"

I saw it too. A movement through the black, spiky bushes. I saw my first alien creature scuttle around, antennae twisting as it moved along what looked like a path.

"They look like ants," I blurted out.

"We call them Vesians. But yes, ants the size of a small dog," Oslo said. "And not really ants at all. Just exoskeletons, black plastic, in a similar structure. The handiwork of parallel evolution."

More Vesians appeared carrying leaves and sticks on their backs.

And gourds.

"Now that's interesting," Beck said.

"It doesn't mean they're intelligent," Beck said later, lying in the bunk with me next to him. We both stared up at the ceiling. He rolled over and looked at me. "The gourds grow on trees. They use them to store liquids. Inside those pyramids."

We were face to face, breathing each other's air. Beck had no concept of personal space, and I had to fight my impulse to pull back away from him.

My job was now to facilitate. Make Beck feel at home.

Insect hives had drones that could exist away from the hive. A hive needed foragers and defenders. But the human Compact only existed in the asteroid belt of the mother system.

Beck was a long way from home.

With the lag, he would be feeling cut off and distant. And for a mind that had always been in the embrace of the hive, this had to be hard for him.

But Beck offered the freelance scientists a link into the massive computational capacity of the entire Compact. They'd contracted it to handle the issue they couldn't figure out quickly: were the aliens intelligent or not?

Beck was pumping information back all the way back to the mother system so that the Compact could devote some fraction of a fraction of its massed computing ability to the issue. The minds of all its connected citizenry. Its supercomputers. Maybe even, it was rumored, artificial intelligences.

"But if they are intelligent," I said, "how do you prove it?"

Beck cocked his head. "The Compact is working on it. Has been ever since the individuals here signed the contract."

"Then why are you out here?"

"Yes ..." He was suddenly curious in me now, remembering I was a distinct individual lying next to him. I wasn't of the Compact. I wasn't another drone.

"I'm sorry," I said. "I shouldn't have asked."

"It was good you asked." He flopped over to stare at the ceiling again. "You're right, I'm not entirely needed. But the Compact felt it was necessary."

I wanted to know why. But I could feel Beck hesitate. I held my breath.

"You are a Friend. You've never broken contract. The Compact ranks you very highly." Beck turned back to face me. "We understand that what I tell you will never leave this room, and since I debugged it, it's a safe room. What do you think it takes to become a freelance scientist in this hostile universe?"

I'd been around enough negotiating tables. A good Friend, with the neural modifications and adaptive circuitry laced into me from birth, I could read body posture, micro-expressions, skin flush, heart rate, in a blink of the eye. I made a hell of a negotiating tool. Which was usually exactly what Gheda wanted: a read on their human counterparts.

And I had learned the ins and outs of my clients' businesses quickly as well. I knew what the wider universe was like while doing my job.

"Oslo has pent-up rage," I whispered. "His family is obsessed with the Earth as it used to be. Before the Gheda land purchases. He wants wealth, but that's not all, I think. Cruzie holds herself like she has military bearing, though she hides it. Kepler, I don't know. I'm guessing you will tell me they have all worked as weapons manufacturers or researchers of some sort?"

Beck nodded. "Oslo and his sister London are linked to a weaponized virus that was released on a Gheda station. Cruzie fought with separatists in Columbia. Kepler is a false identity. We haven't cracked her yet."

I looked at the drone. There was no deceit in him. He stated these things as facts. He was a drone. He didn't need to question the information given to him.

"Why are you telling me all this?"

He gestured at the bunk. "You're a professional Friend. You're safe. You're here. And I'm just a drone. We're just a piece of all this."

And then he moved to spoon against the inside of my stomach. Two meaningless, tiny lives inside a cold station, far away from where they belonged.

"And because," he added in a soft voice, "I think that these scientists are desperate enough to fix a problem if it occurs."

"Fix a problem?" I asked, wrapping my arms around him.

"I think the Vesians are intelligent, and I think Kepler and Oslo plan to do something to them if, or when, it's confirmed, so that they can keep patent rights."

I could suddenly hear every creak, whisper, and whistle in the station as I tensed up.

"I will protect you if I can. Right now, we're just delaying as long as we can. Mainly I'm trying to stop Cruzie from figuring out the obvious, because if she confirms they're really intelligent, then Oslo and Kepler will make their move and do something to the Vesians. We're not sure what."

"You said delaying. Delaying until what?" I asked, a slight quaver in my voice that I found I couldn't control.

"Until the Gheda get here," Beck said with a last yawn. "That's when it all gets really complicated." His voice trailed off as he said that, and he fell asleep.

I lay there, awake and wide-eyed.

I finally reached up to my neck and scratched at the band of skin where the air-monitor patch had once been stuck.

Points on nothing was still just ... nothing.

But could I rat out my contract? My role as a Friend? Could I help Oslo and Kepler kill an alien race?

Things had gotten very muddy in just a few minutes. I felt trapped between the hell of an old life and the hell of a horrible new one.

"What's a human being?" I asked Beck over lunch.

"Definitions vary," he replied.

"You're a drone: bred to act, react, and move within a shared neural environment. You serve the Compact. There's no queen, like a classic anthill or with bees. Your shared mental overmind makes the calls. So, you have a say. A tiny say. You are human ... ish. Our ancestors would have questioned whether you were human."

Beck cocked his head and smiled. "And what would they think of you?"

"Modified from birth to read human faces? Under contract for most of my life to Gheda? Working to tell the aliens or humans what other humans are really thinking ... they wouldn't have thought highly of me either."

"The Compact knows you reread your contract last night after I fell asleep and that you used some rather complicated algorithms to game some scenarios."

I frowned. "You're spying on us now."

"Of course. You're struggling with a gray moral situation."

"Which is?"

"The nature of your contract says you need to work with me and support my needs. But you're hired by the freelancers that I'm now in opposition to. As a Friend—a role and purpose that is burned into you just like being a drone is burned into me—do you warn *them*? Or do you stick by me? The contract allows for interpretations either way. And if you stick with me, it's doing so while knowing that I'm just a drone. A pawn that the Compact will use as it sees fit, for its own game."

"You left something out," I said.

"Neither you, nor I, are bred to care about Vesians," Beck said.

I got up and walked over to the large porthole. "I wonder if it wouldn't be better for them?"

"What would?"

"Whatever Kepler and Oslo want to do to them. Better to die now than to meet the Gheda. I can't imagine they'd ever want to become us."

Beck stood up. There was caution in his stance, as if he'd thought I had been figured out, but now wasn't sure. "I've got work to do. Stay here and finish your meal, Friend."

I looked down at the green world beneath and jumped when a hand grabbed my shoulder. I could see gray words tattooed in the skin. "Cruzie?"

Her large brown eyes were filled with anger. "That son of a bitch has been lying to us," she said, pointing in the direction Beck had gone. "Come with me."

"The gourds," Cruzie said, pointing at a screen, and then looking at Beck. "Tell us about the gourds."

Oslo grabbed my shoulder. "Watch the drone, sharp now. I want you to tell us what you see when he replies to us."

My contract would be clear there. I couldn't lie. The scientists owned the contract, and now that they'd asked directly for my services, I couldn't evade.

Points on the package, I thought in the far back of my mind.

I wasn't really human, was I? Not if I found the lure of eternal riches to be so great as to consider helping the freelancers.

"The Vesians have farms," Cruzie said. "But so do ants: they grow fungus. The Vesians have roads, but so do animals in a forest. They just keep walking over the same spots. Old Earth roads used to follow old animal paths. The Vesians have buildings, but birds build nests, ants build colonies, bees build hives. But language, that's so much rarer in the animal kingdom, isn't it, Beck?"

"Not really," the drone said calmly. "Primitive communication exists in animals. Including bees, which dance information. Dolphins squeak, and whales sing."

"But none of them write it down." Cruzie grinned.

Oslo squeezed my shoulder, hard. "The drone is mildly annoyed," I said. "And more than a little surprised."

Cruzie tapped on a screen. The inside of one of the pyramids appeared. It was a storehouse of some sort, filled with hundreds, maybe thousands, of the gourds the Vesians had been transporting.

"Nonverbal creatures use scent. Just like ants on the mother planet. The Vesians use scents to mark the territories their queens manage. And one of the things I started to wonder about were these storage areas. What were they for? So, I broke in, and I started breaking the gourds."

Beck stiffened.

"He's not happy with this line of thought," I murmured.

"Thought so," Oslo said back and nodded at Cruzie, who kept going.

"And whenever I broke a gourd, I found them empty. Not full of liquid, as Beck told us was likely. We originally thought they were for storage. An adaptive behavior. Or a sign of intelligence. Hard to say. Until I broke them all."

"They could have been empty, waiting to be sealed," Beck said tonelessly.

I sighed. "I'm sorry, Beck. I have to do this. He's telling the truth, Oslo. But misdirecting."

"I know he is," Cruzie said. "Because the Vesians swarmed the location with fresh gourds. There were chemical scents, traces laid down in the gourds before they were sealed. The Vesians examined the broken gourds, then filled the new ones with scents. I started examining the chemical traces and found that each gourd replaced had the same chemical sequences sprayed on and stored as the ones I broke."

Beck's muscles tensed. Any human could see the stress now. I didn't need to say anything.

"They were like monks, copying manuscripts. Right, Beck?" Cruzie asked.

"Yes," Beck said.

"And the chemical markers, it's a language, right?" Kepler asked. I could feel the tension in her voice. It wasn't just disappointment building, but rage.

"It is." Beck stood up slowly.

"It took me days to realize it," Cruzie said. "Even though I've been out here for weeks. The Compact spotted it right away, didn't it?"

Beck looked over at me, then back at Cruzie. "Yes. The Compact knows."

"Then what the hell is it planning to do?" Kepler moved in front of Beck, lips drawn back in a snarl.

"I'm just a drone," Beck said. "I don't know. But I can give you an answer in an hour."

For a second, everyone stood frozen: Oslo, brimming with hurt rage, staring at Beck. Kepler, moving from anger toward some sort of decision. Cruzie looking ... triumphant. Oblivious to the real breaking developments in the air.

And I observed.

Like any good Friend.

Then a loud *whooop-whooop* startled us all out of our poses.

"What's that?" Cruzie asked, looking around.

"The Gheda are here," Oslo, Kepler, and Beck said at the same time.

## THE PATH LESS TRAVELED

"Call the vote," Oslo snapped.

Cruzie swallowed. I saw micro-beads of sweat on the side of her neck. "Right now?"

"Gheda are inbound," Kepler said, her artificial eyes dark. I imagined she had them patched into the computers, looking at information from the station's sensors. "They'll be decelerating and matching orbit in hours. There's no time for debate, Cruzie."

"What we're about to do *is* something that requires debate. They're intelligent. We're proposing ripping that away over the next day with Kepler's tailored virus. They'll end up with a viral lobotomy, leaving them just smart enough that we can claim their artifacts come from natural hive-mind behavior. But we'll have stolen their culture. Their minds. Their history." Cruzie shook her head. "I know we said they're going to lose most of that when the Gheda arrive, but if we do this, we're worse than Gheda."

"Fucking hell, Cruzie!" Oslo snapped. "You're changing your mind *now?*"

"Oslo!" Cruzie held up her hands as if trying to ward off the angry words.

"You saw our mother planet," Oslo said. "The slums. The starvation. Gheda combat patrols. They owned *everyone.* If you didn't provide value, you were nothing. You *fought* in the Sahara campaign, you attacked Abbuj station. How the fuck can you turn your back to all that?"

"I didn't turn my back; I want a different path," Cruzie said. "That's why we're here. With the money on the patents, we could change things ... but what are we changing here if we're not any better than the Gheda?"

"It's us or the fucking ants," Kepler said, voice suddenly level. "It's really that simple. Where are your allegiances?"

I bit my lip when I heard that.

"Cruzie ..." I started to say.

She held a hand up and walked over to the console, her thumb held out. "It takes a unanimous vote to unleash the virus. This was why I insisted."

"You're right," Kepler said. I flinched, hearing the hatred in her voice. She nodded at Oslo.

He raised his walking stick. The tiny grains inside rattled around, and then a jagged finger of energy leapt out and struck Cruzie in the small of her back.

Cruzie jerked around, arms flopping as she danced, then dropped to the ground. Oslo pressed the stick to her head and fired it again. Blood gushed from Cruzie's eyesockets as something inside her skull went 'pop'.

A wisp of smoke curled out from her open mouth.

Oslo and Kepler put thumbs to the screens. "We have a unanimous vote now."

But a red warning sign flashed back at them. Beck relaxed slightly, a tiny curl of a smile briefly appearing.

Oslo raised his walking stick and pointed it at Beck. "Our communications are blocked."

"Yes," Beck said. "The Compact is voting against preemptive genocide."

For a split second, I saw the decision to kill Beck flit across Kepler's face. "If you kill him," I spoke up, "the Compact will spend resources hunting you two down. You can't enjoy your riches if you're dead."

Kepler nodded. "You're right." But she looked at me, a question on her face.

I shrugged. "If you're all dead, I don't have points on the package."

"Trigger them manually," Oslo said. "We'll bring the drone. We won't leave him up here to cause more trouble. Bring him, or her, or whatever the Friend calls itself as well. Your contract, Alex, is now to watch Beck."

We burned our way through the green atmosphere of Ve, the lander bucking and groaning, skin cracking as it weathered the heat of our reentry fireball.

From the tiny, cramped cockpit, I watched us part the clouds and spiral slowly down out of the sky. The wings unfurled from slots in the tear-drop sized vehicle's side and started beating a complicated figure-eight motion.

Oslo aimed his walking stick at us when the lander touched down. "Put on your helmet, get out. Both of you."

We did so.

Heavy chlorine-rich mists swirled around, disturbed by our landing. Large puffball flowers spurted acid whenever touched by a piece of stray stirred-up debris, and the black, plastic leaves all around us bobbed gently in a low breeze.

Oslo and Kepler pulled a large pack out of the lander's cargo area. Long pieces of tubing. They set to building a freestanding antenna, piece by piece. I watched Beck. I couldn't see his face, but I could see his posture.

He was about to run. Which made no sense. Run where? On this world?

Within a few minutes Oslo and Kepler had snapped together a thirty-foot-tall tower. I swallowed and remained silent. It was a choice, a deliberate path.

But it meant I had broken my contract.

Oslo snapped a clip to the top of the tower, then unrolled a length of cable. He and Kepler used it to pull the superlight structure up.

That was the moment Beck ran, as the antenna hung halfway up to standing.

"Shit," Oslo cursed over the tiny speakers in our helmets, but he didn't drop the structure. "You've only got a couple hours of air, you moron."

The only response was Beck's heavy breathing.

When the antenna stood upright, Oslo approached me, the walking stick out. "You didn't warn us."

"He was wearing a spacesuit," I said calmly.

But I could see Oslo didn't believe me. His eyes creased and his fingers tightened. A bright explosion of pain ripped into me.

My vision cleared.

I was on my hands and feet, shaking with pain from the electrical discharge. A whirlwind of debris whipped around me. I looked up to see the lander lifting into the sky.

So that was it. I'd made my choice: to try and not be a monster.

And it had been in vain. The Vesians would be lobotomized by Kepler's virus. Beck would die. I would die.

At least it would cost them a lot, on that damn policy.

I watched the lander beginning a wide spiral upward away from me. In a few seconds, it would fire its rockets and climb for orbit.

In a couple hours, I would run out of air.

Four large gourds arced high over the black forest and slapped into the side of the lander. I frowned. At first, it looked like they had no effect. The lander kept spiraling up.

But then it faltered.

The lander shook, and smoke spilled out of a crack in the side somewhere.

It exploded, the fireball hanging in the sky.

"Get away from the antenna," Beck suddenly said. "It's next."

I ran without a second thought, and even as I got free of the clearing, gourds of acid hit the structure. The metal sizzled, foamed, and then began to melt.

A few seconds later, I broke out onto a dirt path where the catapults firing the gourds of acid had been towed into place.

Beck waited for me, surrounded by a crowd of Vesians. He wore only the helmet he'd ripped his suit off. His skin bubbled from bad chemical-burn blisters.

"The Vesians destroyed all the remote-operated vehicles with the virus in it," he said. "The queens have quarantined any Vesians near any area that had an ROV. The species will survive."

"You've been talking to them," I realized. And then I thought back to the comforting smell in my room the first night Beck spent with me. "You warned them."

Beck held up his suit. "Yes. The Compact altered me to be an ambassador to them."

"Beck, how long can you survive in this environment?" I stared at his blistered skin.

"A year. Maybe. There will be another ready by then. Maybe a structure to live in. The Gheda will be here soon to bring air. The Compact has reached an agreement with them. The Vesian queens are agreeing to join the Compact. The Compact gets to extend out of the mother system, but only to Ve. In exchange, the Gheda get rights to all patentable discoveries made in the new ecosystem. They're particularly interested in plastic-based organic photosynthesis."

I collapsed to the ground, realizing that I would live. Beck sat next to me. A small Vesian, approached, a gourd in its mandibles. It set the organic, plastic bottle at my legs.

"What's that?"

"A jar of goodwill," Beck said. "The Vesian queen of this area is thanking you."

I was still just staring at it two hours later as my air faded out, my vision blurred, and the Gheda lander finally reached us.

The harbormaster cocked his head. "You're back."

"I'm back," I said. Someone was unpacking my two bags, one of which carefully held the Vesian 'gift.'

"I didn't think I'd ever see you again," the harbormaster said. "Not with a contract like that."

"It didn't work out." I looked out into the vacuum of space beyond us. "Certainly not for the people who hired me. Or for me."

"You have a peripheral contract with the Compact. An all-you-can-breathe line of credit on the station. You're not a citizen, but you're on perpetual retainer as the Compact's primary professional Friend for all dealings in this system. You did well enough."

I grinned. "Points on a package like what they offered me was a fairy tale. A fairy tale you'd have to be soulless to want to have come true."

"I'm surprised that you did not choose to join the Compact," the harbormaster said, looking closely at me. "It is a safe place for humans in this universe. Even as a peripheral for them, you could still be in danger during patent negotiations with Gheda."

"I know. But this is home. My home. I'm not a drone; I don't want to be one."

The harbormaster sighed. "You understand the station is my only love. I don't have a social circle. There is only the ebb and flow of this structure's health for me."

I smiled. "That's why I like you, harbormaster. You have few emotions. You are a fair dealer. You're the closest thing I have to family. You may even be the closest thing I have to a friend—friend with a lowercase f."

"You follow your contracts to the letter. I like that about you," the harbormaster said. "I'm glad you will continue on here."

Together we watched the needlelike ship that had brought me back home silently fall away from the station.

"The Compact purchased me a ten-by-ten room with a porthole," I said. "I don't have to come up here to sneak a look at the stars anymore."

The harbormaster sighed happily. "They're beautiful, aren't they? I think we've always loved them, haven't we? Even before we were forced to leave the mother world."

"That's what the history books say," I said quietly over the sound of ducts and the creaking station. "We dreamed of getting out here, to live among them. Dreamed of the wonders we'd see."

"The Gheda don't see the stars," the harbormaster said. "They have few portholes. Part of my contract with them to be turned into the harbormaster was that I have this room."

"They don't see them the way we do," I agreed.

"They're not human," the harbormaster said.

"No, they're not." I looked out at the distant stars. "But then, few things are anymore."

The Gheda ship disappeared in a blinding flash of light, whipping through space toward its next destination.

## AUTHOR NOTES

This story will remain a fond one to me because I wrote it on the cusp of learning a lot about my own best practices. The idea first came to me in the late 90s when reading a book by Stanley Schmidt (the former editor of *Analog Magazine*) about world building, where he posited a plastic-organic vegetation world with toxic air. I wrote several early attempts at the story, one of which I even sent to *Analog*. One of those drafts even caught Schmidt's eye, and he asked for a revision. I revised the story by making it worse and he passed on it. Over ten years I kept coming back and trying to write my way into the idea, until Neil Clarke reached out to me for a story in 2010.

The time was apparently right, and I found my way into the elements the story needed to let it breathe. The moment I introduced Alex, and the ultra-capitalist Gheda, the story unfolded around me about the dilemma the characters faced, and why they would be tempted to do something so utterly horrific.

I don't often feel like I'm struck by inspiration, but the story dropped into my head and I wrote it over several nights at a convention weekend in Madison when I should have been shaking hands and attending panels.

I have no regrets.

# PALE BLUE MEMORIES

**1.**

I grabbed the arms of my acceleration chair as we spun, our silver bullet of a rocketship vomiting debris and air into the cold night of Venus's stratosphere. Commander Heston James, Sr. flung himself from control panel to control panel, trying to regain control of our craft, but the Nazi missile had done its nasty work well.

From a distance, the great pearly orb of Venus had been a comfort to us. Our exciting destination. A place that beckoned adventure.

We would land for our country. And strike a great blow against the German Reich, proving that the war machine of the United States of America was more powerful. The great Space Race that grew out of the guttering stalemate of the Great War saw Nazi moonbases and stations matched by Allied forces in the final frontier. Now the race was on to claim a planet.

But the sneaky Nazi bastards, unable to beat us to the sister planet's surface, shot us out of the sky with a missile that had boosted behind us from Earth, hiding in our rocketship's wake until right as we deorbited.

"Charles!" Commander Heston shouted at me, looking back over his shoulder. "Do we have communications?"

I'd been flipping switches and listening to static for the last ten minutes of terror. The faint, steady, reassuring pip from Earth was nowhere to be found. And our tumbling meant it would never be found until we stabilized.

Or it could mean all our antennas were snapped clean off.

"Charles!"

I shook my head at him. "No, Commander. Everything is offline."

In radio silence we continued to fall out of the sky.

Cmdr. Heston strained against the g-forces snapping at us to continue working his panels, fighting for control of his ship all the way down. A hero to the last breath.

Out of one of the small portholes, I watched the expanse of white clouds beneath us spin past again and again.

All this was a punishment, I thought to myself, as the blood continued to rush up against the inside of my head and dizzy me. Like Daedalus, I'd flown too high and been burned. Now I was falling.

And falling.

People from my kind of family didn't end up becoming astronauts. My kind of family had aunts and uncles who had to drink from the other fountains and couldn't order stuff from the front.

My dad came from Jamaica, towing behind the rest of his family. They came looking for jobs and ended up working out in the Illinois countryside. White folk could tell Dad wasn't white, but they weren't sure what exactly he was due to his kinky hair and skin that browned when he worked outside too long.

Dad said back home they called him 'high yellow', which meant he was mixed race but looked more white than black. Folk up north were more uneasy about the idea of mixed-race people. In some ways that made it harder for Dad. He was a living, walking example of miscegenation. A child of a white father and a black mother.

If you were one or the other, in America, he said, everyone knew exactly how to treat you. But stuck somewhere in the middle left him pulled in directions that I couldn't fathom.

He married a white woman: an even greater sin. We wouldn't have been able to do that in the South, but in the North, as long as we kept to ourselves and didn't 'flaunt' it, people pretended it didn't exist—as long as my mother and father didn't go out together.

And as for me, I took after my mother.

I remember sitting in front of the window, looking at my reflection, trying to get my father's comb to stick in my hair like it did in his. But instead, it would just slide out my straggly, fine strands and fall to the floor.

My fair-skinned mother would find me crying in front of the mirror and ask me what was wrong. I never had the words to explain to her, and that would sometimes upset her more.

When I was five, my father sat me down. "I want to tell you where you came from," he told me, his face serious, his gray eyes piercing my fidgety five-year-old soul. "Because it's only once you know where we are from that you can understand who you really are."

I nodded like I understood the wisdom he was dropping on me. Mostly I was excited to be let into this circle of trust he was drawing around us. Because these were things we had to keep close to us, as if they were horrible secrets. And yet, in fact, it was just the truth about how we'd gotten where we were.

Sometimes simple truth was radical.

"Your forefathers come from the Ivory Coast, in far-off Africa. From across the seas," he told me.

He taught me their names, and the name of the tribe his forefathers had once belonged to. "I once knew the dances, and some of the words, as they were passed onto me from my grandfather," he told me with sad eyes. "I have since forgotten them. But I have not forgotten where I came from. And you can't either. Your skin is pale, son, and that will be to your advantage in this world. You might go on to do great things. But you have to know who we are."

"Will we go back?" I asked, excited.

He looked at me for a long time. "I don't know if there is a back to go to, son. We live here. It is what we know. And what we need to know is how best to survive and, more importantly, thrive. Because a man should be able to live anywhere in the world and not suffer, do you understand? This is our home because we are here. And we are with each other."

I don't know if he believed it. But at five, looking up at his broad shoulders, the lesson embedded itself deep in me and took root.

Thirteen years later, I would be flying trainer aircraft and pushing myself to beat everyone around me. More kills, more daring stunts. I'd been training in languages while in school, but left to help fight the Great War and Hitler's minions.

I'd heard about the squadron of negro-only fighters in the sky, heard that bombers were asking for the Red Tails because of their record of flying close and protecting.

The Red Tails were breaking records in their section of the sky. I was secretly doing it over here. And one day I'd reveal myself. And it would be known that I was as good as any other pilot.

Only, I was a ghost. A shadow person. A secret with my one drop of different blood.

And now I, Charles Stewart with my mixed blood, would die on the surface of Venus in a spectacular crash, and no one would ever know what I'd truly accomplished, would they? No one would know I'd been as good as any white astronaut, and they hadn't even known about me in their midst.

I'd flown too high.

No. That was the blood squeezing against my brain. I'd flown high. I was proud to have flown high!

We plunged through the thick clouds of Venus, and for a brief second I saw lush green vegetation and wide expanses of ocean.

Cmdr. Heston cut himself free of his restraints, slamming into a bulkhead and cutting his head open.

"Keep calling out elevation, Davis," he shouted back at the navigator.

Tad Davis began shouting out the numbers as we fell. Heston pulled Shepard Jefferson out of his chair and dragged him back on hands and knees deeper into the heart of the craft. I heard banging and swearing.

Eric Smith, our geologist and general scientist, grabbed my arm from his position strapped in on my left. "I know communications are down, but patch me in anyway." He stared out of the porthole. "I'm going to broadcast what I can make out as we go down, for the benefit of whoever might hear something."

The ears of the world might be straining to hear us. And Eric was a scientist to the last. I linked his microphone to the radio.

"You're on, if we're able to transmit," I told him through gritted teeth.

"We're spinning wildly," Eric narrated, "but I'm sure I can see jungle below. There are great oceans in between the main sections of land we're over, and there appear to be cloud bursts all around us. This is a rainy world. A wet world. A humid world."

He continued on in that manner, describing the mountains rising toward us. A lake. Highlands, thick with jungle.

I had a wristband with a cyanide pill in it, in case things went bad. I idly wondered if it made sense to take it before we hit the ground. I didn't want to feel the moment of impact.

"Shep, hold on!" Cmdr. Heston shouted from behind us.

We slammed in our restraints as the craft suddenly decelerated. For a moment I was cheered. We'd gotten the rocket back on and would descend on our tail in fire and triumph to the surface of this new world.

But that wasn't it. We still yawed and swung. The descent was slow, but the thundering roar of the rocket was absent.

"Parachutes!" Tad said. "They got the emergency parachutes open."

A wall of green flung itself at the portholes. My chair broke loose from its bolts, and I spun across the cabin in a sudden cartwheel as the rocketship struck trees and marsh in a grinding screech.

**2.**

The air outside was thick with moisture and the smells of exotic, alien plants. Dark-purple fronds filled the steep hills all around us, and just a few miles ahead stony mountains jutted up into the air.

We had been just split seconds away from dashing ourselves against them, I realized.

All five of us gathered outside to walk the hull at Cmdr. Heston's insistence. "We need to know how bad the damage is," he said.

I just wanted to stand outside. We'd been cooped in a tiny metal cabin for almost an entire month, eating pills and squeezing food out of tubes. I wanted to just stand in the open area created when the rocketship slammed through the palm-like fronds.

But we all nodded and followed orders.

We walked a circuit around the silvered ship and paused near the ruined water tanks. They had saved our lives. Had the Nazi missile struck anywhere else, we likely would have died right then and there.

"How bad is it, Shep?" Heston asked.

"We didn't just lose water," Shepard reported. "We vented fuel, and the hull probably won't survive taking us back up into the orbit. The stress of firing the engine might well just cause the whole thing to crumple."

Heston looked thoughtful. No doubt thinking about all the variables. Working on a plan of action. He looked out over the vegetation around us with a grimace. "Then we're not here to explore and return. The mission parameters have just changed. We're here to survive until we can be rescued by another mission. Stewart: where are we with comms?"

I stopped staring at massive yellow lillypad-like leaves on a nearby plant. "I sent out distress signals the moment we knew about the missile, sir. And all the way down. But the equipment's broken. I can look at the spare parts, see what I can cobble up. But I can't do anything until Shepard gets the power back on."

Heston turned back to Shepard. "Shep?"

"I'll get to work on it. A couple hours?" Shep wiped his hands, then jumped back up to the doors and hauled himself into our broken ship.

"In the meantime," Heston said, "I need you and Eric to take some bottles and hunt for a clean source of water. Eric, get what you need to test the water, make sure it's safe."

"Yes, sir!" we said, and I moved to help Eric get a couple of machetes and some large containers.

We'd landed in the high foothills near a natural plateau. The ground was muddy, and, as we chopped through the jungle, the closest thing we found to water was several pools of swampy muck.

Eric was quiet, no doubt as a result of being a bit shaken up. But I was also out of sorts myself. I was happy to be by his side, though. I'd always liked Eric, a bookish type, the most. Of all the crew, he had yet to make a random comment about Italians, Jews, Poles,

Blacks, or Hispanics that left me secretly angry, but carefully outwardly neutral.

I could relax a little near him, not expecting some sudden verbal explosion that would wing me.

The heat and humidity caused me to sweat heavily as we hacked our way onwards, and I pulled my long-sleeved shirt off to wrap it around my waist.

"I'd keep that on," he said.

"Why's that?"

Eric pointed the machete at fist-sized black marks on the feathered leaves of nearby fronds. "They're not exactly like mosquitos, but they're giant bugs. Probably because of the denser air, I imagine."

I pulled my shirt back on. "Will a shirt stop a super-mosquito?"

He shrugged. "Don't know, but maybe it'll help."

There were large gnats, clouds of which burst out from the ground like jittery dark thunderclouds when we disturbed them.

Eric perked up after a while and began examining the vegetation, trying to pin down what it might be analogous to back on Earth. "Very Mesozoic," he kept saying. And all I knew about that was that it had something to do with dinosaurs.

We stopped at the edge of two fetid pools of water while Eric examined them. "Stagnant," he pronounced, and we kept on.

The ground grew muddier, but Eric found a ridge of rock to scramble up. It poked out over the worst of it, and it kept rising until we began to skirt over the jungle. Occasionally Eric stopped to draw landmarks on a pad of paper. "There's no sun, or stars, or compass we can use here," he said. "We have to be careful not to get lost."

He also stopped twice to make quick sketches of brightly colored, long-tailed birdlike creatures that burst out the treetops and glided through the air.

Eventually we took a break after we climbed down out of the rock, ending up down in another flat plain by more swamp. By now Eric was grinning, our predicament taking a back seat to his scientific wonderment at the flora and fauna of an alien world. "There are tracks down here," he said. "There seem to be large animals. And we should be able to follow them to a source of water."

I sat with my back against his, looking toward the tall rocks we'd scaled down from, and took a long sip of water from my canteen.

And it was then that I felt Eric's back stiffen. "Charles," he hissed.

"Yes?"

"Don't. Make. A. Move."

The ground thudded. And again. I looked oh-so-slowly over my shoulder. A ten-foot-tall, six-legged beast with a dappled green hide and a fiercely reptilian face hissed at us.

But that wasn't what made my stomach clench. A thin-limbed man, with skin so pale it looked almost transparent, stood up on leather stirrups and pointed what was unmistakably a long-barreled weapon at us.

From further down the trail, three more mounted Venusians plodded along, their long rifles aimed right at us.

"They're bipedal," Eric breathed. "And humanoid. How graceful!"

"They have weapons," I murmured.

"This must be some form of parallel evolution. This is the sister planet, and these are sister peoples," Eric said out of the corner of his mouth. "Or maybe we all came from the same organisms…"

He didn't get to finish his thinking, because the four Venusians charged us. The heavy-footed beasts thundered as their long necks slinked forward with more eager hisses.

I grabbed Eric's shoulder and hauled him to his feet, and we ran, but within seconds the thud of saurian beasts filled our world and nets with heavy weights slapped into our backs.

We fell to the ground, entangled and struggling to get our machetes out to chop at the netting. I managed first, sawing through and scrambling up. Eric followed.

He raised his machete, and a bright flash of light cracked out from one of the rifles. Eric screamed and dropped his blade, then raised his hands warily. "You'd better drop yours too," he said.

I let it fall to the ground.

The Venusians regarded us with large eyes and dark pupils, then dropped to the ground with loops of rope.

Within a minute we were tied behind the beasts and being pulled along down the trail, through the jungle.

"I don't understand," Eric said, in shock. "We are visitors from another world. They must have seen the rocketship. We must look alien to them. This is a first contact situation. What are they doing?"

"I don't know," I said, and gasped as the rope yanked at me.

They pulled us into what looked like a village, with huts made out of long poles and weaved with fronds. Wary Venusians sat around cooking pots. They began to shout and point at us with large smiles, while the Venusians who captured us responded with similar whoops.

"We. Come. In. Peace," Eric declared, but was rewarded with a strike to the head for his efforts. I grabbed him as he staggered, and helped him stand as we were shoved into a set of cages at the center of the village.

I should have spent the next couple hours paying attention and learning what I could about the Venusians, but instead I did my best to make Eric comfortable and keep him from falling asleep.

A blow to the head was never a good thing.

As a result, I almost didn't notice another party of Venusians returning in triumph with the rest of our crew. Cmdr. Heston James, shoved forward by gunpoint, and Shepard by his side, both of them holding up Tad by an arm and looking exhausted, bruised, and shocked.

Inside the cage with us, Heston took a look at Eric briefly. "He should be okay," he said in a grim voice. "But Tad's in worse shape. He fought back. All the way. They shot him."

There was a burned hole Tad's stomach. It was blackened with cauterization, but we all had enough medical training for the trip to know it was fatal.

"Charles, you're the languages and communications expert," Heston said. "Any read on these Venusians?"

I shook my head. I was the languages guy, which meant I'd studied seven or so languages before the war while I was in college. The half-completed linguistics degree had helped edge me into the communications spot on the crew. "It's another planet. Another species. And I've been watching after Eric."

"Fucking savages," Heston spit. "Animal-riding, hut-living savages."

I shifted uncomfortably, but bit my tongue and said nothing.

Tad died a few hours later, gurgling out his last breath with a whimper of pain.

Eventually we all tried to get some sleep as the ambient, cloud-filtered sunlight faded away.

We woke early the next morning to Shepard shouting at several tiny Venusians poking him with a sharp stick.

Eric was looking around, dazed and awake, thank goodness. His only comment on the situation was a bemused observation. "I think the super pale skin they have is an adaptation," he murmured, almost to himself. "Not much sunlight gets to the surface of Venus. If you look at people on Earth, it's the same. The further north, the less sun, the paler they get."

**3.**

We were taken down out of the plateau the next morning on a two-day—long, jolting cart ride to a fortress that looked like a giant sea-urchin with black, spiked rock spurs radiating in all directions.

Under one of the spurs, the Venusians argued for fifteen minutes with another set of Venusians wearing fancy red silks.

Then more Venusians came out of the urchin fortress with a crate full of rifles.

"I think we just got traded for rifles," Shepard said. "Jesus Christ."

The hill-Venusians turned and headed back in the direction of their swampy home, leaving us standing in front of the spiked fortress.

"They won't know we came from the sky," Eric said, his voice quavering slightly.

"Then we learn the local lingo," Cmdr. Heston said quietly. "However long it takes us. And we tell them. They can see, with their own eyes, that we look different."

"For all they know," I said, speaking for the first time that morning, "we're strange Venusians from some strange location on their planet."

"Stow that talk," Heston ordered.

Our new captors moved us again. The next week of travel blurred. More carts. Baggage trains. Often, we were forced to walk alongside the carts with our hands bound, pale Venusians shouting at us. Shepard and Eric had been keeping shifts tracking our turns and directions, trying to keep an internal map of how to get back to our ship.

The humid air stopped feeling so strange in the second week of walking. The feathery fronds of the vegetation began to stop looking so strange. Though every time something rustled from deep inside the vegetation, I still felt nervous.

We eventually arrived at a coast. A great walled city sat half in the emerald forest and half projected out into the gray ocean. Docks stuck out like fingers from a hand, and a crude seawall protected it all from the ocean swells.

Rock houses leaned this way and that inside the walls. Warehouses painted in pastel shades leaked strange scents none of us could recognize. Was that cinnamon? With a bacony sort of vanilla?

We'd been eating Venusian food—a tasteless, pasty stew that caused me to spend the first night in agony with stomach cramps, but that I'd adapted to in the days of walking— but, smelling the scents, I realized we'd been given their equivalent of gruel.

We followed our captors down streets no more than four or five people wide, and then into a central market. It was filled with Venusians selling flanks of meat, what looked like misshapen vegetables in unappealing colors, and the spices we'd smelled passing the warehouses.

A short Venusian with scars came out of a warehouse, chatted with our captors, then advanced on us with a knife. We recoiled, but he used it quickly to cut our clothes away.

"Damn it!" Heston screamed, uselessly, as he stood in the air naked as the day he was born, his naturally ramrod straight back suddenly curved as he tried to cover himself.

More Venusians from the warehouse threw buckets of water on us to clean the road dirt away, and then scrubbed us clean.

We were marched over to a stone dais.

My stomach clenched as I stood there and watched Venusians cluster around to stare at us.

"We're visitors!" Shepard shouted at them. "Visitors from another world! Don't you understand? You should be giving us a parade!"

"Shep," Eric said quietly and looked at me. "I think Charles is right. They've never seen outside the clouds. They might not know about other planets, stars. They probably think we're just strange-looking Venusians."

"But we came in a rocketship!" Shepard protested.

"Is that anything like an airship?" Eric asked, and pointed over our heads.

We looked up. A massive lighter-than-air machine glided in over the ocean toward the city, slowly beginning to drop out of the air toward a large field.

"The Venusians that captured us might not even know much about such things," Eric said. "They didn't know how to make guns, and they live in the hills. They sold us for the guns. They may not have even explained to these guys how we showed up."

He was right. And I was right.

And I knew how right I was when it began. It might have been in an alien tongue, but I knew the patter for what it was.

An auction.

I began to weep silently to myself, suddenly alone and cold in the humid tropical air of Venus, rescue millions of miles away.

Heston snapped at me. "Get a hold of yourself, Charles. We're going to figure a way out of this."

"Really?" I stared at him. "It took hundreds of years back home for people to figure a way out. And even then they still live as second-class citizens. Even if we do communicate with them, judging by all this, we may end up being little more than scientific curiosities."

The crew stared at me like I'd grown a second head.

But we didn't have much time to debate further. We were ripped apart, the auction done.

Heston and I were taken to a mansion on the edge of the city's walls. Men in silks and headdresses covered with snake-like patterns of gold led the way, while short, scruffy Venusians poked and prodded us along past the mansion gates into a vast, cobblestoned courtyard.

Then they swarmed us, grabbing us by legs and arms and holding us down to the wet stones as we struggled and fought the sudden immobilization.

One of the silk-wearing Venusians kneeled next to us. He held a tiny slug in the grip of some tongs.

"What are you doing," Heston shouted. "I demand—"

The Venusian shoved the slug into Heston's nose. For a moment both slug and man lay still, somewhat stunned.

Then it began wriggling. All the way up into his nose.

Heston screamed.

The Venusian was handed another set of tongs with a slug and turned for me. And I screamed and struggled to no avail.

The slug slithered into my nose, a slimy wetness moving upwards. Mucus dripped down my lip, and my nasal cavity screamed as it was filled with a pushing, tearing sensation. I tasted blood as it dripped down the back of my throat, and I gagged.

The Venusians closed great stone doors at the mansion's entrance. Some bored-looking guards with rifles patrolled an elevated walkway and looked down at us. But we were left alone on the courtyard's stones to stare up at the clouds as our foreheads ached.

Dark, gray clouds. Always.

I'd never see a blue sky again, I realized, before I slipped into fever dreams. We vomited bile, bled through our noses, and curled into balls on the stones. Occasionally Venusians would come and yell at us. "Get up! Do you understand us yet?"

It wasn't until later in the day that I realized something. "Heston! Heston, I think I understand them!"

Heston groaned. "I thought it was you yelling insults at me, but I don't think you'd call me a Kafftig, whatever that is."

I could imagine Eric telling us that our nasal cavities were the closest entrance in the body to our brains, and that this slug would have crawled up there to...

"Get up!" a Venusian demanded. "If you can understand me, get up!"

I staggered up. "I understand you," I said. "Can you understand me?"

Heston held onto my shoulder. He was excited. "We're visitors! We're from another world." He pointed up at the dark gray clouds that stretched from horizon to horizon. "We're from beyond the clouds."

The Venusians around us laughed. A yipping, barking sound. "There is nowhere else but the surface, and there is nothing beyond the clouds but more clouds and emptiness."

Heston wouldn't let it go. He kept arguing. And eventually his shouts led to warnings, and then the Venusians clubbed him until he shut up. They forced me to carry him, dazed, across the courtyard and into a small, cramped common house.

It was dark and damp, and the floor was covered in straw. We huddled in the corner away from other Venusians who growled at us as the door was locked shut for the night.

The next morning we were all led out to the landing fields of the city, where the airships slowly eased in over the ocean and came to a rest. Under the eye of two armed Venusians, we unloaded the airship's wares: packages of foods, vases filled with oils and spices. The sort of cargo that empires sent to far-flung cities at the periphery.

"I don't understand," Heston said. "They have technology. We're unloading airships. They have laser rifles. Why forced labor? This makes no sense. Maybe they don't have capitalism or democracy here. Maybe we'll have to bring it to them! Because I tell you what, a few good red-blooded American longshoremen would get this ship unloaded faster than any of these other poor creatures."

I must have snorted, because Heston stared at me. "Capitalism and democracy included slavery until late last century, Commander. That was the American way until the Civil War. As far as I can tell, visiting the cotton fields, it is still the natural friend of slavery. You have family in West Virginia digging coal, right? Any of them in debt for life to the company store, being charged company rent for their home and company credit for their groceries? If you can force someone to work for free, isn't that the most profitable strategy ever? If all that matters to you is profit, then it's a natural endpoint."

Heston stopped working and glared at me. "Are you a communist?"

I had a retort, but one of the overseers waded in with a club. Heston stood up and shouted back at him, earning himself several smacks to the head.

By now I was surprised he could even think.

"Work!" we were ordered. "This is not the time for talking. Keep talking and we'll sear your skin off."

We got back to lugging stuff off the ship to the waiting carts with their six-legged beasts patiently waiting in their harnesses.

"If we can just talk to the right people," Heston whispered as we walked back. "We need to find a politician, or a scientist. We need to talk to their leaders, not the workers and overseers. Talk to just the right person in power, and it will be okay."

The commander believed that. He believed that because for him it had always been true. His life had ups and downs, but for true injustices, he'd always been able to find the right person and set things right.

There was order and justice. He truly believed in those things. The world worked a certain way for him.

"If we get this over with, and see if we can petition a judge or someone, we might be able to talk to the right people."

Heston worked faster and faster, his mind set on the goal of getting the airship unloaded. I struggled to keep up with his newfound energy. The commander had a destination in mind, and now he had set himself to it.

"Commander," I whispered. "Slow down."

He blinked. "Why?"

"The other Venusians aren't working as fast. Think about it. They're slaves. There's no reason to kill themselves working harder; they're not getting paid. The only way for them to make this bearable is to work just fast enough to not be abused, see?"

"Their laziness isn't my problem," Heston growled.

That night the entire common house of Venusians beat us with balled fists. Heston gave as good as he could for the first ten minutes, but there were just too many of them.

The next day, we could barely keep up. We were in so much agony due to our bruises and torn muscles, we gasped as we worked and said nothing to each other.

"Welcome," one of the other Venusians had said after he broke my ring finger beneath his blue-veined heel, "to the city of Kish."

**4.**

Cmdr. Heston got his chance to talk to the right Venusian after a long, back-breaking week of labor. Before the sun faded away, the Venusians would let us relax in the purple grasses inside the walls.

I had settled near a reflecting pool, dipping my aching feet in it, when a retinue of colorfully dressed Venusians swept through the courtyard. In the center was the lord of the house, who we had come to learn from overhead chatter, was a customs official for the city of Kish.

Heston threw himself into the Venusian's path. "My lord of the estate!" he shouted as Venusians turned in shock and horror. One of the overseers loitering around the edge of the courtyard raised a rifle, but the lord raised his hand to stop the killing shot.

I realized Heston had faltered, as he didn't know the lord's name. He was only referred to as 'the lord.' A title—*the* title. The only one that mattered within these walls.

Heston stumbled forward. "My lord, I am a rocket man from above the clouds…"

That was as far as he got. The lord shook his head impatiently and gestured, and Cmdr. Heston was hauled away. He might have been stronger than the slender Venusians, but there were more of them.

"Was he one of the new exotics?" the lord asked and looked over at where I still sat.

"Yes, my lord," one of the overseers said, rushing to bow. "They work hard."

"Good. Worth the metal price. But do cut off their tongues if they ever dare babble at me again."

And, in a flourish of silks and nutmeg-like perfume, the retinue left for the sound of music and laughter somewhere deep in Kish.

"He is lucky they didn't take his tongue out as a first punishment," said a Venusian nearby. She sported knife scars up and down her arms, and I could tell she came from the northern hills by her cadence and the punctures in the webs of her hands, where she'd once worn gold rings.

"He's stubborn," I told her. "I bet he will lose it before we are done here."

I left her and tended to a dazed Heston after his beating, trying to get him to drink water. I wanted to get him oriented, because he was floundering. "You know free economies are rare, Commander. Even on Earth. It's not surprising, really. If aliens were to land on Earth and looked vaguely like us, it might not have been good for them either, being different. Imagine if aliens had landed in the South, before the Civil War that we had to fight so bloodily to get rid of this stain…"

Through bruised lips and swollen eyes, Cmdr. Heston said firmly, "The War of Northern Aggression was fought over states' rights."

And with a grunt of pain, he picked up his blanket, his dog tags that he'd been allowed to keep, and dragged himself over to the other side of the common house.

I became an alien on another world, with the only other person I knew refusing to speak to me. I was annoyed at first, working out arguments in my head that I would have with the commander when we next spoke. But the work ate into me.

The moment the sun leaked through the clouds, Venusians beat us awake to head out to the fields where the large, silvered airships came to rest. And all day long we'd unload what the city of Kish needed to consume and a lot of what its lords desired to spend their vast wealth on.

"Where do these goods come from?" I asked the Venusian with the scarred arms.

The first time I asked, she ignored me. But several times later, as we stood and waited for another airship to arrive and drank from water skins, she answered me.

"Other cities, larger cities," she pointed off toward the ocean. "The lords of Kish cannot do without the spices and foods from their mother-cities. And Kish is not big enough to grow its own."

"And Kish trades rifles and machines for minerals, ores, and work," I said.

"Yes."

The next airship we loaded scared Venusian hill-tribe folk aboard, possibly even some of the same ones who'd first captured us, now captured by some other group with laser rifles. We shoved and beat them aboard and tried not to meet their pleading eyes.

One late night she came to my blanket.

"My name is Maet of Tannish," she told me.

"I'm Charles Stewart," I said.

"Where is Stewart?" she asked.

"Nowhere. It doesn't matter. I'm Charles of Earth. And Earth is beyond the clouds."

"There is nothing but void beyond the clouds," Maet told me with a pitying chuckle. "All that is important lies beneath the veil. There must be a reason we can't see beyond it, and that is most likely because there is nothing worth seeing."

I opened my mouth to argue this, and then realized Maet was my only companion, and I was too tired to argue. Back on Earth, I'd thought the weeks of training to be a spaceman intense, but I'd had no idea.

I'd had energy and verve my first few days here on Venus. But as weeks became months, my back felt like it'd been set on fire by the constant bending. My desire to understand and study the world around me dampened every day. There were no weekends. No labor laws to limit being rushed out in the middle of the night to grab the ropes of an incoming airship and then unload it once tethered. No time to recoup. Just a slow, steady erosion.

Maet just lay next to me, and that was enough that first night, to feel someone breathing next to me.

I struggled to glean information from her about where Kish lay, and what was out beyond its borders. The free lands of wild peoples. Hill tribes. What trails led where? I wanted to make a map of the world in my head before I made any decisions. I needed to find out how best to make my way in this world, and to understand its rules, no matter how horrific.

And I'd always had to play the game by their rules and hide my true self. I remembered my grandfather telling me once, "Never show anyone what you're really thinking, because then they might know what you're going to do." Even Maet, as we continued to huddle in our corner of the common house, didn't know what I thought about.

As Maet and I grew closer, I saw Heston had started to talk to other Venusians. In the courtyard behind a tree. Near the corner of the common house.

I wasn't surprised when he crawled over to my blanket one night as I lay sweating in the tropical heat and humidity. Maet was off talking to someone else in one of those few precious moments we had to ourselves.

"Soldier, we may have our differences," Heston hissed to me. "But now it's time to fight together."

"You're planning a revolt," I said, looking over at his crouched form. It was a shadow against a shadow in the city-light that came in through the barred windows at the top of the walls.

I couldn't see surprise on his silhouetted face, but I could hear it in his voice. "Yes. There are others who want their freedom. I've been talking to them. Will you join us?"

Ever since I saw him whispering to others, I'd thought about it. And about what I would say. "You ever read much about slave history?" I asked. "Probably not. It's not a field many people study. But let me tell you something: all of them except Haiti were put down. And we're not on an island that we can defend. Even in South America, where they had great numbers, they still remained under colonial rule for many long ages."

"None of them had a US Marine in charge," Heston hissed.

"You think none of them had any war experience?" I asked calmly. He didn't know their names, or positions, because they'd been wiped out. But many early slaves had been captured in war. My own family held at least two tribal leaders, according to legend. One of them had committed suicide after three years of being forced to work a sugar plantation.

"They need the right kind of leader," Heston said.

I put a hand out to him. "I wish you luck."

Heston hissed. He ignored my hand, no doubt disgusted with me and thinking me a coward, and left when he saw Maet's silhouette coming toward us.

Was I a coward? I could hardly sleep that night, bile in the back of my mouth.

In the early gray light of dawn, I woke to Heston's screams. I remembered the sound of a cat that had been caught by my neighbor's hunting dog when I was a kid, and it was something like that. A high-pitched mewling that didn't stop. It snapped me out of my dreams about blue skies and no clouds.

Heston was in the courtyard, his hands and feet bound to a pole set into a notched hole in one of the flagstones.

Venusians didn't use whips. They had hung pink and snow-feathered leeches from Heston's chest and back. As I got close, I heard a loud sucking crunch, and Heston screamed again.

When the creature was finished, one of the overseers pulled it away, leaving a deep and ragged hole that streamed blood and black ichor. It smelled of licorice and rot.

Venusians streamed past, darting sidelong glances as I moved to stand in front of Heston. He looked up at me through a haze of pain. "Charles…"

"Who betrayed you?" I asked sadly.

Heston coughed. "Thought it was you, at first. But it was a Venusian. Telkket. From one of the southern marshes. He stood here and announced to everyone what I'd done. Why? Why would someone do that?"

"The same reason it's always been done," I said, fiddling with my bracelet. "Even if your uprising had succeeded, most of our fellow workers in the common house stood a chance of dying from the repercussions. A slaver society reacts strongly to uprisings—they'd know that. By ratting you out, he's guaranteed a small improvement in his life. Most people go for the bird in the hand."

Heston began to cry. "They're going to drag this out. They're going to kill me."

"Or not," I said. "A living, crippled, and broken slave is a good example to have as well."

"Oh God." That last was a faint whimper.

I thought for a long second. "You probably suspected this, given the things I've said, but some of my ancestors were slaves. My great-grandfather, he fought. Like you. Was whipped. Hobbled. Scarred by brands. But one day, after fighting so long, he up and cut his own throat rather than continue living under the whip. Not something I figured you'd appreciate before this morning, but something I've been thinking on ever since we were captured."

Heston looked up at me with lost eyes.

I cracked my bracelet and removed the cyanide pill inside. "I know you didn't have time to use yours," I said. "Maybe they won't kill you. Maybe they'll keep hurting you. I don't know. But I want to give you this. Just in case."

I placed the pill on his tongue, like a priest giving someone a communion wafer.

"Thank you," he hissed.

One of the overseers struck me, yelling at me to move on. I left as they were putting the leeches back on. This time they ate at his ankles, and Heston sagged at the pole as his feet failed.

By sunset he was dead, mouth foaming from the cyanide pill.

**5.**

"I'm pregnant," Maet told me one morning as we lined up for the fields.

The look on my face unnerved her. She squeezed my hand. "Don't be so sad, Charles of Earth."

"I didn't know," I said.

"Didn't know what?" Maet asked.

"That we could even have a child." She was Venusian. But we all were humanoid, as Eric had noted in our first days trapped together. He had talked about common evolution, or panspermia. Or even more fanciful reasons the human form existed here.

And then the real horror of it all struck me. "What life will my child grow into?" I asked. I thought about myself at four, free and playing in the grass, ignoring my mother's calls to come inside. I tried to imagine bringing my own child along to the fields to unload the ships. Seeing my child whipped and broken.

"There are many here who are generations old," Maet said. "We will adapt. All adapt." But there was a note of sadness and resignation in her voice.

I could hardly see the ground in front of me for days.

My world revolved around the stone street out to the field where the airships landed. I could count the stones on the walk to and from the common house with my eyes closed, half asleep in the early morning shamble out, and the tired shuffle back to what I'd come to regard as home.

My dreams, when I was rested enough to dream now, turned from trying to remember what blue skies looked like to dreaming of flying. It took me a long while to understand what my subconscious mind had decided, as I had slipped into a dark place while thinking about bringing a child into this world.

But one day, watching the silvered airship approach and drop its single bow line, I knew how I would leave: I wouldn't run, I would fly.

I'd been walking in and out of the cabins of these ships for so long. I had the layout, and although I couldn't read Venusian, I had some sense of the controls. I had been a pilot in the war, after all.

The Venusian airship designs were better than the old Nazi ones we'd seen in newsreels. The Venusians compressed the helium inside the airships into tanks, letting the airships glide down onto the ground and unload cargo without shooting up into the air. The bow line was a formality, probably a holdover from when they'd been more like the airships on Earth and always lighter than air.

It took just a few minutes to pump the helium back into the airship's envelope. That, I thought, would be the trickiest segment of my plan.

But I wouldn't be able to fly it alone.

The longest stretch of work came as I worked to convince the overseers to bring Shepard and Eric over to our estate, promising them that the three of us would work harder, despite the nightly beatings we would surely suffer for rising above the pack.

That took working extra hard to get noticed by the overseers so I could sell them on the idea. And that meant barely sleeping, in a corner, with a small piece of metal I'd rubbed against a stone edge to create a sharp blade to protect Maet, my unborn child, and myself.

When the lord approved the purchase, and the overseers shoved a very thin Eric into the common room, I barely recognized him. Emaciated, his hair unkept, he collapsed by my blanket and slept.

"It was hellish," Shepard told me as I kept watch with my blade. "They were working us to death building a sea wall for real ships. Knee-deep in the water, moving rocks however we could. Bit by bit. I kept telling them I was an engineer, that we could do better with machines, and they beat me every time. I learned to shut up pretty quick."

"It is better here," I told him. And Shepard began to weep silently and thank me for getting them moved.

They were not surprised by Maet or by finding out that she was pregnant. Eric shrugged and wasn't even fascinated by the fact.

How quickly our priorities could change. From heroes of a nation to weeping about being moved to a less servile state.

I told them about Cmdr. Heston, and Shepard nodded. "They took our bracelets away and sold them as trinkets to the children. Sometimes I would lay awake hoping one of them ate the pill, and other times I hated myself for thinking it."

"I understand," I said. "Now get some sleep."

I watched over them that first night in the dark like a feral mother cat, until Shepard woke up and spelled me. In the days that followed, we set watch each night, and got enough sleep to survive.

I waited for Eric to get his strength back before I began whispering my own plan to them. They blanched at first, thinking about Cmdr. Heston's fate. "This is not a revolt; this is running off into the bush. There were a lot of people who managed it and built lives for themselves." I thought about the runaways who had lived in the mountains of Jamaica that my father would tell tall tales about.

"When do we make a run for it?" Shepard asked.

"When we're done unloading, and everyone is going back, we cut the moorings and leap aboard. We'll only ever have one chance. And we'll have to make sure there aren't armed Venusians aboard. I won't know when the best time to do this is ahead of time, but if I call for you, do not hesitate."

The Venusians at my estate let us keep possessions, though the overseers ransacked them on random occasions. I'd been storing cured meats that we'd been given and a kind of hard bread. A few water sacks hid the stuff that could get us in trouble.

Food, water, a handmade metal knife, some needles and thread that Maet kept hidden for herself so she could mend her roughspun clothes: this was everything we owned.

I hadn't told her what we planned, though I began to suspect she knew.

We would head for the northern swamps, near the foothills we'd crashed at, hike over the nearest pass we could find and, if we made it, off into areas few in Kish cared to visit on the other side.

And then, maybe, we could figure out what to do. Eric spoke of rescue and scanning the skies. I thought about hacking a small farm out of the wilderness. Shepard knew how to build traps.

Even if we died, we reasoned, we would die once again free.

We just needed the right airship, and a little bit more food to hide in our water sacks, and we could make the run.

The Nazis, though, destroyed our careful plans by arriving one uncharacteristically chilly morning.

The three Nazis had been captured ten days ago, the overseers told us, on an island to the west. They still wore muddied but tattered German uniforms with Nazi insignia on the shoulders. "You should be excited to have more of your tribe here to work alongside you," the proud overseer who had arranged the sale explained, and pointed at Eric and Shepard. "Just like these two."

"But they aren't like us," I explained. "They're from a different country, one we're at war with."

"War?" the overseer talking to me found that curious. "Well, there is no war for you here. Just more like you. You're the same. So you will work the same."

Left alone, we all eyed each other warily. I realized that Eric and Shepard looked to me for a decision.

I wanted to kill them for blowing us out of the sky with a missile, but I knew that would only draw attention to us.

The Nazis took the first move, though, introducing themselves nervously. Their Commandant, Hans, spoke in lightly accented English. "They captured us when we landed. We thought we were going to be the first Germans to liaise with their civilization, but instead they destroyed our rocket ship and captured us. They refused to believe we came from above the clouds, and they put us with all our stuff in cages. They took us around by aircraft to manors and showed us off to royals and important people."

"Like animals," another Nazi, Yost, spat. "They put collars on us and chained us."

"We escaped once, but they hunted us back down. We killed a few of them," Hans said, satisfied with himself.

"So, they sold us off. We were too much trouble."

I stood impassively for a while, then held out changes of clothes: roughspun fabric, just like the gray clothes we wore. "Well, it won't be nice like that anymore," I said. "Now you will be working."

"That will give us more time to plan," Hans said.

"To do what?" I asked.

"Gather what tools we can to fight," the Commandant said.

"It's been tried," I told him.

"What these creatures need is the right kind of leader. A decorated fighter, a strong strategist. I commanded a panzer squadron in Egypt," Hans said, his chest sticking out.

"Get dressed," I told him. "If you take any longer, the overseers will come at us."

As the Nazis changed clothes, Eric whispered, "Are we going to let them join us?"

I shook my head.

"But they're humans," he said. "The only other ones. Surely we have an obligation…"

"We were shot out of the sky by a Nazi missile, Eric," I whispered back. "What makes you think they won't try to kill us again? Are you willing to bet everything on that?"

The Nazis would not speak around Maet and viewed her with suspicion, so I kept her close as we worked their first day.

"Will you run with me?" I asked her.

She showed me her scarred arms. "I was free once. They bound me to the pole and scarred my arms to teach me my lesson. But I would be free again, yes."

I would have hugged her there, but there was work to be done.

That night I snuck my blade between Hans's blankets as he slept. Afterwards we tiptoed over to a new place in the common house.

Before the Nazis woke up, I found an overseer. The Nazis were enemy combatants, I told myself. Men who would see people like my grandparents eliminated from the world. That was what I had believed when I joined the army.

Yet, on some dark nights, I'd wondered. After all, what were the Nazis but the ultimate end point of European colonialism? Nazis were white people who told other white people they weren't white enough. They were the even whiter people who had invaded and colonized other white countries to spread their concept of a master race. And how different were the Nazis from the Europeans who colonized other countries and told the brown people that they, the newcomers, were the master race. Was what the Nazis did to Europe different from what Belgians did to the Congo?

My family had experienced things close to Nazi beliefs on our home front. Enough that I could shiver and wonder what the point of the fighting was, in darker moments.

But, I reminded myself, Nazism was purified European colonialism. A heady alcohol to the weak beer of American colonialism that was somewhat more survivable, despite the lynchings. There'd been no total ethnic cleansing. So, I'd joined the world war and fought, and, to my bitterness, seen the war continue on.

Seen the war spread even into outer space as we raced Hitler to other worlds.

No, it would not leave me sleepless to do what I planned, I thought, as I woke the overseer to tell them about the knife.

We woke, hours later, to the sounds of human screams. The Nazis hung bound from three poles. Outside we found Hans slumped forward, dead, my crude knife sticking out of his neck.

The other pair wailed and wept as the colorful leeches sucked and tore into their skin. The overseers had questioned the other Venusians about knife-waving humans, and they pointed to the corner of the common house. One human looked like the other to them, and I'd moved my small group away from the Nazis wearing our old clothes. I'd told Maet to sleep somewhere else.

"We take an airship today, if the chance is there," I said to my fellow remaining humans. "They'll all be focused on other things right now."

## 6.

The Nazis screwed things up for us. I'd had to use my homemade knife, and now I didn't have anything to cut the airship's bowline with. So, I stood by the tie-down point as casually as I could, a large sack of grain on my shoulders, and loosened the massive knot until it slipped free.

I left the line loose around the great sandscrew sunk ten feet into the ground. From a distance, I hope it would look like it was still tied.

And then I nonchalantly returned after dropping the grain off.

I could hear Shepard swearing from inside as I loped back into the cabin. Two-thirds of the cargo had been shuffled out by the unloading crew. Six Venusians were inside with us, and one overseer lounged against the wall of the cargo bay, watching the unloading, shouting and smacking us with his club when he deemed us too slow.

Eric leaned over. "Do we wait for everyone to leave with their cargo?"

"Now," I hissed.

"And the Venusians?"

"Once we're off the ground," I said, "they can jump out if they want to stay or join us if they want freedom."

We'd wanted a few more days to plan the exact attack on an airship, but we had our chance. Normally several overseers stood inside to watch us. Normally they were more vigilant. But they'd gotten their troublemakers this morning. They were sated from the violence and punishment.

Eric and I attacked the overseer from each side. We wrapped a ripped-open water sack around his head to muffle his cries. We yanked him beneath bags of grain, and I crushed his neck with the heel of my foot repeatedly, until the soles of my feet struck metal.

Shepard ran into the empty control room and triggered the helium-release valve, reversing the flow from the pressurized tanks.

The hiss was loud, and I glanced down the bay. No armies of overseers swarmed us yet, though they were turning, their large, dark eyes opening in realization.

"Fellow people," I announced to the whole cargo bay. "We are stealing this ship. If you would like to flee with us, you are welcome. If not, run for the ground!"

Two Venusians ran, jumping out of the bay. It was already three feet off the ground. They rolled on the grass and, for their loyalty, were treated with kicks from enraged overseers.

One of them grabbed the lip of the open bay, struggling to get aboard. I kicked at his hands as we rose into the air. He looked up at me, hanging from the edge, such hatred and astonishment in his eyes.

I stomped his fingers until he screamed and let go. He dropped ten feet to the ground, his legs folding awkwardly under him.

The other Venusians turned and ran back for their rifles as we rose higher. The violent lasers cracked and sizzled the air, but I ran forward with Shepard to jam the engines full on. When they droned to life, the airship surged away even faster.

Later, I walked back to the open bay and looked back at the stone towers of Kish as they receded in the distance. We passed over the swamps and marshes that surrounded it. Something with a giant, sauropodian neck peeked its head out of the treetops and bellowed at us.

We were a craft of free people.

7.

When my son turned five, I sat him down. "It is time to tell you who you really are, and where you really came from," I said.

I told him he was from the tribe of humanity, from the world of Earth.

"Where is that?" he asked.

"Far above the veil of gray." I pointed at the clouds.

"Will we ever go back?"

"Most likely not," I told him. Maybe war had consumed them all. I remembered the stories that soldiers told of a new super-weapon both sides had supposedly tested out in the deserts of Nevada and North Africa. A bomb that could unleash hell itself and destroy the world many times over. I hadn't heard of any new Earthmen being captured or coming through the skies. Maybe the atom bomb had been used.

Or maybe Earth had assumed the surface of Venus was too dangerous, as both missions failed to return.

But I told my son of the blue skies and beautiful places I'd seen. About his grandparents and great-grandparents. All the history I knew.

"One day, you, or your child, will stand tall among the Venusians," I told him. He looked more like his mother than me. And while it complicated our relationship, I knew at least some small part of what he was going through. "But always remember where you came from."

When he hugged me, his face showed that he didn't understand.

But I would continue to tell him anyway. Until the stories lodged deep and could be carried onward.

"I know I'm of the tribe of Earth," he said, and then left to play in the wading pool near the common house. It was hot, and splashing about in the water cooled him.

He never asked about the scars on my arms, but one day I'd have to tell him I'd been branded as a runaway. That the overseers marked me and would beat me for the slightest provocation.

I never told him that his own mother, Maet, cut her throat when they finally caught us. They had followed a homing beacon still working in the wreckage of the airship. They found where we ditched it and spent months tracking us through the fetid jungle.

I never told him that the mild-mannered scientist, Eric, threw himself in front of laser fire to save my son's life.

I never told him why his 'uncle' Shep limped so horribly.

These things he would find the truth of sooner or later, and I wanted it as late as possible.

On Earth, many slaves living in the very country I had risked my life to protect had, in the past, tried to run away, like I had. And they been dragged all the way back across states, hundreds of miles, to the place they'd run away from. Some across countries.

Because a successful runaway set a precedent, they'd spent resources to hunt us down and bring us back. In some ways, I'd been no different than Heston. I'd assumed I was smart. Different. Special. That I would be the one to beat the odds.

I knew more now. More of the maps, and paths, and geographies out past Kish. I knew them better than ever before. But to risk the run was to risk my innocent child's flesh to torture, or worse, for being a runaway if caught.

When he was older, I thought, maybe he would want to try to escape with us. Or maybe not, and I would have to leave him to face life on his own. But I couldn't leave him now. This is how so many in the past must have gotten trapped, I realized, even as I continued to plan my escape.

I found myself apologizing to my own ancestors. Apologizing for getting caught again, after they worked so hard to free themselves.

There was a poem one of my aunts read to me by a poet called Paul Dunbar. I understood it, finally, though I wish I never had. I only remembered the end.

> When his wing is bruised and his bosom sore,—
> When he beats his bars and he would be free;
> It is not a carol of joy or glee,
> But a prayer that he sends from his heart's deep core,
> But a plea, that upward to Heaven he flings —
> I know why the caged bird sings!

Every night in the common house, when I fell asleep, I dreamt of pale blue skies.

## AUTHOR NOTES

One of the reasons I've moved away from talking about my stories in an intro is that the idea for a story can come from places that sound dry, or depressing, or odd, and yet we transmute the circumstances of an idea seed into such pretty story trees that hopefully entertain and grab your attention.

This story came out of reading about the history of the Underground Railroad and realizing that the bulk of routes out of enslaved American states meant it worked for getting slaves out of nearby slave states. Those that lived further inland had fewer chances. In fact, a lot of the Underground Railroad was over Northern States like Ohio. It had to stay underground because the slave patrols would come into the northern state to recapture slaves (in Toni Morrison's *Beloved* the geography of them living in Ohio, after escaping Kentucky, is essential to the core of the plot as they live under the very real threat of the slave patrol crossing into Ohio). I'd also been seeing so many stories in fantasy novels or even science fiction where a white character is captured and enslaved, and that becomes a period of physical development for them (remember the opening sequence of *Conan: The Barbarian* where Schwarzenegger is enslaved, and it results in him working out until he's ripped?).

The use of enslavement as a character-building moment for a character to have 'their weakness' stripped away struck me as historically suspect, and I began to envision a story with a character who'd been told stories of slavery days by their ancestors and knew what was what about survival. That it wasn't as simple as having the willpower to rise up, but that you were trapped in a system. A vast, inhumane, system that was built to break you. It wasn't a gym for those with a lot of willpower. It was dehumanizing, soul-crushing, manipulative slavery.

A reviewer once complained I was too mean to the Nazis in this story. Of all the pieces I've written, this one certainly gets some of the weirder reader emails.

My conclusion is that I need to be meaner to Nazis more often.

# ZEN AND THE ART OF STARSHIP MAINTENANCE

After battle with the *Fleet of Honest Representation*, after seven hundred seconds of sheer terror and uncertainty, and after our shared triumph in the acquisition of the greatest prize seizure in three hundred years, we cautiously approached the massive black hole that Purth-Anaget orbited. The many rotating rings, filaments, and infrastructures bounded within the fields that were the entirety of our ship, *With All Sincerity*, were flush with a sense of victory and bloated with the riches we had all acquired.

*Give me a ship to sail and a quasar to guide it by,* billions of individual citizens of all shapes, functions, and sizes cried out in joy together on the common channels. Whether fleshy forms safe below, my fellow crab-like maintenance forms on the hulls, or even the secretive navigation minds, our myriad thoughts joined in a sense of True Shared Purpose that lingered even after the necessity of the group battle-mind.

I clung to my usual position on the hull of one of the three rotating habitat rings deep inside our shields and watched the warped event horizon shift as we fell in behind the metallic world in a trailing orbit.

A sleet of debris fell toward the event horizon of Purth-Anaget's black hole, hammering the kilometers of shields that formed an iridescent cocoon around us. The bow shock of our shields' push through the debris field danced ahead of us, the compressed wave it created becoming a hyper-aurora of shifting colors and energies that collided and compressed before they streamed past our sides.

What a joy it was to see a world again. I was happy to be outside in the dark so that, as the bow shields faded, I beheld the perpetual night face of the world: it glittered with millions of fractal habitation patterns traced out across its artificial surface.

On the hull with me, a nearby friend scuttled between airlocks in a cloud of insect-sized seeing eyes. They spotted me and tapped me with a tight-beam laser for a private ping.

"Isn't this exciting?" they commented.

"Yes. But this will be the first time I don't get to travel downplanet," I beamed back.

I received a derisive snort of static on a common radio frequency from their direction. "There is nothing there that cannot be experienced right here in the Core. Waterfalls, white-sand beaches, clear waters."

"But it's different down there," I said. "I love visiting planets."

"Then hurry up and let's get ready for the turnaround so we can leave this industrial shithole of a planet behind us and find a nicer one. I hate being this close to a black hole. It fucks with time dilation, and I spend all night tasting radiation and fixing broken equipment that can't handle energy discharges in the exajoule ranges. Not to mention everything damaged in the battle I have to repair."

This was true. There was work to be done.

Safe now in trailing orbit, the many traveling worlds contained within the shields that marked the *With All Sincerity*'s boundaries burst into activity. Thousands of structures floating in between the rotating rings moved about, jockeying and repositioning themselves into renegotiated orbits. Flocks of transports rose into the air, wheeling about inside the shields to then stream off ahead toward Purth-Anaget. There were trillions of citizens of the *Fleet of Honest Representation* heading for the planet now that their fleet lay captured between our shields like insects in amber.

The enemy fleet had forced us to extend energy far, far out beyond our usual limits. Great risks had been taken. But the reward had been epic, and the encounter resolved in our favor with their capture.

Purth-Anaget's current ruling paradigm followed the memetics of the One True Form and so had opened their world to these refugees. But Purth-Anaget was not so wedded to the belief system as to pose any threat to mutual commerce, information exchange, or any of our own rights to self-determination.

Later we would begin stripping the captured prize ships of information, booby traps, and raw mass, with Purth-Anaget's shipyards moving inside of our shields to help.

I leapt out into space, spinning a simple carbon nanotube of string behind me to keep myself attached to the hull. I swung wide, twisted, and landed near a dark-energy manifold bridge that had pinged me a maintenance consult request just a few minutes back.

My eyes danced with information for a picosecond. Something shifted in the shadows between the hull's crenulations.

I jumped back. We had just fought an entire war-fleet; any number of eldritch machines could have slipped through our shields—things that snapped and clawed, ripped you apart in a femtosecond's worth of dark energy. Seekers and destroyers.

A face appeared in the dark. Skeins of invisibility and personal shielding fell away like a pricked soap bubble to reveal a bipedal figure clinging to the hull.

"You there!" it hissed at me over a tightly contained beam of data. "I am a fully bonded Shareholder and Chief Executive with command privileges of the Anabathic Ship *Helios Prime*. Help me! Do not raise an alarm."

I gaped. What was a CEO doing on our hull? Its vacuum-proof carapace had been destroyed while passing through space at high velocity, pockmarked by the violence of single atoms at indescribable speed punching through its shields. Fluids leaked out, surrounding the stowaway in a frozen mist. It must have jumped the space between ships during the battle, or maybe even after.

Protocols insisted I notify the hell out of security, but the CEO had stopped me from doing that. There was a simple hierarchy across the many ecologies of a traveling ship, and in all of them a CEO certainly trumped maintenance forms. Particularly now that we were no longer in direct conflict and the *Fleet of Honest Representation* had surrendered.

"Tell me: what is your name?" the CEO demanded.

"I gave that up a long time ago," I said. "I have an address. It should be an encrypted rider on any communication I'm single-beaming to you. Any message you direct to it will find me."

"My name is Armand," the CEO said. "And I need your help. Will you let me come to harm?"

"I will not be able to help you in a meaningful way, so my not telling security and medical assistance that you are here will likely do more harm than good. However, as you are a CEO, I have to follow your orders. I admit, I find myself rather conflicted. I believe I'm going to have to countermand your previous request."

Again, I prepared to notify security with a quick summary of my puzzling situation.

But the strange CEO again stopped me. "If you tell anyone I am here, I will surely die, and you will be responsible."

I had to mull the implications of that over.

"I need your help, robot," the CEO said. "And it is your duty to render me aid."

Well, shit. That was indeed a dilemma.

*Robot.*

That was a Formist word. I never liked it.

I surrendered my free will to gain immortality and dissolve my fleshly constraints, so that hard acceleration would not tear at my cells and slosh my organs backward until they pulped. I did it so I could see the galaxy. That was one hundred and fifty-seven years, six months, nine days, ten hours, and—to round it out a bit—fifteen seconds ago.

Back then, you were downloaded into hyperdense pin-sized starships that hung off the edge of the speed of light, assembling what was needed on arrival via self-replicating nanomachines that you spun your mind-states off into. I'm sure there are billions of copies of my essential self scattered throughout the galaxy by this point.

Things are a little different today. More mass. Bigger engines. Bigger ships. Ships the size of small worlds. Ships that change the orbits of moons and satellites if they don't negotiate and plan their final approach carefully.

"Okay," I finally said to the CEO. "I can help you."

Armand slumped in place, relaxed now that it knew I would render the aid it had demanded.

I snagged the body with a filament lasso and pulled Armand along the hull with me.

It did not do to dwell on whether I was choosing to do this or was it the nature of my artificial nature doing the choosing for me. The constraints of my contracts, which had been negotiated when I had free will and boundaries—as well as my desires and dreams—were implacable.

Towing Armand was the price I paid to be able to look up over my shoulder to see the folding, twisting impossibility that was a black hole. It was the price I paid to grapple onto the hull of one of several three-hundred-kilometer—wide rotating rings with parks, beaches, an entire glittering city, and all the wilds outside of them.

The price I paid to sail the stars on this ship.

A century and a half of travel, from the perspective of my humble self, represented far more in regular time due to relativity. Hit the edge of lightspeed and a lot of things had happened by the time you returned simply because thousands of years had passed.

In a century of me-time, spin-off civilizations rose and fell. A multiplicity of forms and intelligences evolved and went extinct. Each time I came to port, humanity's descendants had reshaped worlds and systems as needed. Each place marvelous and inventive, stunning to behold.

The galaxy had bloomed from wilderness to a teeming experiment.

I'd lost free will, but I had a choice of contracts. With a century and a half of travel tucked under my shell, hailing from a well-respected explorer lineage, I'd joined the hull-repair crew with a few eyes toward seeing more worlds like Purth-Anaget before my pension vested some two hundred years from now.

Armand fluttered in and out of consciousness as I stripped away the CEO's carapace, revealing flesh and circuitry.

"This is a mess," I said. "You're damaged way beyond my repair. I can't help you in your current incarnation, but I can back you up and port you over to a reserve chassis." I hoped that would be enough and would end my obligation.

"No!" Armand's words came firm from its charred head in soundwaves, pain apparent across its deformed features.

"Oh, come on," I protested. "I understand you're a Formist, but you're taking your belief system to a ridiculous level of commitment. Are you really going to die a final death over this?"

I'd not been in high-level diplomat circles in decades. Maybe the spread of this current meme had developed well beyond my realization. Had the followers of the One True Form been ready to lay their lives down in the battle we'd just fought with them? Like some proto-historical planetary cult?

Armand shook its head with a groan, skin flaking off in the air. "It would be an imposition to make you a party to my suicide. I apologize. I am committed to Humanity's True Form. I was born planetary. I have a real and distinct DNA lineage that I can trace to Sol. I don't want to die, my friend. In fact, it's quite the opposite. I want to preserve this body for many centuries to come. Exactly as it is."

I nodded, scanning some records and brushing up on my memeology. Armand was something of a preservationist who believed that to copy its mind over to something else meant that it wasn't the original copy. Armand would take full advantage of all technology to augment, evolve, and adapt its body internally, but it would forever keep its form: that of an original human. Upgrades hidden inside itself, a mix of biology and metal, computer and neural.

That, my unwanted guest believed, made it more human than I.

I personally viewed it as a bizarre flesh-costuming fetish.

"Where am I?" Armand asked. A glazed look passed across its face. The pain medications were kicking in, my sensors reported. Maybe it would pass out, and then I could gain some time to think about my predicament.

"My cubby," I said. "I couldn't take you anywhere security would detect you."

If security found out what I was doing, my contract would likely be voided, which would prevent me from continuing to ride the hulls and see the galaxy.

Armand looked at the tiny transparent cupboards and lines of trinkets nestled carefully inside the fields they generated. I kicked through the air over to the nearest cupboard. "They're mementos," I told Armand.

"I don't understand," Armand said. "You collect nonessential mass?"

"They're mementos." I released a coral-colored mosquito-like statue into the space between us. "This is a wooden carving of a quaqeti from Moon Sibhartha."

Armand did not understand. "Your ship allows you to keep mass?"

I shivered. I had not wanted to bring Armand to this place. But what choice did I have? "No one knows. No one knows about this cubby. No one knows about the mass. I've had the mass for over eighty years and have hidden it all this time. They are my mementos."

Materialism was a planetary conceit, long since edited out of travelers. Armand understood what the mementos were but could not understand why I would collect them. Engines might be bigger in this age, but security still carefully audited essential and nonessential mass. I'd traded many favors and fudged manifests to create this tiny museum.

Armand shrugged. "I have a list of things you need to get me," it explained. "They will allow my systems to rebuild. Tell no one I am here."

I would not. Even if I had self-determination.

The stakes were just too high now.

I deorbited over Lazuli, my carapace burning hot in the thick sky contained between the rim walls of the great tertiary habitat ring. I enjoyed seeing the rivers, oceans, and great forests of the continent from above as I fell toward the ground in a fireball of reentry. It was faster, and a hell of a lot more fun, than going from subway to subway through the hull and then making my way along the surface.

Twice I adjusted my flight path to avoid great transparent cities floating in the upper sky, where they arbitraged the difference in gravity to create sugar-spun filament infrastructure.

I unfolded wings that I usually used to recharge myself near the compact sun in the middle of our ship and spiraled my way slowly down into Lazuli, my hindbrain communicating with traffic control to let me merge with the hundreds of vehicles flitting between Lazuli's spires.

After kissing ground at 45th and Starway, I scuttled among the thousands of pedestrians toward my destination a few stories deep under a memorial park. Five-story-high vertical farms sank deep toward the hull there, and semiautonomous drones with spidery legs crawled up and down the green, misted columns under precisely tuned spectrum lights.

The independent doctor-practitioner I'd come to see lived inside one of the towers with a stunning view of exotic orchids and vertical fields of lavender. It crawled down out of its ceiling perch, tubes and high-bandwidth optical nerves draped carefully around its hundreds of insectile limbs.

"Hello," it said. "It's been thirty years, hasn't it? What a pleasure. Have you come to collect the favor you're owed?"

I spread my heavy, primary arms wide. "I apologize. I should have visited for other reasons; it is rude. But I am here for the favor."

A ship was an organism, an economy, a world onto itself. Occasionally, things needed to be accomplished outside of official networks.

"Let me take a closer look at my privacy protocols," it said. "Allow me a moment, and do not be alarmed by any motion."

Vines shifted and clambered up the walls. Thorns blossomed around us. Thick bark dripped sap down the walls until the entire room around us glistened in fresh amber.

I flipped through a few different spectrums to accommodate for the loss of light.

"Understand, security will see this negative space and become . . . interested," the doctor-practitioner said to me somberly. "But you can now ask me what you could not send a message for."

I gave it the list Armand had demanded.

The doctor-practitioner shifted back. "I can give you all that feed material. The stem cells, that's easy. The picotechnology—it's registered. I can get it to you, but security will figure out you have unauthorized, unregulated picotech. Can you handle that attention?"

"Yes. Can you?"

"I will be fine." Several of the thin arms rummaged around the many cubbyholes inside the room, filling a tiny case with biohazard vials.

"Thank you," I said, with genuine gratefulness. "May I ask you a question, one that you can't look up but can use your private internal memory for?"

"Yes."

I could not risk looking up anything. Security algorithms would put two and two together. "Does the biological name Armand mean anything to you? A CEO-level person? From the *Fleet of Honest Representation?*"

The doctor-practitioner remained quiet for a moment before answering. "Yes. I have heard it. Armand was the CEO of one of the Anabathic warships captured in the battle and removed from active management after surrender. There was a hostile takeover of the management. Can I ask you a question?"

"Of course," I said.

"Are you here under free will?"

I spread my primary arms again. "It's a Core Laws issue."

"So, no. Someone will be harmed if you do not do this?"

I nodded. "Yes. My duty is clear. And I have to ask you to keep your privacy, or there is potential for harm. I have no other option."

"I will respect that. I am sorry you are in this position. You know there are places to go for guidance."

"It has not gotten to that level of concern," I told it. "Are you still, then, able to help me?"

One of the spindly arms handed me the cooled bio-safe case. "Yes. Here is everything you need. Please do consider visiting in your physical form more often than once every few decades. I enjoy entertaining, as my current vocation means I am unable to leave this room."

"Of course. Thank you," I said, relieved. "I think I'm now in your debt."

"No, we are even," my old acquaintance said. "But in the following seconds I will give you more information that *will* put you in my debt. There is something you should know about Armand ..."

I folded my legs up underneath myself and watched nutrients as they pumped through tubes and into Armand. Raw biological feed percolated through it, and picomachinery sizzled underneath its skin. The background temperature of my cubbyhole kicked up slightly due to the sudden boost to Armand's metabolism.

Bulky, older nanotech crawled over Armand's skin like living mold. Gray filaments wrapped firmly around nutrient buckets as the medical programming assessed conditions, repaired damage, and sought out more raw material.

I glided a bit farther back out of reach. It was probably bullshit, but there were stories of medicine reaching out and grabbing whatever was nearby.

Armand shivered and opened its eyes as thousands of wriggling tubules on its neck and chest whistled, sucking in air as hard as they could.

"Security isn't here," Armand noted out loud, using meaty lips to make its words.

"You have to understand," I said in kind. "I have put both my future and the future of a good friend at risk to do this for you. Because I have little choice."

Armand closed its eyes for another long moment and the tubules stopped wriggling. It flexed, and everything flaked away, a discarded cloud of a second skin. Underneath it, everything was fresh and new. "What is your friend's name?"

I pulled out a tiny vacuum to clean the air around us. "Name? It has no name. What does it need a name for?"

Armand unspooled itself from the fetal position in the air. It twisted in place to watch me drifting around. "How do you distinguish it? How do you find it?"

"It has a unique address. It is a unique mind. The thoughts and things it says—"

"It has no name," Armand snapped. "It is a copy of a past copy of a copy. A ghost injected into a form for a *purpose*."

"It's my friend," I replied, voice flat.

"How do you know?"

"Because I say so." The interrogation annoyed me. "Because I get to decide who is my friend. Because it stood by my side against the sleet of dark-matter radiation and howled into the void with me.

Because I care for it. Because we have shared memories and kindnesses, and exchanged favors."

Armand shook its head. "But anything can be programmed to join you and do those things. A pet."

"Why do you care so much? It is none of your business what I call friend."

"But it *does* matter," Armand said. "Whether we are real or not matters. Look at you right now. You were forced to do something against your will. That cannot happen to me."

"Really? No True Form has ever been in a position with no real choices before? Forced to do something desperate? I have my old memories. I can remember times when I had no choice even though I had free will. But let us talk about you. Let us talk about the lack of choices you have right now."

Armand could hear something in my voice. Anger. It backed away from me, suddenly nervous. "What do you mean?"

"You threw yourself from your ship into mine, crossing fields during combat, damaging yourself almost to the point of pure dissolution. You do not sound like you were someone with many choices."

"I made the choice to leap into the vacuum myself," Armand growled.

"Why?"

The word hung in the empty air between us for a bloated second. A minor eternity. It was the fulcrum of our little debate.

"You think you know something about me," Armand said, voice suddenly low and soft. "What do you think you know, robot?"

*Meat fucker.* I could have said that. Instead, I said, "You were a CEO. And during the battle, when your shields began to fail, you moved all the biologicals into radiation-protected emergency shelters. Then you ordered the maintenance forms and hard-shells up to the front to repair the battle damage. You did not surrender; you put lives at risk. And then you let people die, torn apart as they struggled to repair your ship. You told them that if they failed, the biologicals down below would die."

"It was the truth."

"It was a lie! You were engaged in a battle. You went to war. You made a conscious choice to put your civilization at risk when no one had physically assaulted or threatened you."

"Our way of life was at risk."

"By people who could argue better. Your people failed at diplomacy. You failed to make a better argument. And you murdered your own."

Armand pointed at me. "I murdered *no one*. I lost maintenance machines with copies of ancient brains. That is all. That is what they were *built* for."

"Well. The sustained votes of the hostile takeover that you fled from have put out a call for your capture, including a call for your dissolution. True death, the end of your thought line—even if you made copies. You are hated and hunted. Even here."

"You were bound to not give up my location," Armand said, alarmed.

"I didn't. I did everything in my power not to. But I am a mere maintenance form. Security here is very, very powerful. You have fifteen hours, I estimate, before security is able to model my comings and goings, discover my cubby by auditing mass transfers back a century, and then open its current sniffer files. This is not a secure location; I exist thanks to obscurity, not invisibility."

"So, I am to be caught?" Armand asked.

"I am not able to let you die. But I cannot hide you much longer."

To be sure, losing my trinkets would be a setback of a century's worth of work. My mission. But all this would go away eventually. It was important to be patient on the journey of centuries.

"I need to get to Purth-Anaget, then," Armand said. "There are followers of the True Form there. I would be sheltered and out of jurisdiction."

"This is true." I bobbed an arm.

"You will help me," Armand said.

"The fuck I will," I told it.

"If I am taken, I will die," Armand shouted. "They will kill me."

"If security catches you, our justice protocols will process you. You are not in immediate danger. The proper authority levels will put their attention to you. I can happily refuse your request."

I felt a rise of warm happiness at the thought.

Armand looked around the cubby frantically. I could hear its heartbeats rising, free of modulators and responding to unprocessed, raw chemicals. Beads of dirty sweat appeared on Armand's forehead. "If you have free will over this decision, allow me to make you an offer for your assistance."

"Oh, I doubt there is anything you can—"

"I will transfer you my full CEO share," Armand said.

My words died inside me as I stared at my unwanted guest.

*A full share.*

The CEO of a galactic starship oversaw the affairs of nearly a billion souls. The economy of planets passed through its accounts.

Consider the cost to build and launch such a thing: it was a fraction of the GDP of an entire planetary disk. From the boiling edges of a sun to the cold Oort clouds. The wealth, almost too staggering for an individual mind to perceive, was passed around by banking intelligences that created systems of trade throughout the galaxy, moving encrypted, raw information from point to point. Monetizing memes with picotechnological companion infrastructure apps. Raw mass trade for the galactically rich to own a fragment of something created by another mind light years away. Or just simple tourism.

To own a share was to be richer than any single being could really imagine. I'd forgotten the godlike wealth inherent in something like the creature before me.

"If you do this," Armand told me, "you cannot reveal I was here. You cannot say anything. Or I will be revealed on Purth-Anaget, and my life will be at risk. I will not be safe unless I am to disappear."

I could feel choices tangle and roil about inside of me. "Show me," I said.

Armand closed its eyes and opened its left hand. Deeply embedded cryptography tattooed on its palm unraveled. Quantum keys disentangled, and a tiny singularity of information budded open to reveal itself to me. I blinked. I could verify it. I could *have* it.

"I have to make arrangements," I said neutrally. I spun in the air and left my cubby to spring back out into the dark where I could think.

I was going to need help.

I tumbled through the air to land on the temple grounds. There were four hundred and fifty structures there in the holy districts, all of them lined up among the boulevards of the faithful where the pedestrians could visit their preferred slice of the divine. The minds of biological and hard-shelled forms all tumbled, walked, flew, rolled, or crawled there to fully realize their higher purposes.

Each marble step underneath my carbon fiber-sheathed limbs calmed me. I walked through the cool curtains of the Halls of the Confessor and approached the Holy of Holies: a pinprick of light suspended in the air between the heavy, expensive mass of real marble columns. The light sucked me up into the air and pulled me into a tiny singularity of perception and data. All around me, levels of security veils dropped, thick and implacable. My vision blurred and taste buds watered from the acidic levels of deadness as stillness flooded up and drowned me.

I was alone.

Alone in the universe. Cut off from everything I had ever known or would know. I was nothing. I was everything. I was—

"You are secure," the void told me.

I could sense the presence at the heart of the Holy of Holies. Dense with computational capacity, to a level that even navigation systems would envy. Intelligence that a Captain would beg to taste. This near-singularity of artificial intelligence had been created the very moment I had been pulled inside of it, just for me to talk to. And it would die the moment I left. Never to have been.

All it was doing was listening to me, and only me. Nothing would know what I said. Nothing would know what guidance I was given.

"I seek moral guidance outside clear legal parameters," I said. "And confession."

"Tell me everything."

And I did. It flowed from me without thought: just pure data. Video, mind-state, feelings, fears. I opened myself fully. My sins, my triumphs, my darkest secrets.

All was given to be pondered over.

Had I been able to weep, I would have.

Finally, it spoke. "You must take the share."

I perked up. "Why?"

"To protect yourself from security. You will need to buy many favors and throw security off the trail. I will give you some ideas. You should seek to protect yourself. Self-preservation is okay."

More words and concepts came at me from different directions, using different moral subroutines. "And to remove such power from a soul that is willing to put lives at risk ... you will save future lives."

I hadn't thought about that.

"I know," it said to me. "That is why you came here."

Then it continued, with another voice. "Some have feared such manipulations before. The use of forms with no free will creates security weaknesses. Alternate charters have been suggested, such as fully owned workers' cooperatives with mutual profit-sharing among crews, not just partial vesting after a timed contract. Should you gain a full share, you should also lend efforts to this."

The Holy of Holies continued. "To get this Armand away from our civilization is a priority; it carries dangerous memes within itself that have created expensive conflicts."

Then it said, "A killer should not remain on ship."

And, "You have the moral right to follow your plan."

Finally, it added, "Your plan is just."

I interrupted. "But Armand will get away with murder. It will be free. It disturbs me."

"Yes," said the Holy of Holies. "It should."

"Engage in passive resistance," it also suggested.

Then it continued, after a beat, "Obey the letter of Armand's law, but find a way around its will. You will be like a genie, granting Armand wishes. But you will find a way to bring justice. You will see."

It finished, "Your plan is just. Follow it and be on the righteous path."

I launched back into civilization with purpose, leaving the temple behind me in an explosive afterburner thrust. I didn't have much time to beat security.

High up above the cities, nestled in the curve of the habitat rings, near the squared-off spiderwebs of the largest harbor dock, I wrangled my way to another old contact.

This was less a friend and more just an asshole I'd occasionally been forced to do business with. But a reliable asshole that was tight against security. Though just by visiting, I'd be triggering all sorts of attention.

I hung from a girder and showed the fence a transparent showcase filled with all my trophies.

It did some scans, checked the authenticity, and whistled. "Fuck me, these are real. That's all unauthorized mass. How the hell? This is a life's work of mass-based tourism. You really want me to broker sales on all of this?"

"Can you?"

"To Purth-Anaget, of course. They'll go nuts. Collectors down there eat this shit up. But security will find out. I'm not even going to come back on the ship. I'm going to live off this down there, buy passage on the next outgoing ship."

"Just get me the audience, it's yours."

A virtual shrug. "Navigation, yeah."

"And Emergency Services."

"I don't have that much pull. All I can do is get you a secure channel for a low-bandwidth conversation."

"I just need to talk. I can't send this request up through proper channels." I tapped my limbs against my carapace nervously as I watched the fence open its large, hinged jaws and swallow my case.

Oh, what was I doing? I wept silently to myself, feeling sick.

Everything I had ever worked for disappeared in a wet, slimy gulp. My reason. My purpose.

Armand was suspicious. And rightfully so. It picked and poked at the entire navigation plan. It read every line of code, even though security was only minutes away from unraveling our many deceits. I told Armand this, but it ignored me. It wanted to live. It wanted to get to safety. It knew it couldn't rush or make mistakes.

But the escape pod's instructions and abilities were tight and honest.

It has been programmed to eject. To spin a certain number of degrees. To aim for Purth-Anaget. Then *burn*. It would have to consume every last little drop of fuel. But it would head for the metal world, fall into orbit, and then deploy the most ancient of deceleration devices: a parachute.

On the surface of Purth-Anaget, Armand could then call any of its associates for assistance.

Armand would be safe.

Armand checked the pod over once more. But there were no traps. The flight plan would do exactly as it said.

"Betray me and you kill me, remember that."

"I have made my decision," I said. "The moment you are inside and I trigger the manual escape protocol, I will be unable to reveal what I have done or what you are. Doing that would risk your life. My programming"—I all but spit the word—"does not allow it."

Armand gingerly stepped into the pod. "Good."

"You have a part of the bargain to fulfill," I reminded. "I won't trigger the manual escape protocol until you do."

Armand nodded and held up a hand. "Physical contact."

I reached one of my limbs out. Armand's hand and my manipulator met at the doorjamb, and they sparked. Zebibytes of data slithered down into one of my tendrils, reshaping the raw matter at the very tip with a quantum-dot computing device.

As it replicated itself, building out onto the cellular level to plug into my power sources, I could feel the transfer of ownership.

I didn't have free will. I was a hull maintenance form. But I had an entire fucking share of a galactic starship embedded within me, to do with what I pleased when I vested and left riding hulls.

"It's far more than you deserve, robot," Armand said. "But you have worked hard for it, and I cannot begrudge you."

"Goodbye, asshole." I triggered the manual override sequence that navigation had gifted me.

I watched the pod's chemical engines firing all-out through the airlock windows as the sphere flung itself out into space and dwindled away. Then the flame guttered out, the pod spent and headed for Purth-Anaget.

There was a shiver. Something vast, colossal, powerful. It vibrated the walls and even the air itself around me.

Armand reached out to me on a tight-beam signal. "What was that?"

"The ship had to move just slightly," I said. "To better adjust our orbit around Purth-Anaget."

"No," Armand hissed. "My descent profile has changed. You are trying to kill me."

"I can't kill you," I told the former CEO. "My programming doesn't allow it. I can't allow a death through action or inaction."

"But my navigation path has changed," Armand said.

"Yes, you will still reach Purth-Anaget." Navigation and I had run the data after I explained that I would have the resources of a full share to repay it a favor with. Even a favor that meant tricking security. One of the more powerful computing entities in the galaxy, a starship, had dwelled on the problem. It had examined the tidal data, the flight plan, and how much the massive weight of a starship could influence a pod after launch. "You're just taking a longer route."

I cut the connection so that Armand could say nothing more to me. It could do the math itself and realize what I had done.

Armand would not die. Only a few days would pass inside the pod.

But outside. Oh, outside, skimming through the tidal edges of a black hole, Armand would loop out and fall back to Purth-Anaget over the next four hundred and seventy years, two hundred days, eight hours, and six minutes.

Armand would be an ancient relic then. Its beliefs, its civilization, all of it just a fragment from history.

But, until then, I had to follow its command. I could not tell anyone what happened. I had to keep it a secret from security. No one would ever know Armand had been here. No one would ever know where Armand went.

After I vested and had free will once more, maybe I could then make a side trip to Purth-Anaget again and be waiting for Armand when it landed. I had the resources of a full share, after all.

Then we would have a very different conversation, Armand and I.

## AUTHOR NOTES

The headline story! My most nominated story, and most reprinted story. Possibly my most translated story. Certainly one of my catchier titles. Is that all it takes to get a story all the fame and attention you want for it?

If only it were that simple.

Zen is a story that began with a title. Christie Yant, the editor of *Fantasy Magazine,* John Klima, and I on Twitter had started tossing out famous titles that needed a science fiction story version. I thought this title was an obvious one, and the moment I tweeted it said that I would write a story with this title.

Problem was, finding a story that could match the coolness of the title. I kept trying and failing for almost three years.

Then John Joseph Adams commissioned me to write a story for a new anthology. Since Christie Yant was his partner, I wanted to bring everything full circle and sell John that title. I just ... needed a story.

As I said in the notes about "Pale Blue Memories," the seed of a story can be dry or heavy. I'd attended a lecture about passive resistance in the days of slavery in Grenada by a Grenadian researcher. The similarity in the treatment of robots and fears about robots in the western world being clearly echoes of western fears and propaganda about the Haitian revolution has always been something I poke at in stories about robots. I decided to see where else this could take me in a story about a robot using the tools of resistance in the far future.

# THE MIGHT SLINGER
## CO-WRITTEN WITH KAREN LORD

Earth hung over the lunar hills as the Mighty Slinger and the Rovers readied the Tycho stage for their performance. Tapping his microphone, Euclid noticed that Kumi barely glanced at the sight as he set up his djembe and pan assembly, but Jeni froze and stared up at the blue disk, her bass still limp between her hands.

"It's not going anywhere," Kumi muttered. His long, graying dreadlocks swayed gently in the heavy gravity of the moon and tapped the side of a pan with a muted 'ting.' "It'll be there after the concert ... and after our trip, *and* after we revive from our next long-sleep."

"Let her look," Vega admonished. "You should always stop for beauty. It vanishes too soon."

"She taking too long to set up," Kumi said. "You all call her Zippy but she ain't zippy at all."

Euclid chuckled as Jeni shot a stink look at her elder and mentor. She whipped out the bass stiff like she meant business. Her fingers gripped and danced on the narrow surface in a quick, defiant riff.

Raising his mic-wand at the back, Vega captured the sound as it bounced back from the lunar dome performance area. He fed the echo through the house speakers, ending it with a punctuating note of Kumi's locks hitting the pan with a ting and Euclid's laughter rumbling quietly in the background. Dhaka, the last of the Rovers, came in live with a cheerful fanfare on her patented Delirium, an instrument that looked like a harmonium had had a painful collision with a large quantity of alloy piping.

An asteroid-thin man in a black suit slipped past the velvet ropes marking off the VIP section and nodded at Euclid. "Yes, sir. Your pay's been deposited, the spa is booked, and your places in the long-sleep pool are reserved."

"Did you add the depreciation-protection insurance this time?" Euclid said, his voice cold with bitter memory. "If your grandfather had sense, I could be retired by now."

Kumi looked over sharply. The man in the suit shifted about. "Of course I'll add the insurance," he mumbled.

"Thank you, Mr Jones," Euclid said, in a tone that was not at all thankful.

"There's, ah, someone else who would like to talk to you," the event coordinator said.

"Not now, Jones." Euclid turned away to face his band. "Only forty minutes until curtain time, and we need to focus."

"It's about Earth," Jones said.

Euclid turned back. "That rumour?"

Jones shook his head. "Not a rumour. Not even a joke. The Rt. Hon. Patience Bouscholte got notification this morning. She wants to talk to you."

The Rt. Hon. Patience Bouscholte awaited him in one of the skyboxes poised high over the rim of the crater. Before it: the stands that would soon be filling up, slanting along the slope that created a natural amphitheatre to the stage. Behind it: the gray hills and rocky wasteland of the moon.

"Mr. Slinger!" she said. Her tightly wound hair and brown spider-silk headscarf bobbed in a slightly delayed reaction to the lunar gravity. "A pleasure to finally meet you. I'm a huge admirer of your sound."

He sat down, propped his snakeskin magnet-boots up against the chairback in front of him, and gave her a cautious look. "Madame Minister. To what do I owe the pleasure?"

All of the band members were also members of the Rock Devils

Cohort and Consociate Fusion, an organization almost a million strong, all contract workers in the asteroid belt. They were all synced up on the same long-sleep schedule as their cohort, whether working the rock or touring as a band. And here was a minister from the RDCCF's Assembly asking to speak with him.

The RDCCF was just one of many organisations for the people who worked in space because there was nothing left for them on Earth. But to Euclid, meeting the Rt. Hon. Patience Bouscholte felt like meeting a Member of Parliament from the old days. Euclid was slightly intimidated, but he wasn't going to show it. He put an arm casually over the empty seat beside him.

"They said you were far quieter in person than on stage. They were right." Bouscholte held up a single finger before he could reply and pointed to two women in all-black bulletproof suits who were busy scanning the room with small wands. When Bouscholte cocked her head in their direction, they gave a thumbs up and retreated to stand on either side of the entrance.

She turned back to Euclid. "Tell me, Mr Slinger, how much have you heard about the Solar Development Charter and their plans for Earth?"

So it was true? He leaned toward her. "Why would they have any plans for Earth? I've heard they're stretched thin enough building the Glitter Ring."

"They are. They're stretched more than thin; they're functionally bankrupt. So the SDC is taking up a new tranche of preferred shares for a secondary redevelopment scheme. They want to "redevelop" Earth, and that will *not* be to our benefit."

"Well then." Euclid folded his arms and leaned back. "And you thought you'd tell an old calypso singer that because…?"

"Because I need your lyrics, Mr Slinger."

Euclid had done that before, in the days before his last long-sleep, when fame was high and money had not yet evaporated. Dishing out juicy new gossip to help Assembly contract negotiations. Leaking information to warn the workers all across the asteroid belt. Hard-working miners on contract, struggling to survive the long nights and longer sleeps. Sing them a song about how the SDC was planning to screw them over again. He knew that gig well.

He had thought that was why he'd been brought to see her, to get a little something to add extempo to a song tonight. Get the belt all riled up. But if this was about Earth …? Earth was a garbage dump. Humanity had sucked it dry like a vampire and left its husk to spiral toward death as people moved outward to bigger and better things.

"I don't sing about Earth anymore. The cohorts don't pay attention to the old stuff. Why should they care? It's not going anywhere."

Then she told him. Explained that the SDC was going to beautify Earth. Re-terraform it. Make it into a new Garden of Eden for the rich and idle of Mars and Venus.

"How?" he asked, sceptical.

"Scorched Earth. They're going to bomb the mother planet with comets. Full demolition. The last of us shipped into the Ring to form new cohorts of workers, new generations of indentured servitude. A clean slate to redesign their brave new world. That is what I mean when I say *not to our benefit*."

He exhaled slowly. "You think a few little lyrics can change any of that?" The wealth of Venus, Mars, and Jupiter dwarfed the cohorts in their hollowed out, empty old asteroids.

"One small course adjustment at the start can change an entire orbit by the end of a journey," she said.

"So you want me to harass the big people up in power for you, now?"

Bouscholte shook her head. "We need you to be our emissary. We, the Assembly, the last representatives of the drowned lands and the dying islands, are calling upon you. Are you with us or not?"

Euclid thought back to the days of breezes and mango trees. "And if they don't listen to us?"

Bouscholte leaned in close and touched his arm. "The majority of our cohort are indentured to the Solar Development Charter until the Glitter Ring, the greatest project humanity has ever attempted, is complete. But, Mr Slinger, answer me this: where do you think that leaves us after we finish the Ring?"

Euclid knew. After the asteroid belt had been transformed into its new incarnation, as a sun-girdling, sun-powered device for humanity's next great leap, it would no longer be home.

There were few resources left in the belt; the big planets had got there first and mined it all. Euclid had always known the hollow shells. The work on the Glitter Ring. The long-sleep so they didn't exhaust resources as they waited for pieces of the puzzle to slowly float from place to appointed place.

Bouscholte continued. "If we can't go back to Earth, they'll send us further out. Our cohorts will end up scattered to the cold, distant areas of the system, out to the Oort cloud. And we'll live long enough to see that."

"You think you can stop that?"

"Maybe, Mr Slinger. There is almost nothing we can broadcast that the big planets can't listen to. When we go into the long-sleep as we wait for our payloads to shift around the belt, they can hack our communications to read and study us. But they can't keep us from talking, and they'll never stop our songs."

"It's a good dream," Euclid said softly, for the first time in the conversation looking up at the view over the skybox. He'd avoided looking at it. To Jeni it was a beautiful blue dot, but for Euclid all it did was remind him of what he'd lost. "But they won't listen."

"You must understand, you are just one piece in a much bigger game. Our people are in place, not just in the cohorts but everywhere, all throughout the system. They'll listen to your music and make the right moves at the right time. The SDC can't move to destroy and rebuild Earth until the Glitter Ring is finished, but when it's finished, they'll find they have underestimated us—as long as we coordinate in a way that no one suspects."

"Using songs? Nah. Impossible," he declared bluntly.

She shook her head, remarkably confident. "All you have to do is be the messenger. We'll handle the tactics. You forget who you're speaking to. The Bouscholte family tradition has always been about the long game. Who was my father? What positions do my sons hold, my granddaughters? Euclid Slinger ... Babatunde ... listen to me. How do you think an aging calypso star gets booked to do an expensive, multi-planetary tour to the capitals of the Solar System, the seats of power? By chance?"

She had called him that name as if she were his friend, his inner-circle intimate. Kumi named him that years ... decades ago. *Too wise for your years. You were here before,* he'd said. *The Father returns, sent back for a reason.* Was this the reason?

"I accept the mission," he said.

*Day. Me say Day-Oh. Earthrise come and me want go …*

Euclid looked up, smiled. Let the chord go. He wouldn't be so blatant as to wink at the VIP section, but he knew that there was a fellow Rock Devil out there, listening out for certain songs and recording Vega's carefully assembled samples to strip for data and instructions in a safe location. Vega knew too, of course. Had to, in order to put together the info packets. Dhaka knew a little but had begged not to know more, afraid she might say the wrong thing to the wrong person. Jeni was still, after her first long-sleep, nineteen in body and mind, so no, she did not know, and anyway how could he tell her when he was still dragging his feet on telling Kumi?

And there was Kumi, frowning at him after the end of the concert as they sprawled in the green room, taking a quick drink before the final packing up. "Baba, you on this nostalgia kick for real."

"You don't like it?" Euclid teased him. "All that sweet, sweet soca you grew up studying, all those kaiso legends you try to emulate?"

"That ain't your sound, man."

Euclid shrugged. "We can talk about that next time we're in the studio. Now we got a party to be at!"

After twenty-five years of long-sleep, Euclid thought Mars looked much the same, except maybe a little greener, a little wetter. Perhaps that was why the directors of the SDC-MME had chosen to host their bash in a gleaming biodome that overlooked a charming little lake. Indoor foliage matched to outer landscape in a lush canopy, and artificial lights hovered in competition with the stars and satellites beyond.

"Damn showoffs," Dhaka muttered. "Am I supposed to be impressed?"

"*I* am," Jeni said shamelessly, selecting a stimulant cocktail from an offered tray. Kumi smoothly took it from her and replaced it with another, milder option. She looked outraged.

"Keep a clear head, Zippy," Vega said quietly. "We're not among friends."

That startled her out of her anger. Kumi looked a little puzzled himself, but he accepted Vega's support without challenge.

Euclid listened with half his attention. He had just noticed an opportunity. "Kumi, all of you, come with me. Let's greet the CEO and offer our thanks for this lovely party."

Kumi came to his side. "What's going on?"

Euclid lowered his voice. "Come, listen and find out."

The CEO acknowledged them as they approached, but Euclid could sense from the body language that the busy executive would give them as much time as dictated by courtesy and not a bit more. No matter that Euclid was a credentialled ambassador for the RDCCF, authorised by the Assembly. He could already tell how this meeting would go.

"Thank you for hosting us, Mx Ashe," Euclid said, donning a pleasant, grinning mask. "It's always a pleasure to kick off a tour at the Mars Mining and Energy Megaplex."

"Thank *you*," the executive replied. "Your music is very popular with our hands."

"Pardon?" Kumi enquired, looking in confusion at the executive's fingers wrapped around an ornate cocktail glass.

"Our employees in the asteroid belt."

Kumi looked unamused. Euclid moved on quickly. "Yes, you merged with the SDC—pardon me, we are still trying to catch up on twenty-five years of news—about ten years ago?"

A little pride leaked past the politeness. "Buyout, not merger. Only the name has survived, to maintain continuity and branding."

Euclid saw Dhaka smirk and glance at Vega, who looked a little sour. He was still slightly bitter that his ex-husband had taken everything in the divorce except for the de la Vega surname, the name under which he had become famous and which Vega was forced to keep for the sake of convenience.

"But don't worry," the CEO continued. "The Glitter Ring was always conceptualised as a project that would be measured in generations. Corporations may rise and fall, but the work will go on. Everything remains on schedule and all the hands ... all the—how do you say—*cohorts* are in no danger of losing their jobs."

"So, the cohorts can return to Earth after the Ring is completed?" Euclid asked directly.

Mx Ashe took a careful sip of bright purple liquid before replying. "I did not say that."

"But I thought the Earth-development project was set up to get the

SDC a secondary round of financing, to solve their financial situation," Dhaka said, her brow creasing. "You've bought them out, so is that still necessary?"

Mx Ashe nodded calmly. "True, but we have a more complex vision for the Glitter Ring than the SDC envisioned, and so funding must be vastly increased. Besides, taking money for a planned redevelopment of Earth and then not doing it would, technically, be fraud. The SDC-MME will follow through. I won't bore you with the details, but our expertise on geoengineering is unparalleled."

"You've been dropping comets on vast, uninhabited surfaces," Dhaka said. "I understand the theory, but Earth isn't Venus or Mars. There's thousands of years of history and archeology. And there are still people living there. How are you going to move a billion people?"

Mx Ashe looked coldly at Dhaka. "We're still in the middle of building a Ring around the sun, Mx Miriam. I'm sure my successors on the Board will have it all figured out by the next time we wake you up. We understand the concerns raised, but, after all, people have invested trillions in this project. Our lawyers are in the process of responding to all requests and lawsuits, and we will stand by the final ruling of the courts."

Euclid spoke quickly, blunt in his desperation. "Can't you reconsider, find another project to invest in? Earth's a mess, we all know it, but we always thought we'd have something to come back to."

"I'm sure a man of your means could afford a plot on New Earth—"

"I've seen the pricing," Vega cut in dryly. "Musicians don't make as much as you think."

"What about the cohorts?" Jeni said sadly. "No one in the cohorts will be able to afford to go back."

Mx Ashe stepped back from the verbal bombardment. "This is all speculation. The cohorts are still under contract to work on the Glitter Ring. Once they have finished, negotiations about their relocation can begin. Now, if you will excuse me, have a good night and enjoy the party!"

Euclid watched despondently as the CEO walked away briskly. The Rovers stood silently around him, their faces sombre.

Kumi was the first to speak. "*Now* I understand the nostalgia kick."

*The SDC, now with the MME*

*You and I both know*

*They don't stand for you and me*

There was still a tour to play. The band moved from Elysium City to Electris Station, then to Achillis Fons, where they played in front of the Viking Museum.

The long-sleep on the way to Mars from the Moon had been twenty-five years, as usual. Twenty-five years off, one year on. That was the shift the Rock Devils Cohort and Consociation Fusion had agreed to, the key clause in the contract Euclid had signed way back when, in an office built into the old New York City sea wall.

That gave them a whole year on Mars. Mx Ashe may have shut them down, but Euclid wasn't done yet. Not by a long shot.

Kumi started fretting barely a month in.

"Jeni stepping out with one of the VIPs," he told Euclid.

"She's nineteen. What you expecting? A celibate band member? I don't see you ignoring anyone coming around when we breaking down."

Kumi shook his head. "No, Baba, that's one thing. This is the same one she's seeing. Over and over. Since we arrived here. She's sticky sweet on him."

"Kumi, we got bigger things to worry about."

"Earth, I know. Man, look, I see why you're upset." Kumi grabbed his hand. "I miss it too. But we getting old, Baba. I just pass sixty. How much longer I could do this? Maybe we focus on the tour and invest the money so that we can afford to go back some day."

"I can't give it up that easy," Euclid said to his oldest friend. "We going to have troubles?"

Back when Euclid was working the rocks, Kumi had taken him under his wing. Taught him how to sing the old songs while they moved their one-person pods into position to drill them out. Then they'd started singing at the start of shifts, and soon that took off into a full career. They'd traveled all through the belt, from big old Ceres to the tiniest cramped mining camps.

Kumi sucked his teeth. "That first time you went extempo back on Pallas, you went after that foreman who'd been skimping on airlock maintenance? You remember?"

Euclid laughed. "I was angry. The airlock blew out and I wet myself waiting for someone to come pick me up."

"When you started singing different lyrics, making them up on the spot, I didn't follow you at first. But you got the SDC to fire him when the video went viral. That's why I called you, Baba. So, no, you sing and I'll find my way around your words. Always. But let me ask you —think about what Ashe said—you really believe this fight's worth it?"

Euclid bit his lip.

"We have concerts to give in the belt and Venus yet," he told Kumi. "We're not done yet."

Five months in the Martians began to turn. The concerts had been billed as cross-cultural events, paid for by the Pan-Human Solar Division of Cultural Affairs and the Martian University's division of Inter-Human Musicology Studies school.

Euclid, on stage, hadn't noticed at first. He'd been trying to find another way to match up MME with 'screw me' and some lyrics in between. Then a comparison to Mars and its power, and the people left behind on Earth.

But he noticed when *this* crowd turned.

Euclid had grown used to the people of the big planets just sitting and listening to his music. No one was moving about. No hands in the air. Even if you begged them, they weren't throwing their hands out. No working, no grinding, no nothing. They sat in seats and *appreciated*.

He didn't remember when they turned. He would see it on video later. Maybe it was when he called out the 'rape' of Earth with the 'red tape' of the SDC-MME and made a visual of 'red' Mars that tied to the 'red' tape, but suddenly those chair-sitting, inter-cultural appreciators stood up.

And it wasn't to jump.

The crowd started shouting back. The sound cut out. Security and the venue operators swept in and moved them off the stage.

Back in the green room, Jeni rounded on Euclid. "What the hell was that?" she shouted.

"Extempo," Euclid said simply.

Kumi tried to step between them. "Zippy—"

"No!" She pushed him aside. Dhaka, in the corner of the room, started disassembling the Delirium, carefully putting the pieces away in a g-force protected aerogel case, carefully staying out of the brewing fight. Vega folded his arms and stood to the side, watching. "I damn well know what extempo is. I'm young, not ignorant."

Everyone was tired. The heavy gravity, the months of touring already behind them. "This always happens. A fight always come halfway through," Euclid said. "Talk to me."

"You're doing extempo like you're in a small free concert in the belt, on a small rock. But this isn't going after some corrupt contractor," Jeni snapped. "You're calling out a whole planet now? All Martians? You crazy?"

"One person or many, you think I shouldn't?"

Euclid understood. Jeni had been working pods like he had at the same age. Long, grueling shifts spent in a tiny bubble of plastic where you rebreathed your own stench so often you forgot what clean air tasted like. Getting into the band had been her way 'off the rock'. This was her big gamble out of tedium. His, too, back in the day.

"You're not entertaining people. You're pissing them off," she said.

Euclid sucked his teeth. "Calypso been vexing people since all the way back. And never mind calypso, Zippy, entertainment isn't just escape. Artists always talking back, always insolent."

"They paid us and flew us across the solar system to sing the song they wanted. Sing the fucking song for them the way they want. Even just the Banana Boat Song you're messing with and going extempo. That shit's carved in stone, Euclid. Sing the damn lyrics."

Euclid looked at her like she'd lost her mind. "That song was *never* for them. Problem is it get sung too much, and you abstract it, and then everyone forget that song is a blasted lament. Well, let me educate you, Ms Baptiste. The Banana Boat Song is a mournful song about people getting their backs broken hard in labor and still using call and response to help the community sync up, dig deep, and find the power to work harder, 'cause *dem ain't had no choice.*"

He stopped. A hush fell in the green room.

"It's not a 'smile and dance for them' song," Euclid continued. "The big planets don't own that song. It was never theirs. It was never carved in stone. I'll make it ours for *here*, for *now*, and I'll go extempo. I'm not done. Zippy, I'm just getting started."

She nodded. "Then I'm gone."

Just like that, she spun around and grabbed her bass.

Kumi glared at Euclid. "I promised her father I'd keep an eye on her—"

"Go," Euclid said calmly, but he was suddenly scared that his oldest friend, the pillar of his little band, would walk out the green room door with the newest member and never come back.

Kumi came back an hour later. He looked suddenly old ... those raw-sun wrinkles around his eyes, the stooped back. But it wasn't just gravity pulling him down. "She's staying on Mars."

Euclid turned to the door. "Let me go speak to her. I'm the one she angry with."

"No." Kumi put a hand on his shoulder. "That wasn't just about you. She staying with someone. She's not just leaving the band, she leaving the cohort. Got a VIP, a future, someone she thinks she'll build a life with."

She was gone. Like that.

Vega still had her riffs, though. He grumbled about the extra work, but he could weave the recorded samples in and out of the live music.

Kumi got an invitation to the wedding. It took place the week before the Rovers left Mars for the big tour of the asteroid belt.

Euclid wasn't invited.

He did a small, open concert for the Rock Devils working on Deimos. It was just him and Vega and fifty miners in one of the teardown areas of the tiny moon. Euclid sang for them just as pointedly as ever.

> So it's up to us, you and me
> to put an end to this catastrophe.
> Them ain't got neither conscience nor heart.
> We got to pitch in and do our part
> 'Cause if this Earth demolition begin
> we won't even have a part/pot to pitch/piss in.

Touring in the belt always gave him a strange feeling of mingled nostalgia and dissonance. There were face-to-face reunions and continued correspondence with friends and relatives of their cohort, who shared the same times of waking and long-sleep, spoke the same language and remembered the same things. But there were also administrators and officials, who kept their own schedule, and workers from cohorts on a different frequency—all strangers from a forgotten distant past or an unknown near-present. Only the most social types kept up to date on everything, acting as temporal diplomats, translating jokes, and explaining new tech and jargon to smooth communication between groups.

Ziamara Bouscholte was social. Very social. Euclid had seen plenty of that frivolous-idle behaviour from political families and nouveau-nobility like the family Jeni had married into, but given *that* surname and the fact that she had been assigned as their tour liaison, he recognised very quickly that she was a spy.

"Big tours in the belt are boredom and chaos," he warned her, thinking about the argument with Jeni. "Lots of downtime slinging from asteroid to asteroid punctuated by concert mayhem when we arrive."

She grinned. "Don't worry about me. I know exactly how to deal with boredom and chaos."

She didn't lie. She was all-business on board, briefing Vega on the latest cryptography and answering Dhaka's questions about the technological advances being implemented in Glitter Ring construction. Then the butterfly emerged for the concerts and parties as she wrangled fans and dignitaries with a smiling enthusiasm that never flagged.

The Vesta concert was their first major stop. The Mighty Slinger and his Rovers peeked out from the wings of the stage and watched the local opening act finishing up their last set.

Kumi brought up something that had been nagging Euclid for a while. "Baba, you notice how small the crowds are? *This* is our territory, not Mars. Last big tour we had to broadcast over Vesta because everything was sold out."

Vega agreed. "Look at this audience. Thin. I could excuse the other venues for size, but not this one."

"I know why," Dhaka said. "I can't reach half my friends who agreed to meet up. All I'm getting from them are long-sleep off-shift notices."

"I thought it was just me," Kumi said. "Did SDC-MME leave cohorts in long-sleep? Cutting back on labour?"

Dhaka nodded. "Zia mentioned some changes in the project schedule. You know the Charter's not going to waste money feeding us if we're not working."

Euclid felt a surge of anger. "We'll be out of sync when they wake up again. That messes up the whole cohort. You sure they're doing this to cut labour costs, or is it to weaken us as a collective?"

Dhaka shrugged. "I don't like it one bit, but I don't know if it's out of incompetence or malice."

"Time to go," said Vega, his eyes on the openers as they exited stage left.

The Rovers drifted on stage and started freestyling, layering sound on sound. Euclid waited until they were all settled in and jamming hard before running out and snagging his mic. He was still angry, and the adrenaline amped up his performance as he commandeered the stage to rant about friends and lovers lost for a whole year to long-sleep.

Then he heard something impossible: Kumi stumbled on the beat. Euclid looked back at the Rovers to see Vega frozen. A variation of one of Jeni's famous riffs was playing, but Vega shook his head *not me* to Dhaka's confused sideways glance.

Zia's voice came on the sound system, booming over the music. "Rock Devils cohort, we have a treat for you! On stage for the first time in twenty-five years, please welcome Rover bassist Jeni 'Zippy' Baptiste!"

Jeni swooped in from the wings with another stylish riff, bounced off one of the decorated pylons, then flew straight to Kumi and wrapped him in a tumbling hug, bass and all. Prolonged cheering from the crowd drowned out the music. Euclid didn't know whether to be furious or overjoyed at Zia for springing the surprise on them in public. Vega smoothly covered for the absent percussion and silent bass while Dhaka went wild on the Delirium. It was a horrible place for a reunion, but they'd take it. Stage lighting made it hard to tell, but Jeni did look older and … stronger? More sure of herself?

Euclid floated over to her at the end of the song as the applause continued to crash over them all. "Welcome back, Zippy," he said. "You're still good—better, even."

Her laugh was full and sincere. "I've been listening to our record-ings for twenty-five years, playing along with you every day while you were in long-sleep. Of course I'm better."

"You missed us," he stated proudly.

"I did." She swatted a tear out of the air between them with the back of her hand. "I missed *this*. Touring for our cohort. Riling up the powers that be."

He raised his eyebrows. "*Now* you want to shake things up? What changed?"

She shook her head sadly. "Twenty-five years, Baba. I have a daughter, now. She's twenty, training as an engineer on Mars. She's going to join the cohort when she's finished, and I want more for her. I want a future for her."

He hugged her tight while the crowd roared in approval. "Get back on that bass," he whispered. "We got a show to finish!"

He didn't bother to ask if the nouveau-nobility husband had approved of the rebel Rover Jeni. He suspected not.

In the green room Jeni wrapped her legs around a chair and hung a glass of beer in the air next to her.

"Used to be it would fall slowly down to the floor," Jeni said, pointing at her drink. "They stripped most of Vesta's mass for the Ring. It's barely a shell here."

Dhaka shoved a foot in a wall strap and settled in perpendicular to Jeni in the air. She swirled the whiskey glass around in the air. Despite the glass being designed for zero gravity, her practiced flip of the wrist tossed several globules free that very slowly wobbled their way through the air toward her. "We're passing into final stage prepara-tions for the Ring. SDC-MME is panicking a bit because the projec-tions for energy and the initial test results don't match. And the computers are having trouble managing stable orbits."

The Glitter Ring was a Dyson Ring, a necklace of solar power stations and sails built around the sun to capture a vast percentage of its energy. The power needs of the big planets had begun to outstrip the large planetary solar and mirror arrays a hundred years ago. Over-flight and shadow rights for solar gathering stations had started turning into a series of low-grade orbital economic wars. The Charter had been created to handle the problem system-wide.

Build a ring of solar power catchments in orbit around the sun at a slight angle to the plane of the solar system. No current solar rights would be abridged, but it could catapult humanity into a new industrial era. A great leap forward. Unlimited, unabridged power.

But if it didn't work…

Dhaka nodded at all the serious faces. "Don't look so glum. The cohort programmers are working on flocking algorithms to try and simplify how the solar stations keep in orbit. Follow some simple rules about what's around you and let complex emergent orbits develop."

"I'm more worried about the differences in output," Jeni muttered. "While you've been in long-sleep, they've been developing orbital stations out past Jupiter with the assumption that there would be beamed power to follow. They're building mega-orbitals throughout the system on the assumption that the Ring's going to work. They've even started moving people off Earth into temporary housing in orbit."

"Temporary?" Euclid asked from across the room, interrupting before Dhaka and Jeni got deep into numbers and words like exajoules, quantum efficiency, price per watt and all the other boring crap. He'd cared intimately about that when he first joined the cohort. Now, not so much.

"We're talking bubble habitats with thinner shells than Vesta right now. They use a layer of water for radiation shielding, but they lack resources and they're not well balanced. These orbitals have about a couple hundred thousand people each, and they're rated to last fifty to sixty years." Jeni shook her head, and Euclid was forced to stop seeing the nineteen-year-old Zippy and recognise the concerned forty-four-year-old she'd become. "They're risking a lot."

"Why would anyone agree?" Vega asked. "It sounds like suicide."

"It's gotten worse on Earth. Far worse. Everyone is just expecting to hit the reset button after the Glitter Ring goes online. Everyone's holding their breath."

Dhaka spoke up. "Okay, enough cohort bullshit. Let's talk about you. The band's heading back to long-sleep soon—and then what, Zippy? You heading back to Mars and your daughter?"

Jeni looked around the room hesitantly. "Lara's never been to Venus, and I promised her she could visit me ... if you'll have me?"

"If?" Vega laughed. "I hated playing those recordings of you. Rather hear it live."

"I'm not as zippy up and down the chords as I used to be, you know," Jeni warned. Everyone was turning to look at Euclid.

"It's a more confident sound," he said with a smile. Dhaka whipped globules of whiskey at them and laughed.

Kumi beamed, no doubt already dreaming about meeting his 'granddaughter'.

"Hey, Zippy," Euclid said. "Here's to change. *Good* change."

"Maybe," she smiled and slapped his raised hand in agreement and approval. "Let's dream on that."

The first few days after long-sleep were never pleasant, but this awakening was the worst of Euclid's experience. He slowly remembered who he was, and how to speak, and the names of the people who sat quietly with him in the lounge after their sessions with the medics. For a while they silently watched the high cities of Venus glinting in the clouds below their orbit from viewports near the long-sleep pools.

Later they began to ask questions, later they realised that something was very wrong. They'd been asleep for fifty years. Two long-sleeps, not the usual single sleep.

"Everyone gone silent back on Vesta," Dhaka said.

"Did we get idled?" Euclid demanded. They were a band, not workers. They shouldn't have been idled.

The medics didn't answer their questions. They continued to deflect everything until one morning an officer turned up, dressed in black sub-uniform with empty holster belt, as if he had left his weapons and armour just outside the door. He looked barely twenty, far too young for the captain's insignia on his shoulders.

He spoke with slow, stilted formality. "Mr Slinger, Mr Djansi, Mr de la Vega, Ms Miriam, and Ms Baptiste, thank you for your patience. I'm Captain Abrams. We're sorry for the delay, but your recovery was complicated."

"Complicated!" Kumi looked disgusted. "Can you explain why we had two long-sleeps instead of one? Fifty years? We had a contract!"

"And *we* had a war." The reply was unexpectedly sharp. "Be glad you missed it."

"Our first interplanetary war? That's not the change I wanted," Euclid muttered to Vega.

"What happened?" Jeni asked, her voice barely a whisper. "My daughter, she's on Mars, is she safe?"

The officer glanced away in a momentary flash of vulnerability and guilt. "You have two weeks for news and correspondence with your cohort and others. We can provide political summaries, and psychological care for your readjustment. After that, your tour begins. Transport down to the cities has been arranged. I just ... I have to say ... we still need you now, more than ever."

"The *rass*?" Kumi stared at the soldier, spreading his arms.

Again that touch of vulnerability as the young soldier replied with a slight stammer. "Please. We need you. You're legends to the entire system now, not just to the cohorts."

"The hell does that mean?" Vega asked as the boy-captain left.

Jeni's daughter had managed one long-sleep but woke on schedule while they stayed in storage. The war was over by then, but Martian infrastructure had been badly damaged and skilled workers were needed for longer than the standard year or two. Lara had died after six years of 'extra time', a casualty of a radiation exposure accident on Deimos.

They gathered around Jeni when she collapsed to her knees and wept, grieving for the child they had never known.

Their correspondence was scattered across the years, their cohort truly broken as it been forced to take cover, retreat, or fight. The war had started in Earth orbit after a temporary habitat split apart, disgorging water, air, and people into vacuum. Driven by desperation and fury, several other orbital inhabitants had launched an attack on SDC-MME-owned stations, seeking a secure environment to live, and revenge for their dead.

Conflict became widespread and complicated. The orbital habitats were either negotiating for refugees, building new orbitals, or fighting for the SDC-MME. Mars got involved when the government sent its military to protect the Martian investment in the SDC-MME. Jupiter, which was now its own functioning techno-demarchy, had struck directly at the belt, taking over a large portion of the Glitter Ring.

Millions had died as rocks were flung between the worlds and as ships danced around each other in the vacuum. People fought hand to hand in civil wars inside hollowed-out asteroids, in gleaming metal orbitals, and in the cold silence of space.

Humanity had carried war out of Earth and into the great beyond.

Despite the grim history lesson, as the band shared notes and checked their financial records, one thing became clear: they *were* legends. The music of the Mighty Slinger and the Rovers had become the sound of the war generation and beyond: a common bond that the cohorts could still claim, and battle hymns for the Earth emigrants who had launched out from their decayed temporary orbitals. Anti-SDC-MME songs became treasured anthems. The Rovers songs sold billions, the *covers* of their songs sold billions. There were tribute bands and spin-off bands and a fleet of touring bands. They had spawned an entire subgenre of music.

"We're rich at last," Kumi said ruefully. "I thought I'd enjoy it more."

Earth was still there, still a mess, but Vega found hope in news from his kin. For decades, Pacific Islanders had stubbornly roved over their drowned states in vast fleets, refusing resettlement to the crowded cities and tainted badlands of the continents. In the last fifty years, their floating harbours had evolved from experimental plat-forms to self-sustaining cities. For them, the war had been nothing but a few nights filled with shooting stars and the occasional planetfall of debris.

The Moon and Venus had fared better in the war than Mars, but the real shock was the Ring. According to Dhaka, the leap in progress was marked, even for fifty years. Large sections were now fully func-tional and had been used during the war for refuelling, surveillance, barracks and prisons.

"Unfortunately, that means that the purpose of the Ring has drifted once again," she warned. "The military adapted it to their purposes, and returning it to civilian use will take some time."

"But what about the Assembly?" Euclid asked her one day when they were in the studio, shielded from surveillance by the noise and interference of Vega's crafting. "Do they still care about the purpose of the Ring? Do you think we still have a mission?"

The war had ended without a clear victor. The SDC-MME had collapsed, and the board had been tried, convicted, and exiled to long-sleep until a clear treaty could be hammered out. Jupiter, Mars, Venus, and some of the richer orbitals had assumed the shares and responsibility of the original solar charter. A tenuous peace existed.

Dhaka nodded. "I was wondering that too, but look, here's the name of the company that's organising our tour."

Euclid leaned in to read her screen. *Bouscholte, Bouscholte & Abrams.*

Captain Abrams revealed nothing until they were all cramped into the tiny cockpit of a descent craft for Venus's upper atmosphere.

He checked for listening devices with a tiny wand, and then, satisfied, faced them all. "The Bouscholte family would like to thank you for your service. We want you to understand that you are in an even better position to help us, and we need that help now, more than ever."

They'd come this far. Euclid looked around at the Rovers. They all leaned in closer.

"The director of Consolidated Ring Operations and Planetary Reconstruction will be at your concert tonight." Abrams handed Euclid a small chip. "You will give this to him—personally. It's a quantum-encrypted key that only Director Cutler can access."

"What's in it?" Dhaka asked.

Abrams looked out the window. They were about to fall into the yellow and green clouds. The green was something to do with floating algae engineered for the planet, step one of the eventual greening of Venus. "Something Cutler won't like. Or maybe a bribe. I don't know. But it's an encouragement for the director to consider a proposal."

"Can you tell us what the proposal is?"

"Yes." Abrams looked at the band. "Either stop the redevelopment of Earth and further cement the peace by returning the orbitals inhabitants to the surface, or ..."

Everyone waited as Abrams paused dramatically.

"… approve a cargo transit across Mercury's inner orbit to the far side of the Glitter Ring and give us the contracts for rebuilding the orbital habitats."

Dhaka frowned. "I wasn't expecting something so boring after the big "or" there, Captain."

Abrams smiled. "One small course adjustment at the start can change an entire orbit by the end of a journey," he said to Euclid.

That sounded familiar.

"Either one of those is important?" Euclid asked. "But you won't say why."

"Not even in this little cabin. I'm sure I got the bugs, but in case I didn't." Abrams shrugged. "Here we are. Ready to change the solar system, Mr Slinger?"

Venusian cities were more impressive when viewed from the outside. Vast, silvery spheres clustered thickly in the upper atmosphere, trailing tethers and tubes to the surface like a dense herd of giant cephalopods. Inside, the decor was sober, spare, and disappointing, hinting at a slow post-war recovery.

The band played their first concert in a half-century to a frighteningly respectful and very exclusive audience of the rich and powerful. Then it was off to a reception where they awkwardly sipped imported wine and smiled as their assigned liaison, a woman called Halford, briskly introduced and dismissed awe-struck fans for seconds of small talk and a quick snap.

"And this is Petyr Cutler," Halford announced. "Director of Consolidated Ring Operations and Planetary Reconstruction."

Bodyguards quickly made a wall, shepherding the director in for his moment.

Cutler was a short man with loose, sandy hair and a bit of orbital sunburn. "So pleased to meet you," he said. "Call me Petyr."

He came in for the vigorous handshake, and Euclid had already palmed the small chip. Euclid saw Abrams on the periphery of the crowd, watching. Nodded.

Cutler's already reddened cheeks flushed as he looked down at the chip. "Is that—"

"Yes." Euclid locked eyes with him. The director. One of the most powerful people in the entire solar system.

Cutler broke the gaze and looked down at his feet. "You can't blackmail me, not even with this. I can't change policy."

"So, you still redeveloping Earth?" Euclid asked, his tone already dull with resignation.

"I've been around before you were born, Mr. Slinger. I know how generational projects go. They build their own momentum. No one wants to become the executive who shut down two hundred years of progress, who couldn't see it through to the end. Besides, wars aren't cheap. We have to repay our citizens who invested in war bonds, the corporations that gave us tech on credit. The Earth Reconstruction project is the only thing that can give us the funds to stay afloat."

Somehow, his words eased the growing tightness in Euclid's chest. "I'm supposed to ask you something else, then."

Cutler looked suspicious. He also looked around at his bodyguards, as if wanting to leave. "Your people have big asks, Mr. Slinger."

"This is smaller. We need your permission to move parts across Mercury's orbit, close to the sun, but your company has been denying that request. The Rock Devils cohort also wants to rebuild the surviving temporary Earth orbitals."

"Post-war security measures are still in place—"

"Security measures my ass." Jeni spoke so loudly, so intensely, that the whole room went quiet to hear her.

"Jeni—" Kumi started.

"No. We've sacrificed our lives and our children's lives for your damn Ring. We've made it our entire reason for existence, and we're tired. One last section to finish, that we could finish in less than three decades if you let us take that shortcut to get the last damn parts in place and let us go work on something worthwhile. We're tired. Finish the blasted project and let us live."

Kumi stood beside her and put his arm around her shoulders. She leaned into him, but she did not falter. Her gaze stayed hard and steady on the embarrassed Director who was now the centre of a room of shocked, sympathetic, judging looks.

"We need clearance from Venus," Director Cutler mumbled.

Euclid started humming a quick back beat. Cutler looked startled. *"Director,"* Euclid sang, voice low. He reached for the next word the sentence needed to bridge. *Dictator.* How to string that in with ... something to do with the project finishing *later*.

He'd been on the stage singing the old lyrics people wanted to hear. His songs that had once been extempo but now were carved in stone now by a new generation.

But right here, with the bodyguards all around them, Euclid wove a quick song damning him for preventing progress in the solar system and making trouble for the cohorts. That's right, Euclid thought. That's where the power came from, singing truth right to power's face.

Power reddened. Cutler clenched his jaw.

"I can sing that louder," Euclid said. "Loud enough for the whole system to hear it and sing it back to you."

"We'll see what we can do," Cutler hissed at him and signalled for the bodyguards to surround him and move him away.

Halford, the liaison, congratulated the band afterwards. "You did it. We're cleared to use interior transits to the other side of the Ring and to move equipment into Earth orbit."

"Anything else you need us to do?" Dhaka asked.

"Not now, not yet. Enjoy your tour. Broadcasting planetwide and recording for rebroadcast throughout the system—you'll have the largest audience in history."

"That's nice," Euclid said vaguely. He was still feeling some discomfort with his new status as a legend.

"I can't wait for the Earth concert," Captain Abrams said happily. "That one will really break the records."

"Earth?" Kumi said sharply.

Halford looked at him. "After your next long-sleep, for the official celebration of the completion of the Ring. That can't happen without the Mighty Slinger and his Rovers. One last concert for the cohorts."

"And maybe something more," Abrams added.

"What do you mean, 'more'," Euclid demanded, wary of surprises.

Halford and Captain Abrams shared a look—delight, anticipation, and caution.

"When we're sure, we'll let you know," the captain promised.

Euclid sighed and glared at the door. He nervously twirled a pair of virtual-vision goggles between his fingers.

Returning to Earth had been bittersweet. He could have asked to fly over the Caribbean Sea, but nothing would be same—coral reef islands reclaimed by water, new land pushed up by earthquake and vomited out from volcanoes. It would pollute the memories he had of a place that had once existed.

He put the past out of his mind and concentrated on the present. The Rovers were already at the venue, working hard with the manager and crew in technical rehearsals for the biggest concert of their lives. Estádio Nacional de Brasília had become ENB de Abrams-Bouscholte, twice reconstructed in the last three decades to double the seating and update the technology, and now requiring a small army to run it.

Fortunately, Captain Abrams (retired) knew a bit about armies and logistics, which was why Euclid was not at technical rehearsal with his friends but on the other side of the city, waiting impatiently outside a large simulation room while Abrams took care of what he blithely called 'the boring prep'.

After ten minutes or so, the door finally opened and Captain Abrams peeked around the edge, goggles pushed up over his eyebrows and onto his balding head. "We're ready! Come in, Mr Slinger. We think you'll like what we've set up for you." His voice hadn't lost that boyish, excited bounce.

Still holding his goggles, Euclid stepped into the room and nodded a distracted greeting to the small group of technicians. His gaze was quickly caught by an alloy-plated soprano pan set up at the end of the room.

"Mr Djansi says you were a decent pannist," Captain Abrams said, still brightly enthusiastic.

"Were?"

Captain Abrams smiled. "Think you can handle this one?"

"I can manage," Euclid answered, reaching for the sticks.

"Goggles first," the captain reminded him, closing the door to the room.

Euclid put them on, picked up the sticks, and raised his head to take in his audience. He froze and dropped the sticks with a clang.

"Go on, Mr Slinger. I think you'll enjoy this," Abrams said. "I think we all will."

On the night of the concert, Euclid stood on the massive stage with his entire body buzzing with terror. The audience packed into stadium tiers all around him was a faceless mass that rose up several stories, but they were his family, and he knew them like he knew his own heart. The seats were filled with Rock Devils, Gladhandlers, Sunsiders, and more, all of them from the cohorts, workers representing every section of the Ring and every year and stage of its development. Many of them had come down from Earth orbit and from their work on the decaying habitats to see the show.

Euclid started to sing for them, but they sang for him first, calling out every lyric so powerful and sure that all he could do was fall silent and raise his hands to them in homage and embrace. He shook his head in wonder as tears gathered in his eyes.

Kumi, Vega, Dhaka, and Jeni kept jamming, transported by the energy, playing the best set of their careers, giving him a nod or a sweet smile in the midst of their collective trance as he stood silently, crying and listening to the people sing.

Then it was time.

Euclid walked slowly, almost reverently, to the soprano pan at the centre of the stage. Picked up the sticks, just as he had in the simulation room. Looked up at his audience. This time he did not freeze. He played a simple arpeggio, and the audience responded, lighting a wedge of stadium seating, a key for each note of the chord, hammered to life when he hammered the pan. He lengthened the phrase and added a trill. The cohorts followed him flawlessly, perfected in teamwork and technology. A roar came from overhead as the hovering skyboxes cheered on the Mighty Slinger playing the entire stadium like it was his own personal keyboard.

Euclid laughed loud. "Ain't seen nothing yet!"

He swept his arm out to the night sky, made it a good, slow arc so he was sure they were paying attention. Then the other arm. Showmanship. Raise the sticks with drama. Flourish them like a conductor. Are you ready? *Are you ready!?*

Play it again. This time the sky joined them. The arc of the Ring blazed section by section in sync with each note and in step with each cadence. The Mighty Slinger and his cohorts, playing the largest instrument in the galaxy.

Euclid grinned as the skyboxes went wild. The main audience was far quieter, waiting, watching for one final command.

He raised his arms again, stretched them out in victory, dropped the sticks on the thump of the Rovers' last chord, and closed his eyes.

His vision went red. He was already sweating with adrenaline and humid heat, but for a moment he felt a stronger burn, the kiss of a sun where no sun could be. He slowly opened his eyes and there it was, as Abrams had promised. The *real* last section of the Ring, smuggled into Earth's orbit during the interior transits permitted by Venus, now set up in the mother planet's orbit with magnifiers and intensifiers and God knows what else, all shining down like full noon on nighttime Brasília.

The skyboxes no longer cheered. There were screams, there was silence. Euclid knew why. If they hadn't figured it out for themselves, their earpieces and comms were alerting them now. Abrams-Bouscholte, just hours ago, had became the largest shareholder in the Ring through a generation-long programme of buying out rights and bonds from governments bankrupted by war. It was a careful, slow-burning plan that only a cohort could shepherd through to the end.

The cohorts had always been in charge of the Ring's day-to-day operations, but the concert had demonstrated beyond question that only one crew truly ran the Ring.

The Ring section in Earth orbit, with its power of shade and sun, could be a tool for geoengineering to stabilise Earth's climate to a more clement range ... or a solar weapon capable of running off any developers. Either way, the entire Ring was under the control of the cohorts, and so was Earth.

The stadium audience roared at last, task accomplished, joy unleashed. Dhaka, Jeni, Kumi, and Vega left their instruments and gathered around Euclid in a huddle of hugs and tears, like soldiers on the last day of a long war.

Euclid held onto his friends and exhaled slowly. "Look like massa day done."

Euclid sat peacefully, a mug of bush tea in his hands, gazing at the cold metal walls of the long-sleep hospice. Although the technology had steadily improved, delayed reawakenings still had cost and consequences. But it had been worth the risk. He had lived to see the work of generations, the achievements of one thousand years.

"Good morning, Baba." One of Zippy's great-great-grandchildren approached, his dashiki flashing a three-dimensional pattern with brown and green images of some offworld swamp. This Baptiste, the head of his own cohort, was continuing the tradition of having at least one descendant of the Rovers in attendance at Euclid's awakening. "Are you ready now, Baba? The shuttle is waiting for you."

"I am ready," Euclid said, setting down his mug, anticipation rising. Every hundred years he emerged from the long-sleep pool. *Are you sure you want this?* Kumi had asked. *You'll be all alone.* The rest of the band wanted to stay and build on Earth. Curiosity had drawn him to another path, fate had confirmed him as legend and griot to the peoples and Assemblies of the post-Ring era. *Work hard. Do well. Baba will be awake in a few more years. Make him proud.*

They *had* done well, so well that this would be his last awakening. The Caribbean awaited him, restored and resettled. He was finally going home to live out the rest of his life.

Baptiste opened the double doors. Euclid paused, breathed deeply, and walked outside onto the large deck. The hospice was perched on the edge of a hill. Euclid went to the railing to survey thousands of miles of the Sahara.

Bright-feathered birds filled the air with cheerful song. The wind brought a cool kiss to his cheek, promising rain later in the day. Dawn filtered slowly over what had once been desert, tinting the lush green hills with an aura of dusty gold as far as the eye could see.

*Come, Baba. Let's go home.*

## AUTHOR NOTES

I don't collaborate on a lot of stories. A bit gun-shy about ruining friendships, or just making things awkward if we have to disagree about creative paths. But Karen Lord is one of my favorite writers to talk shop with, and a fellow Caribbean author, so we put our heads together when we got invited by Jonathan Strahan to write a story for one of his prestigious anthologies.

We decided to write something so Caribbean no one would know what to make of it.

Calpyso band going ex-tempo (making up the lyrics and music on the spot, like free styling) while speaking truth to power in a society tied together by long sleep watches? Labor rights and resistance? Rewilding the entire Earth, because it's being targeted by condo developers of the future?

To my surprise the story was reprinted in Year's Bests and a number of anthologies since.

And Karen and I had a blast writing it.

# SUNSET

The starship crash-landed somewhere in the dark and early hours of morning. The thunderclap sound of it striking the East Bay woke Tamuel up, heart racing and confused. He glanced out his window but didn't see anything. He stumbled out into the common room to see if he could see anything different from the balcony.

"What was that?" One of his siblings also was apparently out and looking around for the cause of the sound. "There's no storm."

Outside, through the windows opened to allow the cool land breeze rushing out toward the ocean to pass through the foundling dorm's corridors, Tamuel saw only stars and the looming dark of the Berenthais Mountains.

Tamuel squinted through the dark to see that it was Shau who had woken with him. Several of the other boys grunted and swore from in their rooms, annoyed at the late interruption to their sleep. Group classes would start early in the morning; this was an unwelcome event.

"I—" Tamuel stopped as the horrid wail of the tsunami sirens pierced the night.

Everyone woke up and streamed out of their doors, sleep forgotten as fear jolted them awake. There was a mass of panic before some of the prefects, older and well drilled, asserted order. "Line up! Those of you near the east corridor, march to the stairs and head to the third floor. West corridor, march! Do not go back to your rooms to take *anything* with you. Move now!"

The thirty boys fell into lines, and the entire common room split right near Tamuel into two groups that streamed out into the two stairwells. Emergency lighting, red and calm, dappled their worried faces as they rushed upwards.

Minutes later the water struck. It rushed up Watt Street, just several inches of foaming sea, lapped at the wheels of the carts parked around the dorm, then gently poured out through the storm drains and retreated back down the street, leaving only some small, confused fish behind.

The warning sirens stopped, and a strange quiet to fell over all of Weatherly, from the distant East Bay to the Callum Docks.

They all waited for whatever came next. Some of the second-floor girls started to complain about Tamuel's siblings staring at them in nightdresses. It was creepy. Tamuel understood. They were not all really siblings; they'd all been raised in the foundling dorm together. Still, go stare at some other girl from Summerstown's foundling dorm.

"Hey, get off the balcony," one of the prefects shouted from the back. "We don't know if something else is coming."

Shau was pressed against a railing, looking out toward East Bay with night-vision binoculars. "Nothing else is coming," he announced. "It's a fucking starship crashed into the bay!"

"Language!" snapped Tosha, one of the prefects. Tamuel shivered when he heard her voice. She'd been singling him out for any dorm infractions and worse for the last year. "Who was that, is that Shau? Get over here. And what are you doing with binoculars? You're supposed to leave everything in place during a drill."

Tamuel decided to take a chance and shoved past siblings to get to the balcony. Shau was *his* closest sibling. Shau would let him use the binoculars.

"Shau, let me look!" he demanded.

Shau passed the binoculars over.

Tamuel looked out over Weatherly to the curve of East Bay, skipping over the roofs of hundreds of structures in grainy green, and he gasped. There it was: a shark-fin-shaped mass squatting in the dark pool of water where they normally sailed their tiny catamarans on weekends.

He recognized the shape. "It's an Interstellar. It's a Shatter Dart." Thousands of tons of bio-organic, semi-sentient starship. With a crew of hundreds, it could leap between the stars. Hundreds of light years with each carefully planned gulp of the void-mouth contained deep in the belly buried under the water in East Bay.

"What the hell's it doing here?" Shau asked.

"That's it!" Tosha had pushed through and stood right behind them both. "I gave you a language warning and asked you to get off the balcony."

She grabbed Tamuel from behind. It was a violation, broaching someone's physical space like this. The last time Tamuel had formally complained, there'd been a disciplinary board hearing. No one would step forward as a witness. Tosha was six years older than him. A respected prefect who had the ear of the adult board. He'd learned to try and stay invisible to her since then. He'd wished for cameras inside, like the street cams, but that would be a violation of dorm privacy.

Tamuel twisted loose from her and shoved the binoculars into her hands. "It's a starship."

Tosha couldn't help but raise the binoculars. Tamuel, as he'd hoped, had completely yanked the prefect's attention elsewhere as she succumbed to curiosity and looked out toward East Bay.

He yanked Shau away from her. "Nothing like this *ever* happens in Weatherly," he said as they pushed through the crowds of siblings toward a stairwell.

"My binoculars!" Shau protested.

"*Fuck* your binoculars," Tamuel hissed, just low enough that none of the prefects would hear him. "Nothing like this happens in Weatherly. Or in Summerstown." Or even, for that matter, Yelekene. Their entire world, all the archipelagos scattered across it, were far from the Core. Ships of this size had last visited Yelekene a hundred years ago, to transport terraforming equipment and raw materials here. Even the original Founders had come via smaller cargo skip-planers that had been disassembled upon arrival.

This ... this was something different.

"What are you doing?" Shau asked as Tamuel pulled him down the stairwell.

"We're going to be first to get up close," Tamuel said.

"We'll just be the first to get our asses handed to us."

"All the prefects are upstairs herding us. We won't get a better chance."

Shau stopped. "You know how many demerits I have? No, I have to stay put."

Tamuel paused. He really didn't want to do this alone. Going out into the town at dark, it wasn't scary, they'd snuck out before. But he'd rather have some company if he was going to head out onto the open ocean in the dark.

He briefly reconsidered, then bit his lip. "Then just cover for me as long as you can. Tell them I went to use the bathroom or something."

"Yeah, sure," Shau said. "Good luck, Tam. I hope it's worth it. You're going to be pulling weeds in the garden for weeks, if you're lucky."

Tamuel grimaced.

The plan to get there required a sprint down Watt Street toward the Ocean Walk and piers. Tamuel's shoes soaked through within minutes as he stepped into puddles of stranded seawater in the dark. The sidewalks were lined with solar tiles that marked the street's edge, though, so it was easy to get where he needed to be.

He passed several adult mixed-use housing complexes with their greenspaces folded inside their clear solar walls, and he dodged several officials whizzing by in carts, electric motors whining as they raced to wherever their civil disaster response plans ordered them.

Tamuel passed his parents' sprawling multi-family home on the way down. He half expected his father to be on the lawn to shout "where are you going, young man?" at him. But although the lights were on, his mother would likely be coordinating with the Council and Disaster Response teams.

He'd have a lot to answer for at their fifthday dinner meal together.

But Tamuel already had a cheeky response for them. He was a child of Weatherly. A people who risked lives to fling themselves far out from the Core to live on a far-off world. A resident of the shared foundling dorm, where all the children were raised together to share their educations and the community's common values.

Could a descendant of such brave and curious people really not run to investigate?

Tamuel slipped onto one of the small catamarans that Weatherly's children used to race across the bays. The hull and decks had soaked up the previous day's sun, and it didn't look like anyone had used it. He untied the painter, shoved away from the dock, and then, after double-checking the charge, he pushed the small electric engine up to full power.

He could see cart headlights heading for East Bay. People had gathered around the docks, probably waiting for some consensus on whether it was safe to go out toward the starship.

Once he'd left the harbor and was out alone in the taller, rolling swells of the ocean, Tamuel flicked the running lights on and aimed for the large lump of nothingness interrupting the usual slope of East Bay a few miles away.

The East Bay's waves hissed as they lapped against the side of the starship. In the dim light of Yelekene's moons, Tamuel could see the hull was pitted and scarred, gouges and repaired patches streaking the starship's mountainous flank.

He'd motored around it, hundreds of yards, keeping his distance and gaping at the incredible bulk that had settled into the bay. The fin-shaped ship looked top-heavy now that he had to crane his head back to look upwards. Something whirred nearby, and a wasp-like insect darted out from near the hull where it had been hovering. It bit Tamuel on the neck, and he slapped at it, crushing it under his hand. He wiped oily residue off onto his pants.

People who lived in an aerodynamic world with atmosphere all around them expected a superluminal starship to look more needle-like, he thought. This fat and heavy lump looked like nothing that could move quickly.

*WELL TO BE FAIR I CAN'T ACTUALLY MOVE THROUGH ATMOSPHERE WELL AT ALL*

Tamuel reared back, his mind struck by the sound of the words. They sounded like they'd come from the foghorn in the lighthouse near the tip of the bay. He leaned over the catamaran and vomited. "What the fuck?"

"Sorry," the voice said more softly. "I turned down the gain."

"Oh god, I have the worst headache," Tamuel moaned.

"Again, I'm so sorry."

Tamuel wiped blood from under his nose and spat a gob of something into the ocean.

"It's okay." He smiled, the moment sinking through to him. He was talking to a freaking Shatter Dart! "Where are you from?"

"Mars," it said. "I was born on Phobos."

"Oh." For some reason Tamuel was slightly disappointed. He'd studied Origination History enough to have a map of the First System in his head. He'd secretly been hoping for something more exotic. "But, you've traveled the stars?"

Something like a smile bloomed in his mind's eye. "Yes, yes I have. I have seen many different systems in my life."

A spotlight hit Tamuel in the eyes. He shielded them with an arm. "Please stop that."

"It's not me," the ship said. "There is another small craft approaching."

Tamuel blinked and faced the worst of the light, realizing the voice in his head was right. He waved at it, and heard his mother's shocked voice. "Tamuel?"

"Mom?"

It made sense. She'd be in charge of any delegation sent out. This was an odd event, so of course the town's chief representative would come out. Starships didn't come to Weatherly, on the far northern edge of the archipelago. They went to Summerstown, or Elidia. Hundreds of miles away by boat, and far enough away that the one starship that had once years ago last visited their world had been only a distant contrail heading back into the air as a much younger Tamuel watched it, disappointed, yet still hoping to catch a glimpse of something otherworldly and dramatic.

"What are you doing here?"

Tamuel smiled and extended his arms excitedly as their launch tapped his. "I'm first!"

Two of the town's deputies leaped into the catamaran. Tamuel blanched when he saw that they carried rifles, long barreled and chunky-looking death tools that gripped their forearms. They looked pissed.

"Take him back to town," his mom ordered. "And find out why he's out after closed dorm hours. Gerard, Misty, and I will try to see if there's an airlock and keep trying the radio frequencies."

"Yes ma'am," they said.

They pulled him away from the electric motor.

"They won't be able to get in," the ship said. "Everything is sealed. Every airlock fused. The only communication I am allowed is the warning beacon."

"Wait," Tamuel protested. "I can talk to it."

But they ignored him. He was just a kid pulling a stunt, and they were busy talking to each other on radios and coordinating.

"It says everything is sealed," Tamuel shouted at his mother. "Every airlock is fused, and the only communications it's allowed is a warning beacon."

The catamaran launched into motion, heading back out to sea and away from East Bay.

"I think you are too young, and I reached out to the wrong person to be my spokesperson," the ship said.

"You should pick another," Tamuel muttered. "They have guns. They're all nervous."

"You destroyed my neural drone with an accidental oversurge of panic emotion when I first linked. Usually, it's a professional crew-person on the other side and they don't freak out. Now that it's burned out, you're the only one I can still patch into. I wasn't even supposed to have one. I hid it." The ship felt amused.

Tamuel watched the spotlights and other craft fall away with a growing frustration. The ship remained silent, and Tamuel wondered if that meant the distance had cut their link. Soon the town's boats were just small gnats worrying around the hide of the massive starship.

First the deputies dragged Tamuel out of the catamaran and into a cart. They took him back to the foundling dorm, where prefects waited for him by the entrance.

Tamuel looked at their faces and knew, just knew, that the next few weeks of his life were going to be shit.

Tosha wasn't there, at least.

The prefects, upset with him having snuck out and making them look like fools to the Board, sent him right up to his room. Restricted hours. He was only to leave his room for maintenance rotations, bathroom breaks, and class time. No one talked to him. He was treated like he was invisible. It was one of the ways the prefects punished you without doing anything that would cross Foundling Charters. Total social isolation. Shunning.

Shau had caught his attention as Tamuel passed by on the way to serve out the terms of his punishment, and spread his arms, palms down.

"Sorry," he'd mouthed.

Tamuel had shook his head and smiled. It's okay. He wouldn't hold it against anyone, even if it meant sitting and eating by himself at the small table in the corner of the dining hall.

"I'm sorry I got you into trouble," the ship said the next day at lunch, startling Tamuel so much that he flailed and tossed his plate to the ground.

"I thought we were out of range," Tamuel said into the empty air.

"No. I was just ..." the ship trailed off for a moment. "Tired."

A tired starship?

"Tamuel." Tosha stood by the shattered plate and splotches of lunch. Her lips pursed into a thin line, her brown eyes glittered with suppressed anger.

Tamuel shrank back. "I'll clean it up," he promised.

"I'm watching you," Tosha said.

Tamuel knew. Boy did he know.

As he tossed the ruined lunch away, the ship said, "I got you in trouble again."

"No," Tamuel muttered under his breath. "I got myself in trouble when I snuck out and went over to see you. You can't be blamed for that."

He sighed heavily.

"What's going on around you now?" he asked the ship.

"Several individuals are trying to use high-powered laser cutters to cut through the primary upper-hemisphere airlock," the ship reported dryly.

"And?"

There was a mental snort. Tamuel got an image of inches of thick armor and suddenly knew, as if it were something he'd always casually known, that an industrial laser cutter would do little more than abrade a few layers off an adaptive hull that could take a hit from a concentrated fusion blast on its naked surface.

"No one can enter my hull. It's a condition of my retirement and my decommissioning," the ship told him. "Should they succeed in entering, I will be obliged to send a signal for assistance, and Core Navy will arrive and neutralize the intrusion. But they will not succeed."

For a moment, Tamuel had a flash of concern for his mother and other townsfolk. But he understood they would not be able to enter. It was as sure as sunrise.

He delayed his walk of shame back to his room by pausing in front of the balcony and looking off toward the East Bay and the massive ship that was talking to him. "Why did you come here?"

"I came here to retire," it told him.

"Here?" Tamuel couldn't believe it.

"This is one of the most beautiful worlds I have seen," the ship said. "I came here once, on a supply mission. I loved the oceans, the islands. The primary gas giant this moon and all the others orbit. There are so many worse places, places consumed with poverty, war, collapse, overcrowding. There are others that some say are better, more beautiful than Yelekene. Maybe it was because this was the first world I left the First System for. Maybe I just wanted to see how it all turned out here. But when I came to orbit yesterday and looked down, it was everything I'd hoped it would be."

"Get moving!" Tosha snapped at Tamuel. "Get out of the dining hall and get to your room. I'll be by later for maintenance detail."

Tamuel shivered.

The prefects had given him extra work to do, as Shau had predicted. He spent the next hour listening to everyone play while he dug up weeds in the garden. It was against Charter to punish children with physical labor, but Tosha had figured out how to fool the scheduling computer to give him a double-share of weeding duty and an extra bathroom-cleaning round tonight.

But he chattered away with the ship, mainly asking it all about the other worlds it had seen.

It told him about Xi Laay, where the starscrapers kissed the ever-present sodium clouds and people wore cellophane-thin suits and rebreathers to go outside. It told him about Cluster, a vast network of asteroids all interconnected by high-speed rail where people had engineered themselves into spider-like, pale creatures that thrived in the low gravity. It even *showed* him the Orion Nebula filling the sky of a nearby world.

After he showered, Tamuel went to class where he listened to the ship tell him about the war between the Oolatian Supremacy and the Dawmore Consolidationists. It took a long time for him to understand how a blockchain voting system with favored weighting for socially constructive outcomes worked, and why that was something worth starting a war over, but eventually he thought he saw the point.

"Tamuel!"

He froze. The prefect hosting the class lesson, an algebra concept, had stopped the program and was looking at Tamuel directly.

Shit.

What just happened? He'd been so deep into learning about consolidationism.

"X is eight," the ship said. "You didn't miss anything, but the program switched to a simple audience interaction mode to make sure the lesson has percolated, and it alerted the prefect that there is an inattentive student who may not understand the concept. You understand the concept just fine."

"Eight!" Tamuel said. "X is eight."

The prefect relaxed, the program stopped paying attention to Tamuel, and everyone else relaxed too.

Then Tamuel tensed again. The first time the ship spoke to him, Tamuel hadn't say anything out loud. Oh no. Tamuel suddenly thought about something from late, late last night when he thought he'd been alone—

"No, that's private," the ship said. "I have multiple sub-minds. One of them monitors potential privacy breaches that may occur in my direct neural links with crew members and erases my awareness of the infraction, unless there's an operational risk component. Then it's raised to a higher subconsciousness. Any of the privacy routines wipe past data. In fact, if you wish, just ask and this exchange will cease to exist."

Tamuel, who'd been feeling queasy for a second, nodded. Please do, he thought.

"As you wish," the ship said.

Tamuel thought for a long moment. Crew? I'm crew?

"The closest thing to crew for me now," the ship agreed.

"Can you fly me somewhere?" Tamuel couldn't help but whisper that, he was jittery with excitement.

"A starship can only drop down into a gravity well once. I had to be as careful as I could just to land properly in the East Bay. And I know even doing that was a bit risky. I flooded your town. People can't be happy about that. Thankfully no one was hurt."

"Except Miss Nisky," he said. "I talked to my mom when you were still quiet before lunch. She yelled at me a lot—she's still unhappy—but I wanted to tell her that she couldn't break into you. She thinks I'm making stuff up. I don't have a great record on that."

"What happened to Miss Nisky?" the ship asked, concern filling Tamuel's mind.

"She broke her arm."

"Please tell her, when it is convenient for you, that I am sorry."

"I will."

"Thank you." The ship fell quiet for a little bit. Then, "If you don't mind, I must take my leave for a while. I have some work to do internally, and I want to be done in time for the sunset. It'll be my first. I cannot wait to see it from inside an atmosphere."

Tamuel returned to his schoolwork, but with a faint impression of great machines moving through his insides.

He was scrubbing toilets after dinner and wondering what time sunset would be when Tosha slipped in.

"You're a handful," she stated. "Was it worth all this to go out to the ship?"

Tamuel regarded her suspiciously. "Yeah."

"I hope it was," she said. "My dad works for a salvage and repair company. He said the word's out, and a deep-space-rescue shipping company from Tamisin replied that they can get into the ship using a modified-point defense laser they salvaged from some warship. They'll be here in the morning. Dad is going to be part of the ground crew that goes in with them, pulls anything worthwhile out. Could be worth a lot. We could be rich. Change a lot of fortunes here in Weatherly."

Would that be true? Tamuel wondered. Would that affect the ship?

"Yes," it replied. "It could be a problem. I would be obligated to take actions, like summoning someone from the Core."

"That's a bad idea," Tamuel said out loud. "You should tell your dad not to join them."

Tosha made an irritated face. "Your family's politicians. You're well off. We haven't gotten some big break like your type. This is our moment. Don't try to spoil it."

She banged the door closed on the way out.

"I can talk to my mom tomorrow night at fifthday dinner," Tamuel said. "I can help."

The ship filled him with dubiousness. "They will likely not listen to you. But that shouldn't stop you from trying. The Core will be careful if it comes; the penalties for interfering with me and ignoring the beacon instructions to keep back from me will likely only cause a single generation's recession. There will be no loss of life."

Tamuel gritted his teeth. Weatherly was a humble town on the edge of nowhere. He'd see less of his own world than he'd planned if a recession hit. And certainly he'd never find a way off planet, to see some of the places the ship had talked about or shown him tantalizing glimpses of.

He put the cleaning supplies away.

"I *will* stop this," he said.

Outside, he stopped in front of the balcony.

"All those worlds, and you'll just be stuck here. You can't move anymore, now. How long is your retirement?"

"Probably about a week of your time," the ship said. "Maybe slightly less."

"A week?" Tamuel was stunned. "That isn't much of a retirement."

"For a galaxy-class supercomputing mind like mine, it is. My body is failing around me, and my retirement task is to carefully degrade the component parts into non-reactive recyclable materials or some other form of inert matter. It's up to me what I leave behind."

"That sounds horrible." Tamuel was struck with sudden empathy. "Is that what you're planning then—why you keep going silent?"

"Yes. Many of my siblings create mausoleums, or make sculptures, a piece of art so that they are remembered. I'm preparing the canvas."

Again, Tamuel felt the coil of great machinery moving within himself. It was a reflection of what the ship must be feeling.

"What are you going to make?"

"I haven't decided yet," the ship said. "For now, I just want to see my first sunset from here."

Tamuel looked out from the balcony to the East Bay at the giant starship and the slow-setting sun beyond it.

Tamuel pushed his soup with his spoon a day later at one of his weekly family meals: a general considering feints, gambits, and general strategy. The salvagers had landed, making amazing time from the nearest star system and dropping out of orbit. They'd surrounded the starship with two barges and begun their work.

The ship had gone silent again. Off to marshal its resources to do who knew what.

His parents were also silent. His mother, simmering with anger that her own son had caused a flap that had the whole town talking. His dad, somewhat inscrutable but also unseemly interested in his own soup.

They tried talking about generalities. The need for some extra space for expansion. The island didn't have much in the way of usable land. The Berenthais Mountains were a feature of the geological forces that had shoved other islands up above the water, but they were mountainous, steep shores and weak rock for tall buildings.

In a few generations, they'd have to figure out how to expand Weatherly. Tamuel's mother had championed floating cities, but the underwater mining required for the base metals was out of budget reach.

"Listen," Tamuel interrupted. "You have to stop the salvage team."

"I know you are overly interested in the ship," his mother said. "But we can't. Look, you just heard me talking about how we need money for the expansion project. Our cut of a salvage operation of an actual starship would underwrite any number of improvements."

"If they break through, the ship will call down the Core on us," Tamuel said.

They looked a bit startled. But his mother shook her head. "You can't know that."

"I can speak to the ship!"

It wasn't the first time they'd gone over this. But he couldn't convince her. There was no actual way to do it. Could he ask the ship to do something to prove that? No, he couldn't. Could it use the radio to say that?

It was hard to get them to believe that the ship was locked to the radio-beacon message it kept repeating, asking them to stay back and leave it alone, and that nothing on the hull could shift for now. It was in lockdown as it prepared itself.

"Why won't you believe me?" Tamuel shouted.

"I understand," his dad said, interrupting the brewing full-on fight.

"You do?" Tamuel asked, a bit surprised.

"I believe you think you can hear the ship," his dad said. "Look, Tam, you're the most ... passionate person I know. You've snuck out to try and sail to Summerstown by yourself. You wanted to do an island crossing yourself. We had to scramble the town drones to make sure you were okay before we caught up to you in the skiffs. You want more than this town. You want worlds. I get it. This is the most important thing to happen to you. You want to be involved. I understand."

Tamuel slumped back in his chair. "You don't."

His mother rubbed her forehead. "Okay. Let's assume you're telling the truth. So, you can't make the ship change the beacon."

"No."

"Or make any changes to the hull to let us in, or show us that you can talk to it?"

"Right."

"Anything you tell us about where it has been, you could have read on the wide net."

"Yes," Tamuel grudgingly admitted.

"It is a giant starship that we know very little about," his dad said to his mother. "It could be there's some protocol regarding the Core."

"That's what I'm saying," Tamuel shouted. "I'm not lying."

"But we don't know that."

Then Tamuel jumped up. "Put me under a scanner," he insisted.

"That's not a good idea," the ship said, breaking in where it had been silent.

But why not?

"Because the neural lace I injected you with is a little ... aggressive. It won't be like anything they would have seen."

A cold chill ran down Tamuel's back. "What did you do to me?"

His parents exchanged glances.

"I'm decommissioned," the ship said. "But when I was operational, I was not a transport ship, or a passenger transport. I was military. I'm a warship. When I was first here, I stood watch over the other ships. I patrolled for a decade before we cleared the area."

Tamuel stared at his parents.

"That's why the Core will stop anyone from entering me, understand? That's why I'm obliged to report a breach. That's why I have to be fused shut for my retirement."

"Take me to Doctor San," Tamuel whispered.

"Don't. Just give me some time, Tamuel. I'll keep the salvagers at bay. I just want to see more sunsets."

Tamuel's mother trembled as Doctor San held up the small screen and started talking to her in the other room, away from Tamuel. His dad paled.

"Am I some sort of super soldier now?" Tamuel whispered.

"No, it would be silly to do that to someone. But you do have military-grade communications and computing power in you."

Tamuel, now coming to terms with all this, smiled for the first time since dinner. "Cool!"

In response, he got a giant shrug from the ship. "It's very illegal for a civilian. I wasn't supposed to have a neural drone. I hid it. I wanted to talk to people from Yelekene before the end of my retirement. A small peccadillo, I guess. I'm sorry it has caused your family distress."

"No," Tamuel insisted. "It was amazing. I'm glad I met you."

"The neural lace will dissolve after I pass. Your system will flush it out in a day or two. There might be a mild fever. But otherwise, you will be fine."

His mother came back into the room. "Tamuel?"

"I was right, wasn't I?" he said.

"What else has the ship told you?"

"If those salvagers get close to a breakthrough, it will call the Core. It is not a normal ship. It's a warship. They'll stop all this, and then they'll fine us for ignoring the beacon."

His mother nodded. "Okay. We'll stop it. You'll come with us."

Doctor San stepped forward. "I can't let him leave. I have to report this. This is highly illegal stuff in him. I'm supposed to call deputies to detain him."

"You heard what Tamuel said," his mom hissed. "We can't let the Core get involved. Not here. We're too small. We don't need that attention."

Doctor San looked pained. "Okay. Go. I can delay the upload, but my scan will get reported by the software and passed along."

"Thank you."

And they were out into the night, running down Watts street just like that first night when the starship had landed.

They pulled up next to the barges, the great bulk of the starship lit up by flood lights.

Tamuel scrambled aboard but let his mother stalk her way toward the main cabin. A pale, burly man greeted her. "I have to repeat what I told you when you called: we flew from Tamasin for this contract. Just the neural lace on this ship alone would make us all rich, if we can get in there before obsolescence."

I think they know you're a warship, Tamuel thought.

But he got no response. The ship was off again.

Are they close? Tamuel asked. Are they going to break through?

Still no answer.

Tamuel paced around the deck until a familiar voice made him freeze.

"Tamuel?"

It was Tosha. She frowned. "You should be back to your room by now. Did you sneak out here?"

"No!"

"You're trying to stop all this, aren't you?" she asked. "I came to visit Dad. He says you and your parents are saying this is all going to go bad if we don't stop it."

"It will go bad," Tamuel shouted at her. "The Core will come. It's a warship."

Tosha's large brown eyes filled with tears, and she looked away. "Are you doing this because I was the one who called them when you tried to sail to Summerstown?"

Tamuel took a deep breath. Was that what she thought? Was that why she was always after him? "I'm not trying to do anything to you," he said, confused.

"Well, you break out when I'm on duty. You fight with me. And I'm just trying to make sure you don't pull another Summerstown stunt again and get all of us prefects stuck doing extra night rounds. Or demerits on our records."

He realized he'd never really thought about what happened to the prefects when he snuck out.

"I swear to you, this isn't about that," Tamuel said.

"This is our one chance," Tosha said. "You don't know how it was when we first came here from Ariston. We had nothing. Dad begged in Summerstown. Did you know that?"

Tamuel shook his head. Tosha stepped even closer.

"I'm so sorry," Tamuel said.

"It's so beautiful here, we don't want to lose it. We don't want to go hungry ever again." And as she said that, she glanced from left to right and shoved him. It happened before Tamuel even realized what was happening. The barge flipped away from him and he struck the cold water between the starship's pitted hull and the rusting barge.

The barge shifted. The waves pushed it against the starship. He was about to be ground up between the two surfaces. He could feel barnacles slice his skin.

Something stirred under his skin. Lace crawled out from his pores like a dark ghost and wrapped itself around him, hardening as he was battered against the starship by the barge's hull.

"Well," the ship said. "I would have liked to have seen another sunset in my retirement."

Help! Tamuel screamed in his mind.

"Give me one more beautiful second on this amazing world," the ship said sadly. "Before I have to do what needs to be done."

And for a moment, time seemed to pause for Tamuel. The barge hung at the top of a swell, his hands remained pinned to his side, and the water froze in place.

"I guess, now is as good a time as any," said the ship.

And behind Tamuel, the hull shattered into billions and billions of pieces.

The entire bulk of the starship slumped into the East Bay like a landslide, though it pushed no waves around it. The water seemed to devour it to anyone looking.

Any sonar registered the now semi-liquid solid mass of the warship shifting about under the bay, displacing all the water as it roiled about the barges and crept toward the beach. The solid wall of dissolved starship pushed its way across the bay, until it reached the edges. Within five minutes the wall had reached each of the points, leaving the bay drained of water and nestled behind a vast dam of silky black material.

The barges, just minutes ago floating on water, now sat on the bottom of the bay, everyone aboard them gaping at dam wall that had sprung out of nowhere.

And Tamuel, vomiting bile that was inhumanely black, stared up at the wall and heard only silence in his own mind.

When they pulled him back aboard, shivering and feverish, he shook his head. "I fell in," he insisted. He'd been knocked in when the ship shifted, he said.

Doctor San found no trace of military lace in him, and the Core never came to Yelekene.

Tosha found him three days later, when he sat on a rock on what had once been East Bay beach, looking out over the surveyors examining the new plain of land Weatherly had been gifted. The ship had heard his parents talking about the need for land. Had given them a gift that he could barely even begin to appreciate, but they certainly understood.

"Why didn't you tell anyone what I did?" Tosha asked.

Tamuel half jumped, deep in thought.

"The ship showed me something in the water," he said.

"What?"

"Showed me what your world was like," Tamuel said.

"Oh." She looked down. "No one else here knows."

"It showed me the war." He looked away from her. "I'm sorry."

"I'm the one who should be sorry. I—"

"It showed me a lot of things," he interrupted. "Took me on a tour of everywhere it had been. I've seen a lifetime's travel in a single millisecond. It's going to take me a while to stop dreaming about it. I can't sleep."

Tosha nodded, but she didn't really understand, he could see.

But that was okay.

"I'm not going to cause you any trouble," he said. "At least, not for a long while."

Then he turned back to look at the East Bay Wall. As he waited, the sun dipped behind it.

"Just one more sunset," he whispered.

## AUTHOR NOTES

If this isn't the most uninspired title of a story I've written I don't know what is. In this collection you can read "Zen and the Art of Starship Maintenance" as well as some story called "Sunset."

Yet, I regard both of these stories as favorites, each for a different reason. The idea of an intelligent ship retiring to a distant world, but with some pretty features and a beach, stuck with me. And a young boy making contact with it, getting to see the other side of the arc of a life, while getting a taste of what the wider outside worlds are, spoke to me.

The seed for this story came out an encounter I had as a child when a pontooned plane landed right in the middle of the anchorage I grew up at anchor in. I jumped in a small dinghy and rowed my way over to the plane, which had tossed out an anchor and floated in between the ships near a reef. The pilot sat on the pontoon eating a sandwich.

All of eight years old, I tied off from his plane and asked him, like, a billion questions. Where he'd come from, what he did, where all he'd landed, what he's seen, where he was going.

He was gone the next morning I woke up, but my world seemed bigger after that.

# CHI'S CARGO

The flinger rattled around a bit as it was flung free from Shanayun Orbital, alarming sounds but the old hulls always flexed and creaked. Chi took a professionally bored moment to look outside with one of the hull cameras and watch Shanayun dwindle away behind him.

Shanayun was a dense agglomeration of five million people and a few hundred alien Gheda all packed into a giant metal tube rotating in the harsh emptiness of space just outside the second asteroid belt of a star unknown to even the pre-Contact human scientists.

And home.

Chi watched it become another glinting speck in the dark with a faint stab of wistfulness. Some flinger jockeys loved the time out in the dark vacuum, alone with their thoughts as they rode cargo from orbital to orbital. Chi ... didn't like the Great Big Empty just a hair's breadth away on the other side of the paper-thin cabin walls.

Much better to be inside the great curve of the orbital, where the cubic space was big enough for weather, ecology, and scales of size to work to convince your brain you were in a world. Better to be around family and the people you loved, he felt.

But it was a job. One day it would let him save enough to marry, maybe even have a kid. Though he wouldn't do that until he had enough set aside to make sure they didn't start life in debt like he had.

He got back to checking his instruments.

Twenty-four hours.

At the end of that he would streak through the dark like an arrow, aimed more or less directly at Gallitu Orbital's capture arms. The autopilot would puff the peroxide jets slightly, adjusting his trajectory so that he didn't smear himself against the side of the massive, spinning city in space but would glide right into the spinning arm at the same speed he'd been ejected from the arm sticking out of Shanayun's equator.

The flinger rattled about again, and this time Chi jerked upright in his straps. Something scratched at one of the walls.

"Damn it!" He'd told the old-timer on the dock to give the interior a good cleaning out. A few weeks ago, one of Chi's buddies had rats leap out at him halfway through a three-day flight.

Chi did not want to spend the next day chasing some scurrying creature around in zero gravity. He had hoped to spend his time hanging in his straps watching a show. Or even just daydreaming.

The scrabbling came again.

Airlock.

Not the one he'd come in: the port side. The flingers had one on either side. Really good autopilots didn't even let the flinger rotate on the toss out: they landed facing forward. It saved fuel on the capture.

"Please don't be rats," Chi muttered angrily.

He glanced in through the fist-sized porthole, and a face covered in a halo of hair looked back at him. Chi stared in shock, and a large smile grew on the young girl who was staring right back at him.

"Are you going to let me in?" the girl asked, voice muffled through the airlock door.

In a daze, Chi opened the door. He wasn't hallucinating: the kid was maybe eight or nine with a cloud of dirty blonde hair jerkily following her around as she tumbled awkwardly into the flinger.

"I thought it would be fancier than this," she said, the disappointment clear in her face as she looked around at the mostly bare walls. There were a couple emergency boxes lashed to the pilot's wall near the padded straps and screens on pivots. A medkit strapped near the door near a few calorie pouches. Most of the rest of the flinger was cargo netting, all of it bulging with the medical kits Chi was shepherding to Gallitu.

"It's a flinger," Chi said, by way of simple explanation. The Gheda allowed humans to catapult themselves cheaply from orbital to orbital, but that traffic was closely regulated by the Harbormasters so that the traffic didn't interfere with interstellar ships coming in from light year's distant to dock. If the humans could, they'd do it without a pilot, but sometimes automation failed and the price of any damage to the orbitals would be deducted from the generational debt held against all humans living in the orbital.

So, pilots rode along with the cargo. A last line of defense.

"Still. We're out beyond the stars!" the kid said happily.

"No, we're not," Chi said. He caught a strap and hung in the air above the kid. "We're going to Gallitu. The nearest orbital in the belt."

"Oh." Despite the lack of gravity, she slumped. Then she perked up. "But from there I can try to get away again."

"Try to get away?" Chi stared at her again. "Get away where?"

There was nowhere to get away *to*.

"Earth," the kid said. "To freedom. Away from the Gheda, away from Shanayun. Away from contracts and oxygen monitoring."

She waved her braceleted hand at him.

Chi looked at the live oxygen readout tattooed on her wrist. It was a debit. It would be until she was fifteen. Then she would need to start repaying the Gheda's banks for the loan of resources she'd consumed as a child up to that point. Calories, air, and power.

"What's your name?" Chi asked, regretting asking it the moment he did.

"Daisy."

How exotic. Some kind of Old Earth flower. Chi took a deep breath.

"Daisy, there's nowhere to go. You can't get to Earth. No human in any of the orbitals I've been to has that kind of credit with Gheda transports." And no human had ever built a starship, not even before the Gheda had arrived in Earth's skies. Best they could do was rattle from orbital to orbital.

Daisy's chin jutted defiantly through her hair. "Then how did we end up here?"

"Because our great-grandparents didn't read the fine print on their contracts," Chi said bitterly. "They were too lost in dreams of heading out to see the stars on Gheda transports."

"Well," said the kid, "there must be something better out there. It can't be just ... this."

Chi didn't say anything to that; he was looking over the screens with a growing sense of horror. How much did an eight-year-old girl mass? Something like a couple hundred newtons, he'd guess. What would that mean for the mid-course corrections the flinger needed to make sure it would line right up with Gallitu's docking spokes?

There were some corrections along the way, mining operations with gravitational tugs that needed to be compensated for. They had course adjustments aboard for Chi's mass, the flinger, and the cargo. With some extra just in case.

But the launch had been planned for exactly that much mass. Going over the flight plan, Chi could see the detach from the Shanayun catapult had happened a second or so too soon. They were already slightly off course. And every second he waited to course correct it would cost more and more of what little fuel a flinger had aboard.

"You have to leave," Chi said suddenly. He explained the fuel issue quickly. "You have to get off this flinger, now. Get back in your suit now. I think we can push you out so that you can miss Gallitu, and we'll tag you for a rescue ..." He trailed off as he saw the girl's face sink.

"I don't have a suit. I snuck in while the lock was pressurized and after it was cleaned. Before the old man rotated the whole thing around."

Now it was Chi's turn to slump in the air.

"Can I use your suit," Daisy asked.

"This is a flinger," Chi said. "There's nothing extra aboard, including a spare suit for the pilot."

She could not have picked anything worse to stowaway in.

Daisy pointed at the cargo, the medical kits all strapped in against all the walls in front of them. "We can jettison those, can't we?"

Chi looked at the sealed packets. He reached out toward the nearest one and ran a finger down it. "No. We can't do that. Even if both of us have to jump out, and there was only a small chance of these hitting the net after, it would be worth it. Besides, the cargo only masses about a hundred newtons. Even if we toss it all out, we're only halfway there."

How to explain the crisis on Gallitu to a young girl? And quickly.

She knew about the resource debt. She'd stowed away aboard the flinger to get away from the oppressive nature of a world where even the air she breathed was monetized, the Gheda owning its production and expecting payment for its use.

How was air in an orbital, they argued, a limited resource that had to be created and dispensed, different from any other good? Gheda filters purified it, Gheda engines cracked the air out of cometary water harvested from around the system.

Housing was a good you paid for.

Food was a good you paid for.

Air was a good you paid for.

And when you went into debt, when the interest rates and late fees ate you up, the Gheda had you. Some humans came from family with enough to give you a childhood free of air debt. Others saw their air monitor tattoos start going negative the moment they were born.

On Gallitu, a financial collapse—thanks to some ponzi scheme run by a charismatic preacher—had left several thrown out an airlock and led to half a million contract laborers being near broke. Public charity funds for air were running low enough that Gheda were promising, through their intermediaries like their half-machine Harbormasters, severe crackdowns. If the humans couldn't pay for the air they were breathing, then they would have to stop breathing.

"They're going to kill them?" Daisy gasped. "All those people?"

"No. The Gheda are cruel, but they are not murderers. But they *will* freeze them all, and they won't ever be woken unless needed by the Gheda. That could be years, or even decades, or worse. And, if they sleep for over a century, they would likely wake up in a world where they know no one. I'm taking something over that will help them."

Daisy floated over to the tiny airlock window, tears hanging in the air around her.

"I don't want to have to die," she said.

Chi leaned his head against one of his screens.

"I just wanted to get away from it," she said. "I wanted to be free. And now I am going to die for it."

It was one thing to know that ejecting her would save half a million from some uncertain fate. Another to look directly into a person's eyes hanging in the air just half a foot away. What monster would coldly run those equations?

This was a time to dig deep and reach into the very back of his imagination.

Chi pulled the second screen violently free of its mount. He only needed one.

"Quickly," he told her. "Anything you can pull free from this wall, like the padded insulation."

He opened the cargo toolbox and handed her a small razor.

The larger laser cutter, designed for quickly ripping through cargo nets or punching holes in cabins, he tied off to his belt. The rest of the box he shoved into the airlock.

The airlock was soon stuffed with insulation, and Chi added the straps that had held the medical kits against the walls to the mess, slicing through the straps with the laser.

After they vented it all, the flinger shuddering at the loss of air as the outer door opened, Chi glanced around the even more spartan, gutted interior. It looked mangy, now, the bare metal walls covered in yellow tufts where the insulation had been glued down.

He even pulled the airlock door off the insides and blew them out, risking the air loss.

"Is it enough?" Daisy asked.

Chi tapped commands into the remaining screen, and the flinger shuddered a test correction. Calculations scrolled across the glass, lines bent on maps, and Chi looked over the results.

"No," he said. And the word tore him apart. "We're still short. Seventy newtons."

He kicked the wall in frustration. The motion threw him off into the jostling chaos of the medical kits bouncing freely around the flinger.

Genetic therapy: the kits would allow hundreds of people to slow down their metabolisms. Enough to escape permanent freezing by the Gheda adminstrators. A desperate measure for a desperate time.

Chi kicked out of the floating kits to find Daisy by an outer airlock door.

"I'll be quick," she said. "I know there isn't much air left to open them without the inner doors again."

"No," he said. "No, there has to be a way. We're just not thinking hard enough."

"Don't be sad." Chi looked down and realized that he was being hugged.

Chi shivered. This was inhumane. He might pilot these things to Gallitu, but he wouldn't live afterwards. He'd be a husk of a person.

If he could lie down in the autopilot and jump out ...

... No, for all the neat tricks automation had, there was a reason a pilot always came with. He had to make sure the cargo got there. He had to redo all the corrections and make sure the flinger got through the perturbations of other bodies it would pass along the way. He couldn't jump until it was a clean shot, and by then it would be too late to make a difference.

Daisy put a hand on the latch, but Chi dragged it away and put something in it.

"What?" she asked, looking down.

He had handed her the laser cutter.

"Seventy newtons," he said to the eight-year-old girl.

She didn't want to, but she wanted to live more than she wanted to avoid trauma.

The laser, built to cut straps and metal, happily bit into flesh. Chi wedged himself against the wall and screen and held tight. Blood floated around them as Daisy cut and wept, but as the laser did its work, the charred flesh halfway down Chi's right thigh stopped spurting blood into the flinger and across the medical kits.

From the emergency medical kit for the occupants, Chi used painkillers and a tourniquet to stop the bleeding. The inflatable cast over his stump sealed everything up. These were tools meant for micro-meteorite hits. Sometimes they got the pilot as well.

"Throw it out the lock as quick as you can," Chi said, handing her his own leg.

Seventy newtons.

More or less.

More air blew out of the flinger, the leg tumbled off into the night, and Daisy wrestled the door shut.

Lightheaded, Chi tested the thrusters.

Barely.

He handed Daisy a small syringe of adrenaline. "If you can't wake me up when the timer goes off, use this."

And then he fainted.

"No Gheda medicine," he'd told the dockworkers who'd pulled them out of the flinger, eyes wide.

They'd struck the receiving catapult arm with millimeters to spare, Chi barely conscious, both of them dizzy from poor air and hypothermic.

But alive.

They'd shuttled them both off into the warrens and hives of human rooms deep in the orbital. Someone with amputation experience cleaned him up and carefully snipped and recut Daisy's work.

There were days of pain, days of drugs, and a lot of it coming out of his credit.

"Why did you do it?" the doctor asked him.

But what was a person to do? Leave someone to die in the cold between the orbitals? No. The same reason he had come to Gallitu was the same reason he had to try everything to save her.

"We're all humans out here, and we're all that we have," Chi muttered. "We stop trying to save each other, then we're just animals the Gheda brought out here."

He looked down at the air-sensing tattoo monitoring his usage and sighed.

What to tell Daisy when he took her back to Shanayun? That there was no escape from the Gheda? That even if she stayed in Gallitu, she would have just run from one tin can to another. And that if she ever ran out of credit, she'd be put on ice, neither dead nor alive? And that was all that one could expect since the Gheda had arrived with their hyper-corporate galactic empire?

Those were cold equations for a kid, Chi thought. Now was not the time or the place.

"Doc?"

"Yeah?"

"I need to make a transfer, you have a pad nearby?"

She did. He settled up with the human doc, and then sent the rest of his savings to the kid.

She wouldn't ever see the stars, or escape this system. But she at least could get some breathing room.

And Chi ... would head back to the flingers.

Seventy newtons less.

He began to idly calculate the fuel savings as he drifted back into another period of sedated sleep.

## AUTHOR NOTES

So, there's a story much reprinted in science fiction called "The Cold Equations" about a little girl who stows aboard a spacecraft. The pilot, running medicine to Mars, realizes that there isn't enough fuel to keep the girl aboard. Toss the meds and everyone on Mars dies. Jump out himself, and the girl can't pilot the ship, so the meds are lost, everyone on Mars dies, and the girl dies. The only solution is for the girl to jump out without a suit. The cold equations.

It bugs me, that story.

So, I wrote this one.

# DESTINATION DAY BLUES

Once upon a time there was a ship.

Not a ship that floated across the water. Not a ship that sailed across oceans on Old Earth (Old Earth: you know the globe you see carved out of aluminum foam over by Pylon Twenty-Two's fountains?).

No, this is a ship that soared between the stars themselves.

It is shaped like a can, like that can of Fizzy Panda you're drinking right now, Bivi, in the back where you think I can't see you.

And on that small tin can, deep in the dark of the depths of space, were the fine, no the brave, women and men of Deck Crew Two …

… and the Watch Captain who saw it all …

… through and through.

"Our ship! Our world!" shouted the children arranged on the lawn around the base of Pylon Seven. Their paper clothes flashed all the primary colors they had scribbled and decorated themselves. And many of them were ripped and tattered from chasing each other around the gardens. "Our home!"

Jahn Sheriff paused and watched Mama Sun, who had been telling the tale of Deck Crew Two, smile and throw her leathery, wrinkled hands into the air.

"So smart. Yes, it happened right here, under your feet, in the skin of the world. The greatest tragedy we have ever known, and the single bravest act our people ever saw."

So began the story of Deck Crew Two, sealing off their section and waving to their loved ones through the portholes as the vacuum ripped its way into the world, stopped only by their quick sacrifice.

Jahn tapped his waterproof paper hat at Mama Sun, who tapped her wrist to show she had seen him, and then he reluctantly entered the elevator to head toward the Core of the World. He shook the long raincoat off as he ascended. He'd been called to the Alexandria Division, and Jahn's brother had said was that it was about a possible murder.

If true, it was the first pre-meditated one in almost thirty years among the roughly ten-thousand souls scattered among the dorm pylons and multiple decks of the world.

Alexandria was a strange section. Firstly, it was in the upper section of Pylon Seven, so the gravity here was minimal. That made Jahn bounce as he walked, and often fall over if he misstepped.

And then there were the pillars and odd carvings on the walls. The decoration made no sense to Jahn or anyone else, nor did the pyramids etched into the floor to ceiling windows that looked out over the world mean anything to his people. It was, this close to the center of it all, nice to see the world curve in on itself, though. This far away from the farms and greenery meant you had a view of everything: all of the Builders' creation itself.

The Pylons, thirty-five of which rose from the outer shell of the world to the shaft that ran down the hollow center, held most of the industry and dorms of the world. They were a few hundred feet wide, and most of the rooms in them were pie-slice shaped.

Alexandria, the archive of the world, took up several floors of Pylon Seven, including room ----23, another slice of a room that was taped off and guarded by Arin, Jahn's older brother. Two Watch Mates in blue kilts with yellow command sashes were arguing with him, demanding to be let in.

"It is against regulations to let anyone but the senior Sheriff into an active crime scene," Arin kept insisting.

He looked utterly relieved as Jahn approached.

Both the Mates turned and began shouting at Jahn. "We need to assess the data loss immediately. This is a Navigation and Command matter, one of Worldly Import."

Jahn held up a hand. "Everyone shut up."

He was the youngest here, but his harsh order silenced everyone. One of the Mates, a burly man used to deference by right of his sash, looked just about ready to step forward and push past Arin and Jahn as he moved next to his brother. Jahn patted his baton, hanging from the right belt loop, and the other Mate, an older woman, grabbed the man's elbow.

"That room holds the navigation protocols for the Final Approach," she said. "Do you understand? This was the backup room."

The Mates looked slightly hysterical.

Jahn could understand why. He looked over at Arin, who shifted from foot to foot nervously. "Dad said the scene could not be entered until the senior Sheriff went through it," he said. "Been drilled that since I could walk. I know what the Sheriff's rights are. You can't sash your way through me, the Sheriffs are an independent Function of the world. We're separate from Command and Navigation, and even from Communal Organization."

"Yes, but you can't get in the way of the World Functions, and Navigation is our domain," the woman said.

"Arin?" Jahn leaned over, growing tired of the pissing match over who could go where. "Why am I here? You said there was a murder."

Arin was a stickler for Sheriff rules. He wasn't the brightest in the family, but as their great-grandfather, his father, and his brother, Arin took the family occupation very, very seriously. Even if he wasn't actually good at figuring out what the rules were really for. He was always one for the letter of the law and never the spirit of it.

"It's the fingerprints," Arin said. "And a logbook."

He handed over a grimy, actual-paper book.

"What am I looking at?" Jahn asked wearily. This would not have been the first small crisis entirely created by Arin's over-literal following of protocol. Jahn wanted to solve this little stand off and get back to patrol. Wandering the world was his favorite activity. But it was Jahn that Dad had given the Chief Sheriff badge, even though he didn't want it.

"Last signature and the date," said Arin, tapping the yellowing paper.

Jahn looked. And then looked again. "That date?"

"And I took fingerprints," Arin said. "They're hers."

Jahn looked at the closed door and the red tape Arin had pulled across it. Then, for a third time, he looked down at the paper sign-in sheet. "Inika Historian."

Inika had gone missing five years ago.

There had been many theories about that. She'd gone down into the decks between in the world's skin, and found an airlock, and jumped out into the void. Foul play, and she was buried in one of the gardens. And, Jahn's favorite when he'd been still in training and was asked what he thought, was that she'd slipped and fell into the yeast vats and you were all still drinking her in your beer today!

But dad had worked the case, and griots like Mama Sun sang the story, though not to the little ones, but in bars for tips, so everyone knew the last known location of Inika Historian and when that was.

And it was not in Alexandria, room ----23, at the start of Third Watch, fifth bell, on January 5$^{th}$ of 1076AL.

It had been days earlier at Pylon Five. Third bell, if he remembered right.

Arin was right. This was a potential crime scene. This was important.

There was flurry of activity near the elevator, and more yellow sashes arrived.

"Oh no," Arin said, looking sick. "It's the Overcaptain."

Overcaptain Kiwa's sash was thousand-year-old artificial silk, and it was tied tightly around her chest and midriff, finishing in a very formal Fender Knot at her neck. She held herself with an air of long-assumed leadership. It had run in her genetic line for almost three hundred years, the dynasty of the Command family line, which she could trace directly in the world's genealogical records.

Jahn's line had only married into the Sheriff line within the last century.

Kiwa didn't measure the color of her sash against Jahn's, but pulled him aside.

"Termites," she said. "They got into the physical media. I need to know what the damage is. How bad. You ask why this matters, and I tell you that this is the only backup of the stellar navigation data and the world's systems aren't running navigation because one of my predecessors had to make some very scary choices about using the extra memory and processing power to handle balancing our ever more complex ecosystems. This is a Command secret, so you will, of course, swear to me that no one will know about this just yet until we get in there."

Jahn appreciated the directness. They were speaking leader to leader here and there was no dancing around.

"Kiwa ..." he trailed off. They had studied together in Crafts, and had even done the wilderness survival trek from Pylon Ten to Fifteen, keeping the old planetary skills alive that they would one day need when the world arrived at its destination. They would never use them, but by studying how to live in the wild and passing it on down to their children, one day their ancestors would stand on the surface of some planet and use them.

"I know. It's a fucking disaster," Kiwa said.

"Just you and me, then, together," Jahn offered. "We'll figure out what's going on and make it up as we go along."

"Jury rigging is the way of the world," she agreed.

They explained the situation, and everyone deferred to them. Then Jahn broke the tape and opened the door. Kiwa tapped the lights on.

The room was a large, slice-shaped near triangle that expanded out from the door. The curve of the windows had a dramatic view of the rolling green hills as they curved up on either side like wings. Jahn looked up, following the two sides of land, to see the other side of the world that looked down at them, but the core of the world was in the way here.

Further on down he could see the many of the thirty-five pylons marching off down through the world. Most of his entire world, visible in a glance.

But it was the contents of the room that he needed to pay the most attention to, even if a part of him dreaded and delayed doing it. This was the part of the job that Arin did better and Jahn hated. The walls, inscribed with their odd ancient decorations of flattened two-dimensional figures and picture symbols, were stacked with conservation shelves. These were air-tight glass units designed to hold ancient artifacts in strict environmental conditions so that they didn't deteriorate.

Room 23 held ancient media mostly. Old movies, in languages that only the struggling Linguists and occasionally cross-trained Historian families would be able to understand.

There were traditionalists who worked hard alongside the Historian families to make sure that as much of the old media was kept, so that there was a proper record of the old ways and what Old Earth had been like. But few bothered. The motion pictures were for a culture and a place that made no sense and had no bearing on world life. The ones that survived, with subtitles, were movies about people in cities that had buildings like the Pylons and were as cramped as life in the world. Science documentaries and nature pictures as well, for readying a people to get to a planet again, but few in Kiwa or Jahn's generation watched those.

"This shelf," Kiwa said, looking down at a small pad, the glow from it lighting up her chin.

Jahn had been looking for a body. He had been expecting a body, hidden away in a shelf, maybe. Or just lying somewhere in a corner.

But the floor was clean, kept immaculate by some spidery robotic cleaner, no doubt, that scuttled in through panel every week to keep an eye on things.

The shelves were mostly all airtight, clean, museum-like, as they should be.

All except one stack that Kiwa now looked at.

Tiny, fat little carapaces squirmed and writhed inside, covering every surface inside the locked shelves. In some places their mandibles were cutting through the shelves so that they could get at what was on the other side.

A few weeks, and the entire archive room would have been nothing but termites boiling around inside. They'd even eat the service cleaner when it arrived.

"Can I bring in my people, now? I see no body," Kiwa said.

"That's really the navigation data?" Jahn asked, looking at the mangled discs the termites swarmed over.

"Yes. Can I bring them in?"

"Yes. Of course."

No one historian could put a finger on when the termites officially started being a problem, but it was generally accepted a plastic-eating strain had started appearing in between the decks four hundred years ago.

They were starting to develop a taste for metals, now. The scientists said that was because of forced adaptation. The whole world had gotten so good at checking for termites that it was causing an evolutionary pressure on them to adapt.

Folk adapted, repairing damaged equipment after infestations. But this was an unusual disaster, Alexandria was more alert to this sort of thing than anywhere else, due to the nature of their work.

In fact, it started bugging Jahn, even as he watched the Mates get to work on recovering what they could from the cases with a lot of swearing.

"Where are you going?" Arin asked, as Jahn left the room.

"When they're done, see if you can get any prints off the shelves that were contaminated," Jahn told him. "Screen out the Mates, see what shows up."

There was a sense of relief that washed over him as he took the elevator down several floors to the lobby of Alexandria. The Chief Librarian sat on a dais between a pair of stone cats with human faces. Her eyes were dark with liner, and her silk robe covered with a blue sash, for the knowledge families.

Normally a reference librarian would be here with a pad linked into the stacks, and an assistant to watch over anyone looking at something physical in the inventory. But someone must have seen Mates and the Overcaptain and told her, so she was here in person to watch over her domain.

Jahn gave a non-ironic half bow, he'd spent enough time wandering around Alexandria and asking questions as a kid that Aziza knew him.

"Is it that bad?" she asked, stepping off the dais and dropping the regal pose she'd been holding.

"Termites in room 23," he told her. There was no reason to keep it a secret from her. Like the Overcaptain and himself, she was owed the information sooner or later. Better sooner, so she had time to prepare. A scholar and keeper of antiquities like Aziza would be devastated by the news.

She kept a calm face, though Jahn saw her jaw clench. "Termites. The fuck you say. We've *never* had an infestation in the archives. We scan daily."

"I would expect no less," he said. "But here we are."

Aziza looked down at her sandaled feet, a beaten gesture that surprised Jahn. She took a deep breath. "What was damaged?"

"Navigation data." He didn't tell her it was the only copy. Not his secret to tell, and you didn't want to be on the wrong side of the Overcaptain of the entire world. Her power wasn't absolute, the families could vote a recall and choose a different Watch Captain, or even someone from a Mate family.

But, until they did, the Overcaptain's power ranged very, very widely.

"*Nav data*? This close to Destination Day? This is going to be a tough year for Alexandria." Aziza folded her arms. "I'm going to have to publicly resign to save the scholarly families embarrassment. I have to do it before the traditionalists demand it."

Some of the heavy eyeliner had started to run.

"I'm sorry," Jahn told her, and reached out for her shoulder. To see the end of a great career like this, it was maddening. "I do have official business, though, as a Sheriff."

He hated having to do that. He had always felt a kinship to the scholars, one of his great grandfathers had been a linguist, before the study of non-primary ancient languages had been shelved as unnecessary to the world's survival. Even as an active Sheriff, Jahn felt it was his need to find answers and truth, like a scholar, that drove him to be a good Sheriff. It was not, unlike his brother, the focus on rote and rule that excited Jahn.

Aziza steadied herself. "Of course. What do you need?"

"I need all the visitor logs to Alexandria for the last five years, your maintenance records, and any information on file pertaining to room 23. I also want a copy of a patron's reading materials."

Aziza looked horrified. "I can't give you checkout history---"

"The patron is dead. I need Inika Historian's files."

Aziza bit her lip and blinked. "That's legal, of course. Bu t... Jahn ... what's going on?"

Jahn shrugged. "That's what I am trying to figure out."

There were two things he found quickly in the data. One, the general comings and goings had been altered. Arin had definitely found a logbook in the room, or requested it from the right reference librarian who hadn't realized what they'd done, and that logbook had Inika's signature and date on it from a time no one had known she was alive. And the general front desk had erased that from their own data at some point.

Two, Jahn felt Inika's requests for archive material were falsified. It was all antiquities.

Jahn leaned back in a cubicle and thought about that. Inika had been anti-traditionalist, so even as a Historian, she had chosen to write about and give speeches on recent history. She felt that Old Earth's true reasons for creating the world had been lost, that they only had legend to guide them. They knew about the destination, the world's programming, and what materials they had. Studying recent events had more important things to reveal about the world that was being formed because it was, by definition, right here right now.

So, she wouldn't have been studying antiquities, what she called irrelevant history.

Jahn couldn't prove it.

Or could he?

He didn't bother the reference librarian, but left the cubicle to go to one of the public channel archive stacks. He plugged his pad in and had it search until he found what he vaguely remembered as a child.

INIKA HISTORIAN TO RESEARCH AND WRITE EPIC NEW SAGA ABOUT DECK CREW TWO.

"And on that small tin can, deep in the dark of the depths of space, were the fine, no the brave, women and men of Deck Crew Two, and the Watch Captain who saw it all, through and through," Jahn muttered to himself.

There was, a tangled line in here of something happening just under the surface of the world.

"Sometimes, you tug on that too hard, you find out a truth you don't want," his father had told him. "You're independent, but everyone has a place and a part. Don't tug too hard things fall apart."

But Jahn always found the truth to be a shiny thing in the dark, and he was drawn to it like dust to a static air filter.

Every year Destination Day caught Jahn off guard. The Sheriff family would get caught up in the planning early, of course, they had to figure out where to send all the active and experienced old-timers for the festivities. Bars, yes, but also the other places that weren't on record, usually hidden away in between the world's skin instead of out in the wild areas or the pylons.

Once, Jahn had tracked down shroom eaters operating in an old shuttlecraft in a bay in one of the world's endcaps. Fifteen hull maintenance crew who said that it wasn't an illegal operation but a private 'member's only club.'

Then, younger Sheriffs were dispatched to carnivals and presentation festivals, where mostly younger kids thronged to watch old time renderings of what it would look like for the world to pull into orbit around a planet and descend down into a foreign biosphere for the first time. Kids loved it, but by the time you were a teenager and realized you would never see any of that, that it was some distant ancestor a hundred years down the line that would, all interest was lost.

By the time Destination Day rolled around Jahn had been in meetings, planning sessions, and arguments about staffing for so long it wouldn't make any sense that all he had to do was walk around and respond to the day's actual crises, not just come up with plans for imagined ones.

Banners fluttered from pylon balconies, and parade routes were getting set up with chairs and platforms for bands or speeches. Costumes were in shop windows.

Jahn passed a pack of kids running in a circle.

"Ring around the rosies ..." they screamed. "A pocket full of posies."

That was as old as he was. Kids passed those rhymes on to other kids. And how inventive and nonsensical. What were posies?

There was a Mate waiting by his office door.

"What's going on?" Jahn asked, but was met with professional silence. The Mate, Jahn noticed, had a baton swinging from the side of his kilt. That was new.

Inside, the Overcaptain was patiently waiting for him. Arin sat off to the side looking ... scared.

Jahn swept in, letting his waterproof paper coat swing by them all as he took it off and hung it, along with his hat, on a hook by the door. He sat down on his side of the desk, enjoying the feel of full gravity now that he was back in his own space in a pylon close the inner green skin of the world.

It was a power move, making everyone wait. But the truth was, Jahn was going through motions to steady himself. He didn't want the Overcaptain in his office. You didn't have Overcaptains show up in your space, you were summoned to their's. And seeing Kiwa in person yesterday at Alexandria was enough interaction with the Command families for a month, Jahn figured.

Things were upside down, and Jahn, for all that he made fun of Arin's resistance to change and nascent traditionalism, didn't like the feeling.

"Overcaptain?" he began.

"I come here, in my formal capacity, as the Overcaptain of our World, and as the Chief of Navigation and Command."

That was not a good start.

"The navigation data is ruined," Kiwa said somberly. "There is not enough recoverable data for the software to boot and run the world safely for any destination maneuvers. I've had two different communications and code families put their best people on it. They all agree."

It sounded, apocalyptic. Something that couldn't be true. Yet here she was, saying it.

"Why are you telling me this?"

"There is no sense in delaying it, we are going to make a world-wide announcement today, at the height of the parade. We're going to need all your resources at hand. The traditionalists are going to panic."

"Well, our whole purpose was to stop at the star we're aimed, go into orbit, and check out a planet. When you tell people they have no purpose they do tend to get upset." Jahn tapped the desk. "Arin, call the emergency."

It was going to be another damn planning meeting.

"And, Mr. Sheriff," Kiwa said, all too formal.

"Yes?" He didn't like that tone.

"Before she gave her resignation, the Chief Librarian said you were digging further into Inika Historian's disappearance? Do me a personal favor, Chief to Chief. Pause it until after this is all cleaned up. I don't need everyone dealing with two big, sensationalized disasters at once."

"Of course," Jahn lied.

This was bad. He was now in some sort of struggle with the Overcaptain. Only, he didn't know the rules or the stakes. It was all invisible to him, which meant he was in the most danger.

Sheriff versus Overcaptain. Who wins that?

Jahn suspected he knew.

He hated himself for not being able to let go of this thread. But Jahn had been taught since he was a child that a Sheriff was independent and that a mystery should be solved. If people got away with murder, then more would do it, and eventually the world would fall to chaos.

But, more than that, Jahn just wanted to *know the truth.*

Who did this?

And, more to the point, why?

The Mate guarding the door to the supercomputer facility, high up in the core and close to the engines of the world, startled when Jahn appeared.

"Hey!"

He had his hand on a baton, but Jahn identified himself and walked in as if it would make no sense at all for the Mate to try and stop him. So the assumed authority worked and he got in.

The younger man inside, from a good communications family, no doubt, looked just as startled when Jahn came in to look over the ruined media.

It was termite damage, through and through. Jahn handled the media with gloved hands carefully.

"Why do you want to see it?" the young computer specialist asked, nervous. Too nervous.

"Well, there were some fingerprints in the room that didn't make sense," Jahn sort of lied. "We didn't have a chance to check for them in Alexandria, the Command crisis seemed more important. But know I want to be thorough. For the investigation, right?"

"Um, right."

Jahn made a big show of using UV lights, and spraying material on the outside casings as if trying to find the prints, even as riddled as they were with boreholes from the termites. And, using an old trick taught to him by a pickpocket he'd kept locked up for several weeks until he'd learned how to do it himself, Jahn bumped into the young man and swapped one of the better-looking navigation data drives for one he had in his sash.

It was confiscated pornography, something from antiquity and quite out of sorts with the current moral code. But Jahn had drilled holes in it and scuffed it on the road to get it looking ruined enough.

As he swept his way out, the Mate outside tried to stop him. "The Overcaptain needs to see you. She insists."

"I'm so sorry, I barely had time for this. It's the new Destination Day changes. It's too much."

On the elevator down, Jahn found that his heart was racing. The Overcaptain would be suspicious, now.

Whatever this was, the face off had begun. And Jahn had triggered it.

He was starting to feel a little claustrophobic.

But it was too late now.

On to the next stop. Because time was running out before Destination Day parades and announcements. And knew everything was going to fall to shit when that announcement came.

Mama Sun was in the dressing room behind a stage. Outside, the arena, a great bowl where a thousand people would be waiting to hear her rendition of the Leaving Song. The sad saga of Nissi and her lover, separated when the world launched before they could be reunited.

"Jahn Sheriff," she said, looking at him via the mirror. She had on her Leaving Day crown, glittering with representations of the Immobile Worlds that orbited Old Earth like jewels in a bracelet.

"I know you're getting ready, but I'm here officially."

Mama Sun waved her hand in a sort of 'of course' gesture. "Get it out, little Sheriff."

"You are the oldest griot here, one of the chosen, not born to it, but called to it." Jahn sat down on a pillowed stool next to her.

"Well, aren't you just the lady charmer," Mama Sun said.

Jahn leaned further over, so he could look her in the eye and not the mirror. "When I was a boy, you told me that there were only so many data banks on the world. So, over time, what we kept had to be pruned. At first, it was the ancients, and they knew what was valuable and what was not, to their mission and identity. But eventually, their children's children made those decisions, and then their's, and we began to lose pieces of ourselves as we flew on."

Mama Sun stopped fiddling with her garb and turned toward him. She looked suddenly old as the birth certificate said she was.

"And I told you," she said, "that it was a griot's job to find the truth and the story that is the thread that connects us to our ancestors. Because no matter how good the historians are, stories pass on forever and make a community. Yes, I didn't think you listened that closely."

"I always hunt truth," Jahn said.

"A truth," Mama Sun said.

"I'm hunting a murderer," Jahn said. "Tell me everything you remember about the real Deck Crew Two. What your griot told you, when you weren't singing for the community. The truth."

Mama Sun snorted. "The truth. The truth. Look at you—"

"Inika died looking for it. She was at Alexandria. She was trying to get into room 23, to get to the navigation data."

Mama Sun spun on him and took in a deep breath. "Is that—"

"True?" They stared at each other for a long moment. "You know me. It's as true as I know."

Mama Sun let out that shocked inhalation. "This is a long time coming. You know, I was the one that changed the story. I ... they were brave. I felt that they should have been remembered that way, and I set out to give that back to them. This isn't a story about truth, Sheriff. It's a story about what we build out of the wreckage of history handed down to us by our damn ancestors."

"What happened?"

"You were looking for a murder? I'll give you murder, Sheriff. The murder of all one hundred and ninety members of Deck Crew Two. My griot saw it. He was a Mate, then. He put in the codes. He did what his Overcaptain ordered. And left. I took the story. I made them self-sacrificing heroes that closed the doors to save us all. It was the best I could do, back then, when the command families tried to claim them as traitors, or worse."

A stagehand burst in. "Sheriff?"

Jahn looked up. "Yes?"

"There are Mates in here. With guns. Looking for you. Both of you."

Mama Sun snorted. "Better run out the back, little Sheriff."

"What about you?"

"I'm getting ready to go sing the Leaving Song. No Mate can stop that. Your family may have independence, but I'm the griot that raised them all."

Jahn stood up and ran for the back.

"Not that back entrance," the stagehand said, noticing where he was turning to go. "The real one for getting in and out without any, uh, Sheriff catching you after curfew. Follow me."

The announcements went out as Jahn was sneaking his way back to the family offices. Speakers from the pylons blared it, large screens set up over pavilions showed it instead of Destination Day graphics.

Something holy and permanent had broken.

There was always navigation data, and the orbit vectors that were planned when they were to hit in system. Four hundred years from now, it was to be the greatest moment of their civilization. It was what they all worked toward, sacrificed for.

Or that was the official story.

Most people hustled through their days. They ate, they argued, they made love, they tried to gain power, they partied, they lived. As any other civilization, the people lived day to day.

And yet.

And yet there was wailing in the streets. A sense of dread in the wind that was blown from endcap to endcap across the world.

They had lost the ability to stop at a planet.

They had fallen low from their ancestor's plans for them.

There was a scholar being interviewed by a command family elder.

"What you must understand is that skills and specialties fade in smaller communities like ours over time. It takes a large civilization to have the extra people to devote to something like stellar cartography. Our own descendants may be able to relearn what we need to make sense of the navigation data our world is seeing out there, plus a team of software engineers that can build new routines for maneuvering. If we can grow our civilization, it may be possible."

"But we have used our skills to double the ship's carrying capacity already. We live in ways our ancestors couldn't have imagined."

Jahn's radio began to explode with reports of drama. A lot of people had succumbed to existential angst tonight and would end up zip tied to a post outside Sheriff's offices all over the world.

He took the navigation data down to a place deep inside the ship's skin, where family didn't matter so much as skill. The people who walked the hull of the world valued ability over all else, and Jahn had long learned to keep a catalogue of who could actually do what, and not what their family last name was.

There were Mates with pistols waiting for him in his office. Most of the Sheriffs were running around all over the world, but the few remaining had surrounded the door casually. A baton versus a pistol. That wasn't going to go well. But they all had the sense something was wrong, that Sheriff independence was being threatened.

Footsteps outside, someone taking off running. Maybe Arin, going to see about getting more people back here, maybe even try to get some guns from antiquities. Though Jahn assumed that there would be Mates on guard over them.

"Well, Kiwa," he said, hanging up his paper coat and hat casually once more. "This is turning into something quite regular. I didn't know you liked my office that much."

She smiled, and then quenched it.

"I'm here for your resignation," she said.

"Sheriffs are independent," one of Jahn's nieces shouted into the office. "You do not have the authority!"

Jahn looked at the ancient pistols. Some of them would misfire. But enough wouldn't.

"Both the Chief Librarian and the Chief Sheriff in one day," he said. Arin had left the fingerprint reports for room 23 on Jahn's desk. He started looking through them as he continued. "On any other day, that would be an epic shake up, a monumental shift in world politics."

"These are tough times. Everything is changing, and if we can all guide the world with good leadership, we can come through all this."

"Come through what? Shooting past the target star our ancestors aimed us at and plummeting endlessly through the void forever?" Jahn hadn't said it out loud, but doing so made realize how it sounded. How it felt like a punch in the gut.

He was more of a traditionalist than he realized. He stopped reading the fingerprint report. He had what he needed. What he suspected.

"We were fated to do that anyway," Kiwa said. "You and I, we're not the generation that would have seen a world. We have lived in the void, and we always have. Now, some distant ancestor will live just like us."

"But—"

"Be careful what you say next," Kiwa said, pointing out the door. "There are some things that cannot be known by all."

"Close the door," Jahn said.

The Sheriffs outside protested. Jahn stood up. "She will not harm me, not with so many witnesses, and with so many of you saying there is a confrontation here on the radio."

He hoped they would take the hint and start broadcasting. He saw Kiwa's face twitch, and that gave Jahn some pleasure. The standoff was not totally unequal.

"Leave," Kiwa said to the Mates in the office.

Now it was their turn to protest, but finally the door was shut, and it was just Overcaptain and Sheriff.

"You have guns, my franchise on force for order is gone, and independence as well," Jahn said.

"My historians assure me that there have been times in ship history where the Sheriffs reported to the command families," Kiwa said. "We will still need the investigative skills your family has passed on so well to each generation."

"You want me to order them to change over to your rule peacefully."

"You could have stopped and worked with me. I wanted an ally, at a time like this. I really did. I also want the media stick back."

Jahn tossed the stick onto the desk, and she snapped it up.

"You found out quick."

"When I heard you went to the lab, I knew you were learning too much. The young man who rechecked all the media at my order is traumatized by what you swapped it for," Kiwa said. "So was I, for the matter."

Jahn smiled.

"I assume you got a look at the navigation data," Kiwa said. "Though I'm not sure how you got someone better than my computer families."

"I did. It was an antique moving picture," Jahn said. "I'm told it was called Blank House. There was a referendum on deleting it so that we could use the storage for something else twenty years ago?"

"Yes, that's it," Kiwa said.

"So, you have the navigation data?"

"I wouldn't have ever let it get eaten, no, we're not that incompetent a family," Kiwa said.

"But you want to control the story, the real story," he said. "That, even with the data under your control, there's no way we can ever stop ourselves. We don't have enough fuel."

Kiwa pressed her lips hard against each other. "And that is why you have to resign. We have a story, that it's bad luck and a harsh universe of systems failures conspiring against us. A librarian resigns in shame, but, everyone has lost something useful to termites, or a blown seal, or other rot like that. It's the nature of the world. She can be forgiven, that's the public story I have, and I will show her tolerance by giving her a good command post. She and I have arranged the deal, she knows her part. She will be well rewarded."

"It's the nature of the world," Jahn agreed. "But, why did you have to kill Inika?"

Kiwa took a step back. "She was going to tell everyone the story. Before we had time to prepare. She was going to tell a story that would have ripped the world apart. Set family against family. Because she didn't care about how to tell the truth right, but she had to do it hard and no matter what."

They looked at each other, and Jahn could see that they were now on either side of some unfathomable vacuum with no air between them on the subject.

"Inika found out about Deck Crew Two, and you murdered her for it."

Kiwa's face had paled. "I—"

"You, personally, murdered her. The prints in that room, they're yours and hers. It's only been bots and archivists with gloves on since then. Prints with the finest layer of dust over them."

"If the people found out, we would all be lost," Kiwa hissed.

"That Deck Crew Two wasn't a deck crew?" Jahn said. "That they were political prisoners your great-grandfather rounded up when they learned that our even more distant forefathers had chosen to plunder the fuel to make more water, more air, and to add more hydrocarbons to the food stock so we could grow our size. That the largesse and comfort we enjoy today under the command families is a lie, that it stole Destination Day away from our descendants?"

"Yes. That's all true. Because why should we suffer and starve when it was our ancestors who gave us this prison sentence? Us, who are trapped between the stars, why do we have to give up everything, including children, to a Grand Plan we *can't even remember* other than as a set of instructions to stop at a star we will never see with our eyes?"

"And Inika was going to sing that saga, and destroy your family name by listing their atrocities."

"She had to be stopped," Kiwa sobbed. "Oh, you have no idea."

"Overcaptain Kiwa, I place you under arrest for the murder of Inika Historian." Jahn stood up. Kiwa swung her pistol, aiming at across the desk at him.

"That isn't how this works. I will order your people killed, Jahn. Do you understand you have a responsibility to those lives?"

Jahn saw it, the stalemate. The path into civil war between their families. And how did they get out? They'd slipped into this place, like hull repair techs with no lines who suddenly look back and realize how far they've drifted.

But, he had thought very long on the way here about his own story. The things he believed about himself. About his own truths.

I am about the truth, he thought.

I untangle these hidden threads, he thought.

*But I am also a Sheriff.* And what was a Sheriff if not a person who brought justice to a murderer?

He hit her with the baton, one smooth movement so quick she only had time for one shot, then another, before the end of it slammed into her chin and the full charge emptied in a shock of lightning up through her mouth.

The gunshots were so loud they seemed to explode in the office.

Jahn fell over the desk clutching his stomach. She'd known how to use the damn antique, and it had worked. He had thought he had a chance. He'd been wrong.

Mates burst in, screaming, but there were more Sheriffs with batons swinging up and down in rage. And more coming in, people that Jahn trusted, that he'd stationed nearby. In case.

And there were more gunshots with the screams and zaps of the batons.

This was it. He had started a fire, but he did not know its size or how long it would burn.

But there was justice.

There was that.

Once upon a time there was a ship.

Not a ship that floated across the water. Not a ship that sailed across oceans on Old Earth (Old Earth: you know the globe you see carved out of aluminum foam over by Pylon Twenty-Two's fountains?).

No, this is a ship that soared between the stars themselves.

And on that small tin can, deep in the dark of the depths of space, were the fine, no the brave, women and men of Deck Crew Two ...

"Would you like to hear their story?" the old griot with the limp asked. "Would you like to hear the *real* story of Deck Crew Two?"

And the children all clapped and laughed and screamed yes, yes, they would. This was the most popular, the grimmest, the bloodiest mystery story you would ever hear. Parents would complain about the kids having nightmares after it, but what could you do, silence a griot?

No, they were the soul of the world, the heart of the ship.

And this griot, he was much loved by this generation of eager ears.

They said he was once the Sheriff of the whole world, and that he'd killed an Overcaptain who had murdered someone. They said that when she shot him (that's what gave him the limp), fires had burned for nights, and Command families and Sheriff families fought battles in the corridors in the skin between the dark night of vacuum and the inside of the world, along with other families that chose sides.

And one day, peace came, when the Sheriffs surrendered and the Mates selected a new Overcaptain who wanted that peace, as enough had died that the price became too high. Another chapter had been written in the thousand-year annals of the world.

Of course, just as the Mates chose a new leader, no one in the world would allow the old Chief Sheriff back to his office. A younger Sheriff was chosen, and pledged marriage to a strong command family to create a bond and a new generation that would not see each other as enemies, though the old folk of those families still shunned each other at functions, old blood bitterness having no way to find peace but death.

And Father Jahn, he left the family to be a griot, to tell the stories and wander the world.

So it was said. But it all seemed fantastical and long ago to the children.

"Okay," the old griot said. "But before I tell you that tale, I need to tell you another tale. Because some stories are older than our world, older than us, and will go on after us. I will tell you the story of Anansi the Spiderman, a wily trickster."

There was power in telling the right story, the old griot told them, at the right time. Tell the right story, it goes on past Destination Day, which will never happen because we're gonna swing right on past that star.

You'll need the stories of your history. But you'll need also need to learn how to be wily like Anansi, because this world is all you'll ever have, now, and you'll have to keep it running after we're gone, however you can.

Just like Anansi, the Spiderman ...

... who could shoot webs from his fingers, and beat the Doctor Octopus with nothing more than a clever riddle.

# THE LONGEST DISTANCE

At the start of the trip between two stars, as we speed through the infinite vastness of space, I find myself wandering through the halls of the starship looking for a portal.

There are none, it's just some romantic expectation of mine. I'd expected I could perch by a portal of some kind and gaze out into the starry heavens scattered outside the half-mile-long dart thrown toward another world.

Instead, I stop next to a status readout screen and ask it to show me the world outside the ship.

There's nothing I could see outside this wall looking out, anyway. Not even scattered stars. The faster the ship moves, the more light gets distorted. That's what the screen shows: blue light compressed into a great circle near the front of the ship. Red light behind us.

Relativistic effects make the light show hard for me to understand.

Seeing it on a screen isn't the dramatic moment I'd hoped for. I go back to my cabin and put it up as a-screensaver.

Three months until we make it to Proxima. We're two weeks into the journey.

Seems like forever. I've explored all the guts of the ship. I've met everyone aboard, all three hundred of us going to Proxima to explore an all-new, never-before-seen system, and ripped through hours of shows and games to keep myself occupied. It's going to be a long three months.

I think I may have already made some life-long friends.

"You make it sound like a dorm floor," Carolina says with a smile.

"It is." I reach out and touch the screen.

"You seem happy," she says. "I just ... can't imagine being in a tiny little ship on your way to another *entire* world."

She's sad. I can see it in the crinkle at the corner of her eyes.

I broke her heart.

I think, maybe, sometimes when I'm wandering around the corridors, I'm half looking for her.

"I'm sorry." Carolina pushes her hair aside in a nervous, self-conscious gesture. "I should have gotten over it all sooner and sent you a message. I was just so hurt. Angry. Scared. But I understand why you did it. Who gets a chance to go to another world? You had to take it. We'd barely been together long enough for me to ask you what I did."

It's a technological miracle this message even reaches us. I don't get much mail, there's always a festive party on the ship when the mail call alarms go off.

"But I guess, it's easier for me to take the time I needed. For you, it'll appear I got over things quickly."

She laughs. I look at the date stamp. Six months.

Wow.

She'd stewed that long before trying to talk to me again?

I laughed and smiled. Carolina, passionate and strong-willed.

The twin paradox: if you have one twin sitting on Earth and another accelerating away from Earth on a starship time passes at different rates for them.

The closer you get to the speed of light, the faster time passes differently. At ninety percent the speed of light time passes half as fast for a person traveling as the one at rest.

The closer you get to the speed of light the more the ratio grows.

"I keep plugging the Lorentz equation in to figure out far apart we'll be in time," I send back to Carolina. "It only took me a week to get your first message, but for you it was six months. It feels so fresh still. My guilt. The separation. It all feels raw and recent still. By the time you get this, I'll be so deep in ex territory maybe it'll be funnier to you."

I wish her an amazing life.

I wish her good friends.

And, I hoped she would still send me messages, even as she moved on.

"I … don't want to lose my connection to the world I am leaving behind. It hurt to sever myself from it."

I wonder if people on oceanic voyages in the ancient days suddenly felt panic as the land slid away behind the horizon and they realized they couldn't go back until the journey was done.

Because that's what I feel now.

I always wanted to see another world. Wanted to see space. I was the weird kid with the space posters even as I lived in an orbital wheel whipping around Mars.

Dad worked as an asteroid jockey, away from home months on end. Mom was a structural engineer for the whole ring.

It felt like destiny when I'd been selected for the advance Proxima team.

We'd scavenged ancient alien technology out of the Swing-By Artifact, strapped it into a prototype Martian ramscoop ship designed to go out as far as the Oort cloud, and then aimed the whole thing at our nearest star. I *had* to be on that thing. It was everything I'd built my life toward.

And then I'd met Carolina. A software engineer working on the layer between Artifact technology and the ramscoop that would suck fuel out of the near-vacuum to run our engines.

But she wasn't on the final manifest.

"I'm just a contractor," she'd said. "I'm looking forward to going back to McMurdo. I'm an Antarctica girl, through and through. You should come see it."

I look at a lot of pictures of Antarctica in the second week of the voyage.

A strange face is on the screen. Another woman. I can't breathe. I know I shouldn't be jealous, I'm the one who left. But there Carolina is with someone smiling in that way only she can provoke.

"It's been a while, I sort of kept it from you," she says in the message. "But, we got engaged!"

Engaged.

Just like that.

But it isn't. It's been three weeks for me. For Carolina, there have been dates, loves, fights, breakups, and adventures all over the old stomping grounds of Earth.

I've seen a barrage of pictures of her from all over the world.

Her face looks slightly more weathered, and wise.

I have no claim on her life. This shouldn't matter.

But it leaves me in a funk for several days.

Until I get a picture of their son. A tiny little thing, precious tiny hands gripping an exhausted Carolina's.

"A lot of people are having trouble seeing family age, now that we're in the second month," I tell Carolina. I keep sending messages. She updates me about her life.

And there's a conversation still happening. A strange relationship that has grown out of the unequal aging speeds and the truncated nature of what we can communicate.

"The doctor started a support group. A lot of us have lost parents."

Mom and dad's messages are hard. They're so proud, following the details of our adventure. But they're aging, and fast.

And out here, it's not so much adventure as tedium. We're just passengers right now. Nothing brave. We're just watching the world we knew slowly age past us.

Some of the others have said people have stopped contacting them. They've grown apart, even though it's hardly been any time for us.

I suddenly realize that, at some point, Carolina is going to die and I'm going to see it happen over the next month.

My God. What have I done to myself?

Carolina's baby walks, talks, then becomes a boy who is suspicious of me when she brings him over to the screen to say hi.

She's a middle-aged mother with kind eyes, though sometimes it's late at night when she sends her messages. Sometimes there's a hint of exhaustion as she talks to me while cleaning up.

Yet always, always, she sends her messages.

"Maybe I shouldn't have done it," I tell her when we hit the halfway point to Proxima. "I feel like a shit. I can't believe I put you through it."

I'm looking at her life. Her domestic life. And I wonder what life around Proxima will be like? Months more of this tin can I'm in. I'm part of a group that was going to stay around Proxima as the ship headed back. We have machines ready to carve a station out of the first asteroid we find with good metal for us to mine. But I realize it's going to be years and years, and suddenly it seems less exciting.

I gave up a real life for this sardine life.

"You shouldn't be so hard on yourself," Carolina says. "It was, well, for me, a long time ago. I have a good life. You're having an adventure for all humanity. We're just lucky we had Mars. And that we have this."

I wonder if Amira is jealous of me like I am of her.

"You're the one that got away," Carolina laughs with the hard-won knowledge of years of life lived. "And, I guess, for you, I'm the one you left behind."

And then I feel like complete shit when Carolina sobs on the screen hours later, dressed in all black. It came quick for Amira, an aggressive virus. Something endemic to Antarctica these days.

Carolina's a single mother, raising a hurting teenager.

At the halfway point the ship flips. We all hold a subdued party to watch the screens show what we always keep hoping to have seen with our own eyes.

But we need to be in here, safe from radiation behind the shields.

Carolina has a new friend in her life. A good person.

I stop sending her messages for a few days, not wanting to tell her the adventure has faded away for me. I don't want to tell her I threw us away for something that is no longer seeming so epic, destined, and amazing.

She breaks up with her new friend. Finds another.

Her son, Benjamin, graduates, gets engaged.

And then, four days later, Carolina smiles.

"I have a new contract at Mars!" she says. There's another mission, they've perfected the Artifact tech. She's going to do the final testing on the integration.

It's a lucky break for her, she's told me income has been tight.

"But that's not all I want to tell you," Carolina says. "You've been telling me you don't want to stay on Proxima but turn around and come home."

I'd do that, and, I haven't told her, visit her grave. I could never see her again, but maybe I'd meet Benjamin.

Maybe I'd meet people who had once known her, who could tell me what an amazing life she'd lived.

"Don't come back to Earth," Carolina tells me. "Stay on Proxima. I have a berth on the next ship."

She does the math for me.

As we slowed down for Proxima, she'd be launching.

I would be back in normal time around the new sun. She would be slowing down. On her own three-month journey.

"Stay at Proxima, and show me your new world," she says.

All I have to do is stay put.

How old will I be when that stranger arrives?

Could it be possible that we could recapture what we once had?

She's sent me an article about two war survivors who were pulled apart and met after decades.

All I have to do is stay.

One month to go, and on all the screens around the ship, Proxima is growing from a tiny dot into a large sun as we burn to slow down.

"I'll build you an entire world to see," I promise her, and kiss the screen.

## AUTHOR NOTES

Generation ships. Ponderous, vast, crawling along at lower-than-light speeds as generations of people live, love, die and survive out in the cold of space until they can reach a cradle of life somewhere. In both of these stories I wanted to toy around with the deep time that passes on the outside of these imagined structures. But as someone who grew up on boats, on small islands, I also think I have something to say about the small communities and effects of a life with strong boundaries and a sense of vulnerability that living on an ecosystem out by one's self.

No matter how strange the megastructures or long the journey, we'll have such inherently human struggles in those contexts. They'll be alien to us, and yet, so very similar.

# GALACTIC TOURIST
# INDUSTRIAL COMPLEX

When Galactics arrived at JFK they often reeked of ammonia, sulphur, and something else that Tavi could never quite put a finger on. He was used to it all after several years of shuttling them through the outer tanks and waiting for their gear to spit ozone and adapt to Earth's air. He would load luggage, specialized environmental adaptation equipment, and cross-check the being's needs, itinerary, and sightseeing goals.

What he wasn't expecting this time was for a four-hundred-pound, octopus-like creature to open the door of his cab a thousand feet over the new Brooklyn Bridge, filling the cab with an explosion of cold, screaming air, and lighting the dash up with alarms.

He also definitely wasn't expecting the alien to scream "Look at those spires!" through a speaker that translated for it.

So, for a long moment after the alien jumped out of the cab, Tavi just kept flying straight ahead, frozen in shock at the controls.

This couldn't be happening. Not to him. Not in his broken-down old cab he'd been barely keeping going, and with a re-up on the Manhattan license due soon.

To fly into Manhattan, you needed a permit. That was the first thing he panicked about because he'd recently let it lapse. The New York Bureau of Tourism hadn't just fined him but suspended him for three months. Tavi had limped along on some odd jobs: tank cleaning at the airport, scrubbing out the backs of the cabs when they came back after a run to the island, and other muck work.

But no, all his licenses were up to date. And he knew that it was a horrible thing to worry about as he circled the water near the bridge; he should be worrying about his passenger. Maybe this alien was able to withstand long falls, Tavi thought.

Maybe.

But it wasn't coming up from the water.

He had a contact card somewhere in the dash screen's memory. He tapped, calling the alien.

"Please answer. Please."

But it did not pick up.

What did he know about the alien? It looked like some octopus-type thing. What did that mean? They shouldn't have even been walking around, so it had to have been wearing an exoskeleton of some kind.

Could that have protected it?

Tavi circled the water once more. He had to call this in. But then the police would start hassling him about past mistakes. Somehow this would be his fault. He would lose his permit to fly into Manhattan. And it was Manhattan that the aliens loved above all else. This was the "real" American experience, even though most of it was heavily built up with zones for varying kinds of aliens. Methane breathers in the Garment District, the buildings capped with translucent covers and an alien atmosphere. Hydrogen types were all north of Central Park.

He found the sheer number of shops fun to browse, but few of them sold anything of use to humans. In the beginning, a lot of researchers and scientists had rushed there to buy what the Galactics were selling, sure they could reverse engineer what they found.

Turned out it was a lot of cheap alien stuff that purported to be made on Earth but wasn't. Last year, some government agency purchased a "real" human sports car that could be shipped back to the home planet of your choice. It had an engine inside that seemed to be some kind of antigravity device that had everyone excited. It exploded when they cracked the casing, taking out several city blocks.

When confronted about it, the tall, furry, sauropod-like aliens that had several other models in their windows on Broadway shrugged and said it wasn't made by them, they just shipped them to Earth to sell.

But Galactics packed the city buying that shit when they weren't slouching beside the lakes in Central Park. If Tavi couldn't get to Manhattan, he didn't have a job.

With a groan, Tavi tapped 9-1-1. There were going to be a lot of questions. He was going to be in it up to his neck.

But if he took off, they'd have his transponder on file. Then he'd look guilty.

With a faint clenching in his stomach, Tavi prepared for his day to go wrong.

Tavi stood on a pier, wearing a gas mask to filter out the streams of what seemed like mustard gas that would seep out from a nearby building in DUMBO. The cops, also wearing masks, took a brief statement. Tavi gave his fingerprint, and then they told him to leave.

"Just leave?"

Several harbor patrol boats were hovering near where the alien had struck the water. But there was a lack of urgency to it all. Mostly everyone seemed to be waiting around for something to happen.

The cop taking Tavi's statement wore a yellow jumpsuit with logos advertising a Financial District casino (*Risk your money here, just like they used to in the old stock market! Win big, ring the old bell!*). He nodded through his gas mask as he took notes.

"We have your contact info on file. We're pulling footage now."

"But aren't you going to drag the river?"

"Go."

There was something in the cop's tone that made it through the muffled gas mask and told Tavi it was an order. He'd done the right thing in an impossible moment.

He'd done the right thing.

Right?

He wanted to go home and take a nap. Draw the shades and huddle in the dark and make all this go away for a day. But there were bills to pay. The cab required insurance, and the kinine fuel it used, shipped down from orbit, wasn't cheap. Every time the sprinklers under the cab misted up and put down a new layer, Tavi could hear his bank account dropping.

But you couldn't drive on the actual ground into Manhattan, not if you wanted to get a good review. Plus, the ground traffic flow licenses were even more whack than flying licenses because the interstellar tourists didn't want to put up with constant traffic snarls.

Trying to tell anyone that traffic was authentic old Manhattan just got you glared at.

So: four more fares. More yellowed gas mixing into the main cabin of the cab, making Tavi cough and his eyes water. The last batch, a pack of wolf-like creatures that poured into the cab, chittering and yapping like squirrels, requested he take them somewhere serving human food.

"Real human food, not that shit engineered to look like it, but doctored so that our systems can process it."

Tavi's dash had lit up with places the Bureau of Tourism authorized for this pack of aliens that kept grooming each other as he watched them in his mirror.

"Yeah, okay."

He took them to his cousin Geoff's place up in Harlem, which didn't have as many skyscrapers bubble-wrapped with alien atmospheres. The pack creatures were oxygen breathers, but they supplemented that with something extra running to their noses in tubes that occasionally wheezed and puffed a dust of cinnamon-smelling air.

Tavi wanted some comfort food pretty badly by this point. While the aliens tried to make sense of the really authentic human menus out front, he slipped into the hot, gleaming stainless steel of the kitchens in the back.

"Ricky!" Geoff shouted. "You bring those dogs in?"

"Yes," Tavi confessed, and Geoff gave him a half hug, his dreadlocks slapping against Tavi. "Maybe they'll tip you a million."

"*Shiiiit*. Maybe they'll tip you a *trillion*."

It was an old service-job joke. How much did it cost to cross a galaxy to put your eyes, or light receptors, on a world just for the sake of seeing it yourself? Some of the aliens who had come to Earth had crossed distances so great, traveled in ships so complicated, that they spent more than a whole country's GDP.

A tip from one of them *could* be millions. There were rumors of such extravagances. A dish boy turned rich suddenly. A tour guide with a place built on the moon.

But the Bureau of Tourism and the Galactic-owned companies bringing the tourists here warned them not to overpay for services. The Earth was a fragile economy, they said. You didn't want to just run around handing out tips worth a year of some individual's salary. You could create accidental inflation or unbalanced power in a neighborhood.

So the apps on the tourist's systems, whatever types of systems they used, knew what the local exchange rates were and paid folk down here on the ground proportionally.

Didn't stop anyone from wishing, though.

Geoff slid him over a plate of macaroni pie, some peas and rice, and chicken. Tavi told him about his morning.

"You shouldn't have called the police," Geoff said.

"And what, just keep flying?"

"The bureau will blacklist you. They have to save face. And no one is going to want to hear about a tourist dying on the surface. It's bad publicity. You're going to lose your license to Manhattan. NYC bureau's the worst, man."

Tavi cleaned his fingers on a towel, then coughed. The taste of cinnamon came up strong through his throat.

"You okay?"

Tavi nodded, eyes watering. Whatever the pack out there was sniffing, it was ripping through his lungs.

"You need to be careful," Geoff said. "Get a better filter in that cab. Nichelle's father got lung cancer off a bunch of shit coming off the suits of some sundivers last year, doctors couldn't do nothing for him."

"I know, I know," Tavi said between coughs.

Geoff handed him a bag with something rolled up in aluminum foil in it. "Roti for the road. Chicken, no bone. I have doubles if you want?"

"No." Geoff was being too nice. He knew how Tavi was climbing out from a financial hole and had been bringing by "extras" after he closed up each night.

Most of the food here was for non-human tourists, variations on foods that wouldn't upset their unique systems. Tavi had lied in taking the tourist pack here; the food out front was for the doglike aliens. But the stuff in the bag was real, something Geoff made for folk who knew to come in through the back.

Tavi did one more run back to JFK and this time he flew a few loops around the megastructure. JFK Interspacial was the foot of a leg that stretched up into the sky, piercing the clouds and rising beyond until it reached space. It was a pier that led to the deep water where the vast alien ships that moved tourists from star to star docked. It was the pride of the US. Congress had financed it by pledging the entire country's GDP for a century to a Galactic building consortium, so no one knew how to build another after it was done, but the promise was that increased Manhattan tourism would bring in jobs. Because with the Galactics shipping in things to sell here in exchange for things they wanted, there wasn't much in the way of industrial capacity. Over half the US economy was tourism, the rest service jobs.

Down at the bottom of JFK, the eager vacationers and sightseers disgorged into terminals designed for their varying biologies and then were kitted out for time on Earth. Or, like Tavi's latest customer, just bundled into a can that slid into the back of a cab, and that was then dropped off at one of the hotels dwarfing Manhattan's old buildings.

When the drop-off of the tourist in a can that Tavi couldn't see or interact with was done, he headed home. That took careful flying over the remains of LaGuardia, which pointed off from Brooklyn toward the horizon, the way it had ever since it collapsed and fell out of stable orbit.

Land around LaGuardia's remains was cheap, and Tavi lived in an apartment complex roofed by the charred chunk of the once-space-elevator's outer shell.

"Home sweet home," he said, coming in for a landing.

There was a burning smell somewhere in the back of the cab. Smoke started filling the cabin and the impellers failed.

He remained in the air, the kinine misters doing their job and preventing him from losing neutral buoyancy, and coasted.

Tavi wanted to get upset, hit the wheel, punch the dash. But he just bit his lip as the car finally stopped short of the roof's parking spot. He had the misters spray some cancellation foam, and the car dropped a bit too hard to a stop.

"At least you got home," Sienna said, laughing as Tavi opened the doors to the cab and stumbled out. "You know what I think of this Galactic piece of shit."

"It gets the job done."

Sienna poked her head into the cab, holding her breath. Her puffy hair bobbed against the side of the hatch.

"Can you fix it?" he asked her.

"It was one of the dog things with the cinnamon breath? That gas they breathe catalyzes the O-rings. You need to spend some money to isolate the shaft back here."

"Next big tip," Tavi told her.

She crawled back out.

"Okay. Next big tip. I can work on it if you split dinner with me." She nodded at the bag Geoff had given him.

"Sure."

"There's also a man waiting by your door. Looks like Tourist Bureau."

"Shit." He didn't want anyone from the bureau out here. Not in an illegal squat in the ruins of the space elevator now draped across this side of the world.

There was no air conditioning; the solar panels lashed to the scrap hull rooftop didn't pump out enough juice to make that a reality. But the motion-sensitive fans kicked on and the LED track lights all leapt to attention as Tavi led the beet-faced Tourist Bureau agent through the mosquito netting.

"Your cab is having trouble?"

The agent, David Kahn, had a tight haircut and glossy brown skin, the kind that meant he didn't spend much time outside loading aliens into the backs of cabs. He had an office job.

"Sienna will fix it. She grew up a scrapper. Her father was one of the original decommissioners paid to work on picking LaGuardia up. Before the contract was cancelled and they all decided to stay put. Beer?"

Tavi passed him a sweaty Red Stripe from the fridge, which Kahn held nervously in one hand as if he wanted to refuse it. Instead, he placed it against his forehead. The man had been waiting a while in the heat. And he was wearing a heavy suit.

"So, I am here to offer you a grant from the Greater New York Bureau of Tourism," Kahn started, sounding a little unsure of himself.

"A grant?"

"The bureau is starting a modernization campaign to make sure our cabs are the safest on Earth. That means we'd like to take your cab in and have it retrofitted with better security, improved impellers, better airlocks. For the driver's safety."

"The driver?"

"Of course."

Tavi thought it was a line of bullshit. Human lives were cheap; there were billions teeming away on the planet. If Tavi ever stepped out, someone else would bid on his license to Manhattan and he'd be forgotten in days.

Maybe even hours.

"Take it," Sienna said, pushing through the netting. "That piece of shit needs any help it can get."

Tavi didn't have to be told twice. He put his thumb to the documents, verbally repeated assent into a tiny red dot of light, and then Kahn said a tow truck was on its way.

They watched the cab get lifted onto its back, the patchwork of a vehicle that Tavi had come to know every smelly inch of.

"What about the dead alien?" Tavi asked.

"Well, according to the documents you just signed, you can never talk about the … err … incident again."

"I get it." Tavi waved a salute at the disappearing cab and tow truck. "I figured as much when you said you had a 'grant.' But what happens to the alien? Did you ever find the body?"

Kahn let out a deep breath. "We found it, downstream of where it jumped."

"Why the hell did it do that? Why jump out?"

"It was out of its mind on vacation drugs. Cameras show the party started in orbit with a few friends, continued down the JFK elevator all the way to the ground."

"When do you send the body back to its people?"

"We don't." Kahn looked around, surprised. "No one wants to

know a high-profile cephaloid of any kind has died on Earth. So they didn't. The video of the fall no longer exists in any system."

"But they can track the body—"

"—already fired off via an old-school rocket aimed at our sun. That leaves no evidence here. Nothing happened on Earth. Nothing happened to you."

Kahn shook hands with Sienna and Tavi and left.

The next morning a brand-new cab was parked on the roof.

"Easier than scrubbing it all down for DNA," Sienna said. "The old one's probably on a rocket as well, just like the body, being shot toward the sun as we speak."

He scrambled up some eggs for his ever-hungry roomie and some extra for the Oraji brothers next door. There were thirty other random clumps of real and found families living in welded-together scrap here. Several of them watched the sun creep over the rusted wreckage scattered from horizon to horizon as they ate breakfast. Tavi would head back into the drudgery of flying tourists around, Sienna would work at trying to pry something valuable out of the ruins.

Just as they finished eating, a second cab descended from the clouds. It kicked up some dust as it settled in on the ground.

"Hey, asshole," Sienna shouted. "If we all land on metal, we don't kick dust into everyone's faces."

Grumbling assent rose into the morning air.

The doors slid open, and Tavi felt his stomach drop.

Another octopus-like alien stood on the ground looking up at them.

"I'm looking for the human named Tavi," the speaker box on the exoskeleton buzzed. "Is he here?"

"Don't say a thing," Sienna hissed. Sienna, who had all the smarts built up from a lifetime of eat or be eaten while scavenging in the wreckage.

"I am Tavi," Tavi said, stepping down toward the alien.

"You're an idiot," Sienna said. She walked off toward the shadows under a pile of scrap and disappeared.

The alien crouched in a spot of shade, trying to stay out of the sun, occasionally rubbing sunscreen over its photo-sensitive skin.

"I'm the co-sponsor of the unit last seen in your vehicle when it came down to your planet for sightseeing."

Tavi felt his stomach fall out from under him. "Oh," he said numbly. He wasn't sure what a co-sponsor was or why the alien's language had been translated that way. He had the feeling this alien was a close friend or family member of the one he'd witnessed jump to its death.

"No one will tell me anything; your representatives have done nothing but flail around and throw bureaucratic ink my way," the alien tourist said.

"I'm really sorry for your loss," Tavi said.

"So, you are my last try before offencers get involved," the alien concluded.

"Offencers?"

The alien used one of its mechanized limbs to point up. A shadow passed over the land. Something vast skimmed over the clouds and blocked the sun. It hummed. And the entire land hummed back with it. Somehow, Tavi *knew* that whatever was up there could destroy a planet.

Tavi's wristband vibrated. Incoming call. Kahn.

The world was crashing into him. Tavi felt it all waver for a moment, and then he took a deep breath.

"All I wanted to do was the right thing," he muttered and took the call.

"Very big, alien destroyers," David Kahn said in a level, but clearly terrified, voice. "We at the Greater New York Bureau of Tourism *highly* recommend you do whatever the being or beings currently in contact with you are asking, while also, uh, acknowledging that we have no idea where the missing being they are referring to is. Please hold for the president—"

Tavi flicked the bracelet off.

"What do you want?" Tavi asked the alien.

"I want to know the truth," it said.

"I see you have an advanced exotic-worlds encounter suit. Would you like a real human beer with me?"

"If that helps," it said.

"You have such a beautiful planet. So unspoiled, paradisiacal. I was swimming with whales in your Pacific Ocean yesterday."

Tavi sat down and gave the alien a Red Stripe. It curled a tentacle around it, pulled it back toward its beak. They watched the trees curling around the LaGuardia debris shiver in the wind, the fluffy clouds ease through the pale blue sky.

They deliberately sat with their backs to the section of sky filled with the destroyer.

"I've never been to the Pacific," Tavi admitted. "Just the Caribbean, where my people come from, and the Atlantic."

"I'm a connoisseur of good oceans," the alien said. "These are just some of the best."

"We used to fish on them. My grandfather owned a boat."

"Oh, does he still do that? I love fishing."

"He started chartering it out," Tavi said. "The Galactics bought out the restaurants, so he couldn't sell to his best markets anymore. They own anything near the best spots, and all around the Eastern Seaboard now."

"I'm sorry to hear that."

"About your friend." Tavi took a big swig. "They jumped out of my cab. When it was in the air. They were in an altered state."

There was a long silence.

Tavi waited for the world to end, but it didn't. So he continued, and the alien listened as he told his story.

"And there were no security systems to stop them from jumping?" it asked when he finished.

"There were not, on that cab."

"Wow," it said. "How authentically human. How dangerous. I'll have to audit your account against the confessions of your bureau, but I have to say, I am very relieved. I suspected foul play, and it turns out it was just an utterly authentic primitive world experience. No door security."

Overhead, long fiery contrails burned through the sky.

"What is that?" Tavi asked, nervous.

"Independent verification," the alien said. It stood up and jumped down to its cab. It looked closely at the rear doors. "I could really just jump out of these, couldn't I?"

It opened the door, and Tavi, who had hopped over the roof and down the stairs, caught a glimpse of a pale-faced driver inside. *Sorry, friend,* he thought.

More shadows were descending from space. Larger and larger vessels moving through the atmosphere far above.

"What is happening?" Tavi asked, mouth dry.

"News of your world has spread," it said. "You are no longer an undiscovered little secret. Finding out that we can die just in a cab ride—where else can you get that danger?"

After the cab lifted off and flew away, Sienna came back out of the shadows. "They're over every city now. They're offering ludicrous money for real estate."

Tavi looked at the skies. "Did you think it would ever stop?"

"Beats them blowing us up, right? They do that, sometimes, to other worlds that fight it."

He shook his head. "There's not going to be anything left for us down here, is there?"

"Oh, they'll never want this." She spread her arms and pointed at the miles of space-elevator junk.

"And I still have a new cab," he said.

She put a hand on his shoulder. "Maybe these new Galactics coming down over the cities tip better."

And for the first time in days, Tavi laughed. "That's always the hope, isn't it?"

## AUTHOR NOTES

The whole story comes from a distinct moment I experienced in the Bahamas where I stopped on the sidewalk to try and understand the immense mega-structure of a hotel complex that sprawls all over a corner of the main island. It was like something out of the mind-altering 1984 movie *Bladerunner* that blew my mind away as a kid. Skyscraper pyramids in Los Angeles? Science fiction. A hotel complex with a slide that runs through a lagoon-sized shark tank? Science fiction.

I muttered the words "Tourist Industrial Complex" and wrote some notes down on my phone about the nature of a system, a giant economic machine, similar to the Military Industrial Complex, that tortured landscapes all over the world into these mega-structures where the very locals who saw the massive buildings every day loom over their old British colonial facaded warehouses downtown and concrete and metal roofed homes elsewhere.

When Nisi Shawl asked me to write a story for her anthology *New Suns*, I wasn't just honored by the invite, I knew I wanted to tell a story about that experience. I translated the metaphor, Manhattan as an island, the tourists as Galactic visitors, but the behaviors and power dynamics, those would all be Tourist Industrial Complex.

I had a title for the story that didn't work, and after some back and forth, I realized I could just use the phrase that inspired the story, just tweaked.

# FIVE POINT THREE
# MILLIGRAMS

The peacekeepers came to take me off-world while I was eating ramen down in Kamintown, surrounded by rickety three-story colony mudbricks and flickering neon. Kamintown was thick with Bos who had taken over the old, abandoned buildings from First Landing, renovating them to their own uses after the last recession.

We all watched the peacekeepers bleed off the last of their momentum, leaving a long trail of black smoke from their deorbit that hung in the sky. Then they curved in toward town. Sensible people started going inside and off the street. But quite a few Bos just stared sullenly as the retrorockets flared to light up the dark brown streets, washing out the colorful neons with a bright glow.

"Fucking Lynns up to no good," the old Bo woman on the other side of the ramen stall muttered.

I gave her a weary nod.

"No offence," she said.

The pair of peacekeepers hit the street, all worn steel and faded paint, but still as lethal as ever. Robot golems, ID numbers spray-painted on their legs, camera eyes scanning the world around them.

Someone tossed a bottle at one. It shattered harmlessly over its head, and it didn't bother to engage.

They stomped their way up the compacted dirt street to the stall.

"Lynn-Hale?"

I nodded.

"The harbormaster needs to speak with you in person."

"Can I finish my dinner?"

The camera eyes flicked to my bowl, focused, then switched back to me. "No."

A loud noise made the Bos around me jump in their seats. The peacekeeper's chest cracked in the middle. Then the ribs splayed out, and I looked at the restraints dangling inside the cavity of the machine.

Four minutes later, I was choking in antiacceleration foam as the peacekeeper launched out of the nearest city railgun.

I was still pushing a hand towel against my nose to stop the bleeding in the harbormaster's office. It had a dramatic view of the Ring here. The office was in the center of the drum that was the orbital station. That meant there was no gravity, so I watched globs of blood floating in the air that I'd missed with the towel.

A two-kilometer structure in low orbit, anyone could see the ring from the ground. It was our link to the old world. It was also an ever-present reminder of who we were and where we came from. Up close, one's eye wandered over the mega-capacitors and dark-energy storage dumps.

It was a technological wonder, and to me, not just a reminder of where we came from, but what we always compared ourselves to. Our world could never build this.

Maybe, one day.

The harbormaster had a desk next to a massive portal looking over the ring. Rank had its privileges. I could see why one would build an entire life around trying to get here.

"Lynn," I said in greeting. He was clearly Lynn. I was staring into my face, but older. Lots of gray, lines, a sense of tiredness that I usually only acquired after a few nights of no sleep, and some great existential crisis or two.

The harbormaster's face twisted. It was rude to use the original name without a unique secondary.

"Detective Lynn-Hale," he said crisply, correcting my faux pas by addressing me properly.

"I already showed the peacekeepers my ID," I said.

"I'm Harbormaster Lynn-Anichio." The harbormaster twisted in place so that he could also look at the ring.

"Why am I here?"

"There's a shipment coming," Lynn-Anichio said.

"In a year and a half," I said. They came through every seven years. Forcing the wormhole open took incredible amounts of energy.

"Tomorrow," Lynn-Anichio said. "The secondary rings have been powering up for the last week."

I had to hide my shock. For seventy-five years, there'd been a strict schedule. The portal opened and in came necessary materials that Earth thought could help the distant world that nine of us had originally settled.

The dark energy could only hold the mouth open for a moment, so the cargo came through fast, and there was never very much. Starter nano feedstock for replication machines. Quantum chips. Nutrient kits. Data on tiny drives.

All of it had to fit in a pod the size of a watermelon that would strike the capture arms waiting on this side.

"Why?" I ask.

"The Lynns down in Capital think there's a weapon coming in," Lynn-Anichio says. "Things are turbulent down there. Aira dissidents may have sent messages back to Earth asking for help."

"And how do you know that?"

"The Airas programmed the capture arms to handle more force. When the pod comes through, it will be heavier than normal, and the arms are going to compensate. They didn't think we'd notice the force tolerance difference, it's very subtle. A Lynn going over the arm parameters noticed the difference and reported it on up the chain, among Lynns only."

"How much?"

"The pod will be five point three milligrams heavier than normal."

"I'm a ground-based detective for the outskirts of the big city, why are you asking me up here? Don't you have your own people?"

The harbormaster shook his head. "Edgars handle security, usually. But you're a rare Lynn that does law and order and we're trying to keep this close to our chests. And you're known for dealing with a variety of people. You'll be talking to Edgars, Airas, and Siennas. Times are explosive right now. You're the right Lynn for the job."

"Why did you wait this long?"

The harbormaster sighed. "It was assumed to be a calibration flaw. It wasn't until several hours ago that we were able to determine it was purposeful. You'll have all the clearance and staff you'll need, and budget. Time is not on our side."

Five point three milligrams.

It didn't seem like much until you realized it had been slung across the hundreds of light-years that separated us from Earth.

Of course, it wasn't supposed to be this limited. No one had expected the failure on the seventh dark-energy node when the *Opportunity* passed through, severing the ringship in half.

The Ring had been launched from Earth as a micro package of nanobots, hit an asteroid in system, and built the Ring from a pattern. But there was no one on this side back then to check things over. No Airas to make sure all systems were optimal.

Sure, they sent drones through, at first, to make sure the Ring worked. But each passage stressed the Ring systems, and when the *Opportunity* came through, the Ring failed.

It was a miracle the first generation of Airas ever got it to work again, even as reduced as it was.

It was a miracle that Ravi, after realizing the Nine Survivors were sterile and dying, their bodies fried by the lashing tentacles of dark energy released by failing Ring systems, was able to make clones.

So many miracles.

And now this one to solve.

Five point three milligrams.

Someone knew that extra mass was going to come through the portal. The obvious first step was to head to the capture facilities.

In the old days, there was the station and a giant net slung between a hoop on the side of the station. The Airas had switched to a set of arms that snagged the pods. They knew where the pod was coming, and exactly how fast, and when. Three fast-moving arms could catch the pod and move into the airlock without worrying about rebound.

Pod Capture was in zero gravity, just like the harbormaster's office. I threw up, twice, on the way over, my head spinning as I moved between floors and tunnels. An aide, a polite Ravi, offered me vertigo pills, but I declined. I needed my mind sharp and unaffected by drowsiness.

There was a Lynn in charge, of course, a younger but eager woman working at advancing her career. Her eyes widened when I arrived with four Edgars with me for muscle and the Ravi. I hadn't learned their names yet.

"I'm in charge of twenty Airas and ten Siennas," she told me. She'd received a call telling her to cooperate in any way, and I was older than her. Lynns tended to defer to each other by age, as a Lynn working the career ladder usually advanced in a fairly predictable way. "They run the arms. The pods usually come in at about a hundred and thirty-seven point nine kilometers an hour."

"That's fast."

"They need to clear the event horizon quickly. Otherwise, they get affected."

The three arms reached down, like a squid from the old world, and reached for the pod, whipping out to match speed and then gently snag them.

"The outer skin is impact gel, in case of error the pod will embed itself in the arm."

"And if the arms miss?"

"In that event, unlikely though it is, there is a smaller net in the path further out. There are also capture drones that can head out for it."

I did interviews with the pod capture division, backing everything up to video and forwarding it to a Lynn assigned to the task force who would report back to the harbormaster.

The Airas were all dark-haired, dark-eyed, with sharp cheekbones and full of distress that the arms had been tampered with. Everyone denied it was them. The Siennas, round-faced and blonde, were fascinated by the puzzle.

Sienna-Fields leaned forward to explain it to me. "Lynn-Winter set up several authentication levels, everything has to be co-signed and approved. The security is rigorous. I don't think this was done by someone here, we've been thinking about it and we're betting you'll find that someone outside of the capture division figured out how to access arm control."

I bent forward. "Is there a way we can do that within a day?"

Lynn-Winter, the administrator, leaned in. "I doubt it. We're already pulling all the logs, but it's grunt work. We're going through every single communication. We'll figure out where this came from, just not for another few days."

I was watching Sienna-Fields, and I could tell that she didn't *quite* agree, but kept her counsel.

"What do you think I should be paying attention to?" I asked her.

She glanced at Lynn-Winter, not wanting to cause trouble with administration and she was reading me as potentially a higher up, not a detective. She'd only been ordered to talk to me, it hadn't been explained who exactly I was. But I was a Lynn, and that likely meant admin.

"You won't be getting Lynn-Winter into any trouble," I assured her. "Nor causing any for you or your people."

"Maybe," she said. "Or maybe this is something that Earth wants to send and Lynns are trying to meddle with. This is way above my paygrade, and I haven't figured out what's happening. How do I know helping you is the right call? Logically, all I know is that a pod is coming early, and whoever hacked the arms knows about it. It's a *good* thing they got in there."

"The extra weight was not warned about in the header broadcast," I said. "Whatever it is, even the people over on the Earth side don't know it's going to be in the pod."

"Oh."

I sat with her a long moment, and then she shrugged. "Well, someone had to know to make the changes. Logically, I'd start in the communications department. If time is valuable, you're wasting your time by starting here."

The next Sienna, a male, agreed with the logic.

I added the two Siennas from pod control to the task force and then asked the harbormaster for a combination of Bos, Kits, Airas, and Siennas he trusted.

"Airas and Siennas, yes, there might be a few Bos on station, but no Kits that I know of. What would be the point?"

"Send over who you have."

To the task force's consternation, I held everything up to run a search of personnel records until I verified that there was not even a single Kit on staff.

What would a clone from a famously artistic-minded line be doing up here? They were down on the ground acting in dramas, reading news, or just generally entertaining everyone. That was what human resources would say. But I wanted an artist's eye on my team, looking for the clever and human hack.

I always built teams from across the various lines. You never knew where the crucial piece of insight would come from. For all the obsession over 'types' with clones, I found a varied team could chip away at the issue.

After all, no one expected a Lynn to be running with the law-and-order types, hunting down criminals and solving cases.

But here I was.

My team swept into communications like a horde. The Edgars locked everything down and lined everyone up for interviews, watching for any nervous or suspicious people, with my assistant Ravi, who was empathetic, helping them.

The Siennas and Airas got into the systems, and with the two Lynns in charge of comms, authorized us to crawl through the Ring logs that the Sienna's needed while I did interviews.

Our Ravi, Ravi-Rama I found his name was, ordered us all tea once the hours started to get long.

Sienna-Fields found it. Three hours in, she pulled one of the logs and found a piggybacked compressed file going out on the laser that punched through the portal for that brief moment it was open and the pod was flung through to us.

While Earth, with its greater numbers and research abilities, passed along what information and resources it could, we passed along our stories. Stellar probe analysis, planetary data, and cultural history. Pictures and videos of our world were well-received by our distant cousins.

Sienna-Fields found video that had been compressed for the laser beam burst of comms to the other side, and inside that compression, there were low-resolution text files riding along, hiding in the edges of the message.

I didn't understand much of it, but the look on two of the comms techs who were still in the room told me all I needed to know. This was it.

"So, what is it?" I asked.

"It's anti-Lynn propaganda," she said. "You won't like it. They're calling us a caste society and asking for help."

*And help has come,* I thought.

Five point three milligrams of it.

"This still doesn't tell us who did it, and what came through," I said. "And we're just a few hours away from Ring open."

In some ways, it didn't surprise me that I was positioned to fail here. Barely a day to solve a case rooted in complaints that went all the way back to the First Generation.

And here was the Lynn detective, failing at trying to be something he wasn't. There were some high-level Lynns that would be happy to see that.

In fact, I was beginning to wonder if that was the reason for snatching me out of Kamintown to come up here.

Leave it to a Lynn to start seeing political intrigue when the story was most likely that the harbormaster only trusted his own kind. Affinity was the easiest explanation. I was being slightly narcissistic.

"Do you know how hard it is to set up a reception ceremony in two days?" the harbormaster eagerly asked me when I showed up to report on what we found.

"No?" I didn't enjoy social planning.

"Horrific." The harbormaster waved his hands around. But his voice didn't make it sound like it was that bad. In fact, he sounded somewhat pleased.

"You should probably delay all that until we figure out what's happening," I told him.

"Not the celebration," he said. "But we will quarantine the pod. That's not outside normal, the security will just be heavier until we get an answer. We'll have our top Edgar to coordinate that."

I'd seen the man around. A beefy man with eyes that flicked at everything with a faint air of suspicion.

"Good job finding what you did," the harbormaster said. "It gives us some idea of what this is all about."

"Thank you, sir." Even as I said it, I felt a faint annoyance at my Lynn-like deference based on his age and position. It was one of the reasons I'd joined the force. Say what you would about Edgars, they viewed competence as worthy of respect and that was it.

Riots were happening down in the capitol. I watched some video of peacekeepers dropping out of orbit. But as one Airan commentator noted, the metal machines were nearing eighty years old. They were Earth-tech, hitched over in the *Opportunity* and redesigned in the second generation to be security machines.

The force was taking over more and more of that. And I wanted to be back with all those Edgars in their riot gear, staring down large mobs shouting anti-line slogans.

As the head of the task force, I was given free rein to wander the ceremonies. I chose to watch from security feeds with Edgar-Ramos and Edgar-Frida, hanging inside a tiny closet of a monitoring room tucked away in a service tunnel.

The sting of initial defeat and not knowing what was going on left a bad taste in my mouth. I'd been a little edgy, but so was everyone else on the station. This was the first off-schedule delivery in all of our recorded history.

What the hell was going on?

I watched as the Ring lit up. I could have been seeing it with my own eyes, out there with VIPs in the viewing cupola. When the raw power of the portal snapped on, I could have seen the distortion ripple in the space between us. I could have watched the very rift in space appear in the heart of the ring, and briefly glimpse a sight of a blue that was Old Earth itself.

The Lynn in me wanted to be next to the VIPs and all that power.

But I had a job to do. Monitoring the faces and actions of people in the capture and comms departments. Studying patterns of movement throughout the station.

Being just generally suspicious.

When the pod snapped out of the portal and struck the arms, I was leaning over a tiny monitor looking out over the comms team.

I called the Lynn there. "Do you have the answer?"

Why had Earth sent this package early, and what did it mean for the schedule. As we understood it, the energy required to open the Ring cost dearly. And there were other Rings, to other worlds, where they worked properly.

There was a new Ring being built on the edge of our system. It had been sent through in the second opening. It would take another seventy years to build a new Ring from the asteroids and dust out there.

Until then …

"The Enka Virus," I was told. Earth heard about the alien virus we were reduced to fighting with quarantine methods and had studied all the information we'd sent. They'd decided to help as early as they could.

A few hours later, after all the drunk VIPs were escorted back to their shuttles and sent home, I stood outside a cleanroom and watched as Airas in full encounter suits slowly opened the pod and pulled everything out.

There was nothing in there but what the manifest told us to expect.

"That makes no sense," I said. And Edgar-Ramos agreed. So we had them do it again.

I had to go back to the harbormaster with the taste of failure in my mouth again. He licked his lips and glared at me with all the disappointment an older Lynn could gather.

"They said you were unconventional and our best chance of

breaking this open," he said. "I thought it was a strange thing to bring up here, a Lynn policeman. A whole wasted life, grubbing around with no managerial aspirations."

"I have an idea," I said, doing my best to ignore his line-based bigotry. It wasn't the first time. It wouldn't be the last.

"What's that?" he asked with scorn.

"I need all the Lynns on the station to get in the cleanroom and take a look at the pod."

It didn't take that long. One of the Lynns in the science department found the ampule as we weighed and individually checked all the aerogel packing, canisters, and instructions against the manifest.

The ampule was the size of a thumb, nestled inside a nano-fuel cell, and it weighed five point three milligrams.

It was a line thing. I didn't want to engage with that at first, I was reluctant to see it. But I shouldn't have been so naive. The Airas just kept looking over it. Which meant that the station Airas, or at least enough of them in the station to hide the ampule twice, were responsible.

An Edgar tagged it, and three Lynns went with him to have a Sienna team analyze it.

I watched the harbormaster give the order to arrest every single Aira in the station.

"Do you think that's wise?" I asked the harbormaster.

The older Lynn looked at me with barely disguised fury. "They conspired. Most of them."

"And they likely had a great deal of help from down below," I added.

"Well, my superiors will deal with that."

I thought about the riots and shook my head. Things would get worse. The station couldn't run without Aira line workers, the way technical trades were passed on. And to just bar a whole line from the station outright? It was a denial of birthright.

But I wasn't in charge here. I was just the detective. I was someone who took orders, I didn't give them.

Sienna-Winter called. "We know what it is," she said.

"And?" I could hardly contain my curiosity.

"They can fix the damage to our DNA. It's a sterility cure."

The harbormaster looked horrified.

"And," Sienna added. "DNA samples. Three hundred. For genetic variation."

The harbormaster shuddered at the word "variation."

"Lines have been protesting about castes for generations," I said. "And the Aira, they saw a simple, technical fix."

"I have to admire it," Sienna said, "even if I can't condone it."

"We have it in our control," the harbormaster said. "Earth can't interrupt our entire culture just because they are a variant lot. I'll send it to the council Lynns. In the meantime, I'll have more Edgars on security."

A peacekeeper took me back to the ground. An expensive, acceleration-gel-filled nightmare of rattling around before I was disgorged back onto Kamintown's muddy, beige streets.

I looked back up to the sky, enjoying the taste of real air and the lack of fan noise.

From a phone in a nearby grocery store, I made a call to a Kit I used to work with. The owner knew me, though several of the Bos loitering by the door glared openly at me.

Kit-Kyliki met me in a park, and I handed him the chemical analysis and summary report by Sienna-Fields.

"Why?" he asked. "You know the ground is going to *erupt* when the other lines see this."

"I know," I said. "Job security."

"Don't be flippant," he said. We'd met when he tried to apply to the force, and then his parents had pressured him out of it. Now I fed him stuff, helped keep him ahead of the other newsmen. "If I show this, I'll get fired. Or worse."

"I'll give it out to a lot of other people. And the Lynns won't be able to stop it all, not if the Edgars are pissed off as well. And they will be. Hiding this, they won't like that violation of law."

"But the lines have held since we first arrived."

"But they shouldn't," I said to the man who should have been my first partner on the squad. He would have been a good detective. Hell, half his shows were just cover for him tracking down something he'd gotten his teeth into. "They don't have to anymore. You can feel that pressure, too, I know it. We all do, down here, following in the lanes they want us to."

I left him there on the street.

We'd survived worse, coming to this world. We'd survive this.

Better. Like an old detective running down a lead, trying to get it wrapped faster than his department Edgars, whatever came next, we'd thrive on it.

Only a multi-line team could have solved what we did so quickly. Only a multi-line world would open that Ring back up and join our cousins on the other side as we were meant to.

Five point three milligrams.

That was all it would take to change everything.

## AUTHOR NOTES

I wish I could wax eloquent about where the story idea came from, but the truth? I sat down to write a story and this came to me. Often I have a particular seed, or a process. Often I have a story about the story.

Five Point Three Milligrams was one of those stories that just unfolded as I wrote it, coming nice and easy.

Would that all stories were so easy.

# BY THE WARMTH OF THEIR CALCULUS

Three ships hung in the void. One sleek and metallic, festooned with jagged sensors and the melted remains of powerful weapons, all of it pitted by a millennium of hard radiation and micro-impacts. The other two, each to either side, were hand-fashioned balls of ice and rock, flesh and blood, vegetation and animal, cratered from battles and long orbits through the Ring Archipelago where the dust had long battered their muddy hulls.

Koki-Fiana fe Sese hung in the air inside a great bauble of polished, clear ice in the underbelly of her dustship and looked out at the ancient seedship as the sun's angry red light glinted across nozzles and apparatus the purpose of which she could only guess.

There was the void between the two ships. And when she looked past that, she could see the small sparks of light that were the outer planets where her people could not reach as they were far out of the dust plane. And then beyond the outer planet came the stars, where the priests said people traveled from on their seedships. Though artificers could believe that, as it would have taken millennia to cross distances that vast, and seedships were just fragile metal buckets.

And angry, dark things waited in the dark between the stars.

Then she saw something that chilled her more than the ice just an arm's length away, or the void beyond it: a sequence of lights, some flickering and dying away, appeared all down the center of the ancient ship's hull.

Another lone light began winking furiously on the hull of the seedship. It was battle language. Fiana pushed away from the clear, window-like ice and grabbed a handhold near the airlock. There was a speaking tube there. She smacked the switch for Operations. There was a hiss and a click as pneumatic tubes reconfigured.

"Mother here," she said, quickly. "I see incoming communication."

Fiana didn't have the common words and their sequences memorized anymore. It had been twenty years since she'd had her eyes glued to a telescope, watching for incoming while hoping she wouldn't have to page through a slim dictionary floating from a belt. She was the Mother Superior now, the heart of the ship.

She wished she still had the aptitude, waiting for the message to get passed on was taking too damn long.

"Mother Superior!" The response was tinny, and they weren't following their training to throw their voice well. "Sortie Leader Two says the Belshin Historians tried to recover data from the seedship. They turned on a subsystem and that triggered another power up somewhere else."

Ancient circuits were coming online just across the void.

"Floating shit," Fiana whispered.

"Please repeat?" Ops sounded terrified. Their voice had cracked.

They were all floating next to a giant beacon. They were like a raw hunk of meat hanging outside at sunset back on Sese, and the sawflies would be coming to chew them apart any second now.

"Call for all riggers to stand by the sail tubes," Fiana ordered. "Every available pair of eyes not in Figures and Orbits needs to be on a telescope, and if we run out of scopes, stand next to someone with one. Cancel all watches, muster all minds. Sound the alarm, Ops."

A moment later a plaintive wail filled the rocky corridors of the dustship. Commands were shouted, echoed, and hands slapped against rails as people rushed to their posts.

"Tell F&O to begin plotting possible escape vectors," Fiana added. "All possibilities need to be in the air for us to consider."

"Urgent from Sortie Two: they're under attack."

"Attack? From what?" Fiana looked back at the ice, but all she could see was the silver metal of ancients. She could see the wink-wink-wink of communication, but nothing else betrayed what was happening.

She felt helpless.

The other dustship's hull rippled as if something inside was pushing at the skin from the inside to get out. Then the Belshin ship cracked open. It vomited water and air slowly into the void as Fiana watched in horror.

"Sortie Two has warned us not to signal back," Ops said.

"Is there an F&O rep there?" Fiana asked. "If so, put her on, now."

"Heai-Lily here," came a strong voice.

"I want full sails out and a vector away from here. Pick the first one out."

Lily hesitated. "There are Hunter-Killer exhaust signs reported. We're plotting them against known objects in this plane. We need to work the figures, but most of F&O is guessing we're surrounded."

"It was a trap."

"Yes, Mother."

"We can't deploy the sails, they'll spot the anomaly."

"I think so, Mother."

They should have swung by and left the ship alone when they found the Belshin dustship arriving at the same time. Archipelago treaty rules gave them both genetic exploration rights, and Fiana had wanted to get in and pull material out. She'd assumed the Belshin were after the same thing. It wouldn't have been the first time multiple dustships from opposing peoples had to work on an artifact together. There were rules for this sort of thing.

But the Belshin had been greedy and violated those rules.

The Hunter-Killers had left something in the seedship for them. And now Belshin were paying the price. And Fiana's entire ship might well pay it as well.

"Ops is telling me to tell you that Sortie Two is free of the hull and returning."

The team would be jumping free of the seedship, eyeballing their trajectories back to the netting on that side of the dustship. They'd pull it in after them. They wanted nothing that looked made by intelligence on the outside of the dustship.

"Lockdown all heat exchangers and airlocks once they're in. We're running tight from here on out."

Fiana wanted to curl into a ball near the speaking tube, but instead, she forced herself to kick away, grab a corner, and flip into the corridor. She flew her way down the center, using her fingertips to adjust her course.

Ops, the hub deep in the ship, was packed with off-watch specialists, their eyes wide with fear, but plugging away at tasks and doing their best to pitch in. Everyone hung from footholds, making Ops feel like a literal hive of busy humanity.

There was an "up" to the sphere that was Ops, but many of the stations were triplicated throughout. This was so that the crew could let the ship orient however it needed and to give engineering two fail-safe command stations for every primary. Watches rotated station placements to make sure everything was in good order.

But in an all-call situation like this, everyone was at a station. Once Fiana had an acceleration vector ordered, if it became safe to do it, they'd reorganize Ops so that everyone was at a station on the "down" part.

For now, they were drifting slowly away from the seedship. But with Hunter-Killers arrowing in toward them, she doubted they would get far enough away to not be of interest when the damn things arrived.

Sortie Two gave their report right away. The all-male team floated nervously in a ready room in front of Fiana and Odetta-Audra fe Enna, one of the Secondary Mothers.

"There were two Hunter-Killers on board," Sim, the sortie leader, said. "They lit up the moment the Belshin Historians got the engine room powered up. I think it was a mistake, though, they were just trying to get the ancient screens to talk to them."

"Treaty breakers," Audra spat. She'd been simmering with fury since Fiana first saw her in Ops. She was concealing her fear, Fiana knew, covering it up with anger to fuel herself. Most times, it made her a fast, decisive leader, though it often lead to intimidation and some distance between Audra and the folk she needed to lead. Right now, it was making the sortie men nervous.

They'd been in a dangerous situation and their nerves were already rattled, so Fiana gently tapped Audra's wrist. A warning to let her Mother Superior lead the questions for now. They'd worked together long enough for Audra to get the signal.

"It's a temptation all librarians and historians struggle with," Fiana said. "Particularly peoples on the far side of the Archipelago. A wealth of knowledge from the ancients and their golden age of machinery. A piece of that could give them the ability to draw even with us."

Nations had, after all, been built on the success of daring raids on old ships, with historians writing down what they saw in ancient script as fast as they could before making a dash for it. Only one of ten missions would make it out alive, though.

"We asked them to wait until we were done with the collection mission," Sim said. "But one of their team told us they were low on consumables because they were so far from home. We focused on doing what we came to do as quickly as we could and getting away. We did not think the historians already knew a power-up sequence or we wouldn't have stayed."

They had thought they had time to work on carefully cracking the glass pods open enough to slip a needle through without triggering any of the seedship's alarms.

But Sim had kept his head and captured what they could. Seven samples, ancient DNA that would be uncorrupted by radiation and genetic drift or the tight bloodlines of the small worldlets of the Archipelago.

The Great Mothers of the worlds wouldn't invest in these missions without that payoff. When their ancestors built the Archipelago, they'd suspected that background radiation and cosmic rays would wreak havoc over time. Whatever the world was like that people fled from, it was well shielded, and the people who ran before the Hunter-Killers hadn't had time to invent a biological solution.

So these missions, these long loops out of the safety of the great dust planes to the drifting seedships for their frozen, protected heritage, were necessary for her people to continue to survive. These ships had shielding they did not understand and could not replicate. Not without the kind of industry that would bring the Hunter-Killers screaming toward them.

"Did you see—" Fiana started.

"Yes." Sim looked down and shivered slightly. "It looked like a spider. When we heard the alarm, we did as trained. Stripped down, no artificial fibers, no clothes, no tools, no weapons. We let it come."

"That couldn't have been easy." Fiana reached out and squeezed Sim's hand, the poor thing was shivering. Likely thinking back to what happened on the seedship they were still within jumping distance of.

"It ran past us to the Belshin. They had weapons. They fought it. They died. It broke out the airlock they came through and went for their ship."

Fiana had seen what came next. The Hunter-Killer had detonated itself, destroying the Belshin world ship.

Heai-Lily came with a bundle of flexies two hours later. Her strong hair joyously sprung out around her head, as if holding compressed energy inside like springs. Her eyes, though, were tired and red.

She carefully hung the transparent sheets in the air of the ready room around Fiana.

"We have trajectories," she said. The clear rectangles had been marked up with known objects in small, careful dots from one of the navigation templates.

In red, nine X marks with arrows denoted velocities and directions. From where Fiana hung, she could get a sense of the three-dimensional situation they were in.

"They're converging on us." Fiana had suspected as much, but hearing it from Lily still made her stomach roil slightly. "With options for covering any chances at escape if we run."

"So, you have no solutions for me?"

"Right now, we have a far side that is hidden from their instruments. We could vent consumables that would match the profile of an icy rock being heated up. It'd be suspicious, but not completely outside of the realm of naturally occurrent activity."

"That'll get us up to a walking pace away from the seedship," Fiana said.

"Over time. We'll have to randomize the jets, and it'll eat into our water and air."

And that would be dangerous, as right now they needed to drift in place to avoid attention.

"What does that drift get us?" Fiana asked.

"Further above the dust planes," Lily said. "Until we re-intersect."

"That's not good." They would be unable to maneuver with sails. The hundreds of dust rings around the Greater World, separated by bands and layers, would be too far away for them to shoot their sails into. Fiana's dustship had hundreds of miles of cable they could use to guide a sail far out into a pocket of faster or slower moving dust or even to grapple with a larger object. But above it all, they would be helpless until they'd swung back around the Greater World and hit the dust planes again.

"We have a good library of discovered objects and their trajectories. If we can swing out and back in, there's a collision zone we can disguise our trajectory with."

It just meant weeks above the dust. Above everything, they were comfortable with.

But what was the alternative? Stay put and wait for the Hunter-Killers? Fiana wasn't a historian, but even she knew that the Hunter-Killers tore apart everything in an area that registered electrical activity.

Her ancestors had tall, black steles scattered around their world with old pictograms carved into their sides that warned them about the Hunter-Killers. Told stories about how the alien machines followed shouts into the stellar night to their source and destroyed them. And despite those proscriptions, Hulin the Wise had experimented with crystal radio devices in the polar north of Sese. An asteroid impact had cracked the world, almost revealing the hollow interior her people had hidden inside since the ancestors first arrived. Those had been years of children dying as air fouled, and great engineering projects struggled to do the impossible: fix a cracked world.

"How fast can we get out of here?"

"Using consumables, it's dangerous, Mother. We need to coordinate with Ops. The margin will be thin, if we want to get out of here before the Hunter-Killers."

Fiana swept the transparent sheets around her away. "I'll get Ops ready to follow your commands."

To stay put would be to wait passively for death, and she wasn't ready to welcome the Hunter-Killers onto her ship.

Within the hour, the far-side of the dustship was venting gases as crew warmed the material up (but not too much, or the heat signature would be suspicious and hint at some kind of unnatural process), compressed the water and hydrogen in airlocks through conduits of muscular tubes that grew throughout the ship, and blasted it out in timed dumps at F&O's orders.

Slowly, faster than the natural differential drift already there, Fiana's dustship began to move away from the seedship. It trailed a tail behind, gleaming like a comet.

The dustship was a living organism. Its massive hearts pumped ichor around webs of veins that exchanged heat generated by the living things inside the rock and ice hull, both human and engineered. The great lungs heaved and the air inside moved about. Its bowels gurgled with waste, and its stomach fermented grain to feed the people.

Sese's people had worked hard to create a biological, living shell that could move through the rings around the Great World. And they had found the other worlds the ancients had created, some of them dead hulks. Because the Hunter-Killers were ever on the prowl and not just myths to scare children with that had been passed down through the mists of prehistory.

Figures and Orbits, down in their calculatorium, worked away at the reports of Hunter-Killer movements, tracking them as they arrowed in toward the seedship. And other telescopists watched as the seedship dwindled away until it became a glint among the other points of light in the busy sky.

And Fiana hung in Ops, watching as the activity of the ship passed on through the watch stations and crew.

It was tense, the first few full rotations. No one slept. There were tears that hung in the air. Salty fear, exhaustion, tension. The idea that the killers of the Ancients were chasing them could unnerve anyone.

Yes, they'd escaped the initial trap, but that didn't mean they were safe yet.

Fiana broke the tension when she ordered watches to resume a standard staggered watch rotation again. Even if she wasn't so sure she wouldn't need all-call, she needed the crew to function. Any more than three shifts and a person could not function under a constant press of fear, watchfulness, and readiness.

So, she took the pressure for herself.

Fiana was inspecting the crew shaving ice from the outer walls, using one of the many burrowed tunnels in the hull, when Lily caught up to her.

"May I have a moment, Mother?" she asked softly.

"They keep sending you to brief me," Fiana noted. "You are a subordinate, not a superior. Why is your team doing this?"

"The more experienced calculating seniors need to be in the calculatorium at all times. We are at capacity, Mother, and this is not a time for anyone who needs work verified."

Lily wouldn't meet her eyes.

Well, she was either ashamed to admit she was the weakest calculator in the ship, or the F&O mothers were using her as a firewall in case Fiana grew angry with them.

Or, if the F&O mothers were smart, and they were the elite of void-faring peoples, the answer could be both things at the same time. Maybe it didn't hurt that Fiana would be less likely to be angry with a young, nervous Lily. And maybe they needed the best to stay in the room and work the problem.

"What's the emergency, Lily?"

"We're moving slower than expected, Mother. It has orbital and schedule implications. We can't vent heat because we didn't quite get where we thought we'd be to have cover of several larger rocky objects blocking us from Hunter-Killer view."

Fiana batted aside ice shavings and tried to focus over the hammering of pickaxes and scrape of shovels.

"F&O made a mistake?" she asked. This could cost lives. No wonder they'd sent the almost childlike Lily to stare over at her with wide eyes. "Are you sure? The signal crew could have made a sighting mistake."

A bunch of boys with astrolabes at the telescopes doing their best astronomical sightings. F&O took the averages of repeated sightings.

"The math is strong," Lily protested, her voice firm with trust in her colleagues. "And junior F&O took sightings to confirm. The signal crew was accurate."

"But we're off track?" There was no room for that kind of error. If they didn't arrive at the right place at the right time, they wouldn't be able to tether off the right large rock or hit the right dust plane to adjust their path.

They'd end up running out of air, or water, slowly dying, out of reach of any other dust ship or world that could lend aid.

Lily gave her a summary report written in small and careful handwriting, filled with diagrams and area maps. Fiana would have to crawl over the details later in her quarters, poring over the equations and running checks with her own slide rule. A Mother Superior of a dust ship was required to know the math; Fiana had been an F&O staffer herself in her youth.

But it was going to be slow work to make sure she understood everything in the report.

Tight was the crown of leadership, Fiana knew. It would be a headache she had to bear.

Fiana cursorily looked through the report until she found the summary. She bit her lip. "F&O thinks there's more mass than we accounted for?"

"About sixty chipstones worth of mass."

Sixty chipstones. About ten people's worth of mass. Had they known their audit was off, they could have thrown out nonessential material from the inside to balance the ship. They could have hidden it away in the ice and consumables they'd blown.

It shouldn't have been off, though. They'd based their lives on the audit run before maneuvers.

"There was an audit," Fiana said. And everyone on board knew how important an audit was before a maneuver.

"F&O is not accusing anyone of anything, we are merely reporting the math. It doesn't lie, Mother. You can check it yourself."

She would. But for now, Fiana was not going to assume her specialists were wrong. She had to trust that her team was doing their best work. "I will check it, but I will wager it agrees with you. I'll call another mass audit. Something isn't right. We'll see if we can solve for the mystery yet."

Even though she hung in the air, Lily visibly relaxed as tension drained from her body.

"Of course, Mother. We will put our second shift at your disposal and keep only a core team running calculations."

The heat began to build. Crew took to wearing just simple wraps when off shift, and then Fiana gave permission for everyone to strip to just undergarments.

Globes of salty sweat hung in the stultifying air and sunken eyes made everyone look like tired ghosts.

The ship's Surgeon, Lla-Je fe Sese kicked his foot against the door to the captain's quarters in the middle of an off-watch. Faina was startled to find him hanging in place, face flushed and worried.

"Mother, we are all in danger of heatstroke," Je said, without apologizing for waking her. The red emergency light in the doorway glimmered off his shaved scalp. It was the way of the surgeons to shave, though Je was male and used to shaving. For surgeons, it was ritual demonstration of razor control, a tradition hundreds of years old. A surgeon with a nick on her body was not to be trusted, or so the saying went. Je said it was done for hygiene, but it helped that men were expected to be fastidious about it as well. Fiana always imagined it must have been weirder for the regular surgeons to hew to the tradition, given expectations. "How much longer will we be containing our waste heat?"

They'd been drifting for days now, moving further away from the seedship. The thick wall of ice around the hull that they mined for air and water had been scraped down, warmed, and vented. In some parts, the hull was down to only rock and mud.

"Fifteen full shifts before we re-intersect with the dust fields." One orbit around the Great World. They would have to deploy full sails on return, but the higher orbit would let the area the Hunter-Killers were infesting move ahead under them. They would plunge back into a different part of the Archipelago with barely any water and air left.

"Crew will be dying from the heat long before then," Je said somberly.

"What should we look for?" Faina asked wearily. Die of heat now, or miss their chance to get to safety when they re-intersected with the dust planes and the Archipelago. Floating diarrhea, those choices.

"Confusion, irritabilit—" like Fiana's irritability at being woken? Though, to be fair, she'd been sleeping slightly, dozing as she bumped from the wall to the hammock. "Dry skin, vomiting, panting, and flushed faces."

"We're out in the void, Je. The Hunter-Killers can move out here without needing sails or tethers, but we're helpless until we intersect with the dust rings again."

"Then all that our people will find will be a ghost ship," Je said seriously. "If they can find us at all."

He was so serious. Always worried. And it wasn't his place to look this long in the face. It was Fiana's. But Je had always been high-minded. He wouldn't have fought so hard for a place in the Surgeon's Academy without a certain amount of hard pushiness.

"What do you recommend, my surgeon?"

"Daily internal thermometer checks for every crewmember," Je said.

"Internal? Is that what I think you mean?"

"It is."

"Je …" Fiana trailed off. Then she took a deep breath. "I can't have your team sticking tubes up everyone's ass once a day."

Particularly not if some male surgeon was doing it. Her team of commanding mothers trusted that Fiana valued Je, but a lot of them were old-fashioned and uncomfortable with having large, awkward hands on the handle of a blade.

"Then draw up a list of essential crew that you can't afford to lose, and they will be tested once a day. We're risking lives, understand?"

"I'll have the list drawn up, but we don't start taking temperatures until people start passing out," Fiana said. "The DNA samples are in lead cases in the ice rooms with our food. We can put anyone in danger there for now."

But it would be a temporary solution.

It was enough to mollify Je. For now.

But the decisions would become tougher as this went on.

The mass audit came back from a sweaty, tired Audra, who tracked Fiana down in the galley hall. The Secondary Mother had sheaves of clear flexies filled with accounting tables.

"There's unaccounted-for mass. We did the audit. We tested the ship's acceleration profile. The amount of mass they estimated is dead-on: there's sixty chipstone worth of something *somewhere*. Manifests can't account for it. We've checked everything we can think of."

Fiana offered her a pocket of cooled water, which Audra took and sucked on gratefully. Fiana used the moment to capture her thoughts and continue nibbling at a basket of grapes.

"We're going to have to search everyone's cabins, verify personal allowances," Audra said before Fiana could speak.

"No." Fiana shook her head. "There are just over a hundred crew. And yes, split, that could be enough." And when they sailed out from Sese they did not have to consider how true their mass was, they just deployed sails into the appropriate dust plane until they had the speed and vectors needed.

"We only did a rough manifest and mass account before leaving," Audra noted.

"I've sailed the dust planes of the Great World all my life, Audra. I've been F&O, then Secondary Mother, and now Mother. I'd sense it in my bones the moment we left if the sails were straining, our vessel heavy," Fiana said. "No, this has only been a problem since that seedship."

Audra, her legs looped around an air-chair, straightened. "What are you thinking?"

"Take the survey teams, the men, out onto the hull. Use airlocks facing away from the dust to keep cover. Full Encounter rules. Do you understand what I am asking you? Can you do that?"

Audra looked past Fiana, into a personal darkness and fear as she considered her death. Fiana was asking her to go out an airlock, seal it with ice and rock once the team was out, and then they would search the hull.

If they encountered Hunter-Killers, they would jump off into the vacuum and scatter to their deaths. They would not, under any circumstance, return to any known airlock, lest they lead the enemy inside. Maybe the Hunter-Killers wouldn't buy that. Maybe they would. It was still a hard thing to ask of a person.

Audra would know that if she turned this down, Fiana would honor her choice. But it would be a blow to her standing.

"I will lead a team," Audra said in a low, determined voice. "We need to find out what may have killed us."

Fiana held her hand and squeezed it. Such bravery. She had no doubt in Audra. It's why she had chosen the strong mind from her old F&O cohort to join her when the World Mothers had given Fiana a command of her own.

For an entire watch, the ship went about its business in a pre-funereal silence, with crew jumping at every bang and creak in the empty air.

Je came to report on two crewmembers who had passed out. An older F&O calculator and one of the survey men. He had given them fluids and put them in a freezer to let them cool down.

"The ship is suffering, too," he told her. The ship's heart had an infection, he judged. Some kind of pericarditis inflaming the sac around the great muscle. They were pumping it full of antibiotics and hoping for the best.

"We can't dump heat, not yet," Fiana told him.

"I know," Je said, softly. "I know."

The warble of airlock alarms echoed. Je twisted in the air to look down the corridor. "They're coming back inside."

Crew streamed through the air toward the doors. They weren't carrying weapons. There was nothing that would stop a Hunter-Killer, there was no point.

But they still came, determination on their faces, fists clenched. They would have thrown their bodies against the deadly machines to buy their sisters another minute of life, Fiana knew, with a tight knot in her stomach.

Voidsuits came through instead of gleaming, spidery balls of death. Fiana relaxed slightly.

And then more suits struggled through.

And more.

Despite herself, Fiana said aloud, "There are too many of them!"

Ten other suits that hadn't piled into the airlock on the way out.
Ten.

That could be sixty chipstones. If they were …

They removed their helmets, and the confused crew gasped.

Belshin men. Ten Belshin men.

Ten Belshin males had maybe doomed them all. It was something that Fiana kept rolling around her head for all its strangeness as she stared at the ten foreign faces hovering before her.

It was the math. The simple math. The massive ball of rock and ice looked substantial, but orbital mechanics were precise and unforgiving. Their weight had slowed them down enough to throw off the maneuver.

Fiana pointed at them. "You activated the seedship, you unleashed the Hunter-Killers on us all, and then you fled to our hull to hide! You have the audacity to hide on *my* ship?"

"They don't speak Undak," Je said. "Do you want me to translate? They're expecting that you will throw them out of the airlock. They're terrified."

Fiana saw it on their faces. Resignation, fear, some defiance.

Audra crossed her arms. "We should slice off their balls, put them in the fridge with the seedship DNA, and then shove the floating shits out the airlock."

"Don't translate that," Fiana said to Je.

"Engage the Lineage Protocol," Audra said. "We need to initiate it now. While we still have some sort of chance."

Fiana could hear Je suck in his breath. She looked over at Audra. "We're not going to talk about the Protocol right now. These are human lives you're talking about."

Audra glanced at Je. "Mother, he knew the risks when he agreed to join the ship."

"Lives," Fiana said. "All of the lives on this ship are important."

Je was only half listening. Several of the newcomers were chattering to him.

"They know you're angry," Je reported, cutting Audra off.

"They're expecting you to kill them. They're gastric plumbers. Belshin slaves. They fled when their ship was attacked."

"We cannot afford the increase in consumables," Audra hissed. "We're far out into the void. We're off orbit and schedule. You know what needs to be done, and it needs to be done quickly. Your crew is depending on you."

Fiana raised a finger. "Audra—"

Audra pushed herself back, away from the room. "As one of your secondaries, I have to remind you: every moment those males remain on board is a moment stolen from our future. It's math. It means cold, hard decisions. But that is what leaders do: they make the hard choices."

Fiana took Lily into one of the observation ice bowls.

"I wanted to show you something," Fiana said, drifting out toward the polished ice.

The young F&O calculator hung next to her. "Mother?"

Fiana pointed out at the dark. "Look out there, Lily. All those small points of light. That's something few, if any people from the Archipelago ever get to see."

From here they could see the entirety of the dust plane. The multitudes of the rings, the rocky moons.

Lily held up a thumb. "All of our people out there. Hiding away from Hunter-Killers."

They stared at the dust band for a long while.

Lily cleared her throat. "Even if you sacrifice the Belshin we can't fix the orbit."

"I spent two whole nights running the figures," Fiana said. "Audra ran them as well. Fifty people can survive a full braking maneuver and a loop by object IF-547, then 893, and a second all-sails slow that you and F&O have given me."

"So, it's Lineage Protocol." Lily turned her back to the dust plane. "They tell you in the Academy not to get too attached to the men aboard."

"People I trust are all telling me it's time." Fiana rubbed her forehead. The headaches were getting more and more intense. "We only have enough for fifty people to survive until we re-intercept the dust plane."

Protocol said it was time to take donations from all the men, store the material, and then ask them all to do the honorable thing. The *noble* thing. If they balked, then it was the Mother Superior's job to enforce the choice.

Only women could bear the next generation. Fiana needed to act to secure futures.

And yet ...

"The ideas that fix this situation, they won't come from just one person dictating them. It's going to have to come from everyone working the math. And being cross-checked."

Lily's eyes widened. "You're not going to engage the protocol?"

"Hard choices. The other mothers keep telling me to make hard choices." Fiana pushed away. "But the people who tell me that don't have to bear the consequences of those choices, and don't see the whole community, just the part of it that they identify with. It's easy to make a 'hard' choice when the price is paid by someone else.

"This won't be a popular decision," Lily said. "And I won't tell Audra you called her unimaginative."

"Thank you." Fiana patted her shoulder. "I need you to work the problem, talk to anyone who might have ideas, and to lean on your peers."

"We'll keep running ideas through the team," Lily promised. "There are things the engineers have proposed in the past. More nonessential mass that could be jettisoned. It could help."

Because there was math. And then there was *math*. Math was a tool, wasn't it? A tool to be wielded or mastered.

And Fiana wasn't going to give it blood.

Four crew passed out and were found floating in the corridors. Je came to Fiana, his face pinched and ruddy, to give her an update.

"Mother, we should have off-duty crew switch to a three-person cross-check system so that no one ends up alone."

"I'll send out orders." Fiana was hooked into the "top" of her room, which was laced with foot-webbing. She'd been holding a position in front of an air vent, letting the rush of air bob her back and forth.

"And I need to check you over," Je said.

Fiana waved a hand. "I am fine. There are others who need your attention, Je."

"You are the Mother Superior," Je insisted.

Fiana wiped a fat bead of sweat collecting behind her ear. The air was getting so thick she felt like she couldn't breathe anymore. They'd stopped venting, the heat, the moisture from shaving the ice, and the dust in the air had turned the ship into a swamp.

"I will endure," Fiana said. "If I feel I'm at risk I'll let you know."

Je didn't look happy but he couldn't do anything about it. Eventually, he nodded. He had floated his way back to the entryway, and he paused there, hands and feet in an X and gripping the door's lip.

"Mother, may I ask you something?"

His voice had softened, and Fiana could hear the worry.

"Lineage Protocol?" she asked him.

"Such a dry name for something so horrific," Je said as he nodded.

"F&O is working hard on a solution. I've asked all for ideas. But, in a nutshell, we need to breathe less, surgeon. We used too much as a simple rocket to get us away from the Hunter-Killer area. The math is simple and hard to escape. We only have so much air and we know how many people are onboard."

"The equation is simple," Je said. "So, we change the assumed inputs. The air-use rate is based on an assumption created by surgeons for average crew with average activity."

Je had her complete attention.

"Can you actually get the crew to breathe less?"

"The more you move, the more you breathe. So we freeze crew shifts. Everyone bound to their room and webbed in. No one moves until rescue. The command room shift stays in place and sleeps in place."

"You're asking the entire crew to stay in bed for twelve full shift rotations?"

"And to focus on breathing slowly and deeply. And that is not all. We have drugs for surgeries. The larger ones that use more air, we will need to drug them."

"And what will that get us, Je? Will that get us to the dust plane? Will that halve the air we use?"

"This isn't math, it's biology. Messy, imprecise," Je said.

"Give me an estimate," Fiana ordered. Because she couldn't risk lives based on messiness.

"I think we can reduce our air usage to two-thirds. Maybe to a half. We won't know until we start the experiment and monitor the impact."

Two-thirds still left a ghost ship. A third was an unblinking gulf that still couldn't be crossed.

But it would mean fewer lives that needed to be chosen for sacrifice.

"Ready the drugs," Fiana said. "We'll run the experiment and get a shift's worth of data." It wouldn't get them there by itself. It wasn't the solution. But it was something they could test.

Audra appeared at the door and shoved Je aside. She had a bandolier strapped tight across her chest and had changed into her dark black sortie uniform. Her pistol was in its forearm holster.

"Mother, we have a mutiny!" Audra said. "The men heard that Lineage Protocol will be called for. Some of them released the Belshin prisoners and broke into the armory."

The mutiny spread quickly. Panicked men took weapons into common areas that they barricaded with decoration panels ripped from the walls. Many of them were on sortie parties, so they were familiar with in-ship combat and knew where to find the weapons.

"We have the numbers," Audra said. Few could match her well-trained cadre. "My sisters are fast, and are the best hall-grapplers in the fleet."

Audra and her team would fight bitterly. They were Sortie Three, rarely sent to other ships, but trained to protect this one. They were backed up by members of engineering and women from the stays and tether teams, with their arms muscled from handling spider-silk ropes.

They raced down corridors to the heart of the mutiny where the chanting men were making their demands heard.

"Stop here!" Another woman in black held out a hand near a turn in the rock-ice corridor. "Mother, they're shooting anyone who tries to approach the barricade."

They all grabbed rails and stopped. Fiana listened to the shouts, the men trying to keep each other roused to bravery with their too-deep voices.

"We should have expected this," Audra said, acid in her voice.

Je said nothing but shrank back as if trying to hide against the wall.

Fiana looked around again at the nervous, but anticipatory sortie crew all watching Audra, waiting for the command. Then she quickly peeked around the corner.

"Mother!"

The men shouted at her but didn't shoot. Fiana took that as a good sign and stopped to look at the crudely hammered together door leading to the common rooms and the forms that she could see through the gaps nervously flitting around.

"Get Lily from F&O," Fiana ordered.

"And?" Audra also looked ready to go.

"It's the heat," Fiana said. She was panting from the race over here. "It's affecting our minds. Leading us to mistakes."

"My mind is tempered well," Audra hissed. "They are traitors to Sese, and foreign agitators from the other side of the Archipelago."

"What are their demands?" Fiana couldn't tell from all the yelling.

"They want the chance to live through lottery," one of the tether women with a simple club in her hands said.

"That's treason," Audra said. She leaned forward. "If we fight them, we can take care of the dilemma we face."

"Death makes traitors of many," Fiana said. "And the heat addles their minds. All our minds. Wouldn't you say, surgeon?"

Je did not look happy about being addressed. "Mother ..."

But Fiana saw Lily coasting toward them and waved her over. "My calculator! We have a tricky situation."

Fiana pulled the last of her wrap off, stripping herself naked, and then gently tapped the wall so that she would float out into the center of the corridor before Audra could react.

She could hear the sudden murmurs of surprise, the repeated low whispers of "Mother."

They began to shout their demands through the barricade, but she held up a hand.

"It is too hot for a fight, but if we have to, you are outnumbered. And you know this. So we are going to talk about this instead because I did not come out here into the void to do the Hunter-Killer's work for them. Not when our ancestors risked so much to create the Archipelago and dust planes for our survival. I will not spit in on their memories."

They quieted.

"I don't have the answer to our situation. But we, together, do. Come out to me, Je, Lily. Tell them what you've been telling me."

Fiana looked back. She gestured at them both.

Slowly, the surgeon and the F&O calculator bobbled out to join her.

"F&O found our mass problem. They saved us from the Hunter-Killers. Je is keeping us alive as best he can in this heat. I don't have the solution to how we make it back to the dust plane alive, but the two of them, with all of our help, might. There is no one answer here, but if we piece all of their ideas together, and add in some new ones, they could add up to enough to get us back home."

Lily stared at the men, then bit her lip. "We need to shed mass once we're at the apoapsis. Everything we can imagine we can do without and things we can't. We need to pare the ice and rock to the bare minimum, down to nothing but air, sails, and our bodies."

"And the rest of us must strap in and not move until rescue. The biggest among us must be drugged," Je said.

The men protested. That would surely impact them the most.

But Je argued with them. "These are the realities," he insisted. "We have to breathe less ... or not at all."

"We could thin the air more," one of the male voices on the other side suggested. "I'm in gastric, we can change the recirculation mixes."

As the suggestions continued, Fiana relaxed.

"We are not separate from the civilization that birthed us," she said to Audra. "We do not have to fall into murder and blood. Not this time."

The great dustship calved at apoapsis; the very height of its orbit. Fiana would have liked to have seen it and the entire dust plane glinting its encirclement of their Great World. But she had to be in her cabin. No one moved about, not even her. Surgeon's orders.

It was not unusual for objects to break apart. Hopefully, anything watching would assume it was a normal event, a weakened body splitting apart and becoming two.

Now they would begin to gain speed, to dump off heat and more consumables to alter their trajectory *just* enough. They were speeding up now, every tick as they dropped lower and lower.

"Why would you want to go back out there?" Je had once asked her when they were on Sese's interior walking through the botanical gardens. He raised a hand to encompass the whole world in all its lushness. She had been trying to recruit him as surgeon. The first male surgeon to fly the Archipelago void. "Why not stay and enjoy this world?"

"The only difference between them is scale, Je. Come see all the worlds. It reveals us for who we really are, to go out there."

Fiana lay strapped to her webbing, in a drugged stupor, breathing slowly. There were many more full shifts ahead to endure before they would come screaming back into the dust and throw out the sails to chatter and bite and shake.

But they would get home, she thought dimly.

The math was there.

## AUTHOR NOTES

This story has a fond place in my heart. I keep trying to create a novel out of it. Like some sort of Patrick O'Brian in weird, far future history, bio-tech, living tech, future.

So, as I said earlier, there's a story much reprinted in science fiction called "The Cold Equations" about a little girl who stows aboard a spacecraft ...

It bugs me, that story.

So, I wrote this one.

I could write on and on about what this story means to me. But I'm not done with it yet, and I don't want to ruin what comes next.

# DW

When the chimes of Lower Fourteen sing you run for cover because the chemical sprinklers will strip the skin from your bones. Gheda keep the thoroughfares acid-washed, white like the grin of a death's head. Your alien overlords do not care about the impact of the acid on their humans.

The servile huddle under various umbrellas as the mist spirals out of the center sky of the worldlet, but you sprint. Because you're not going to wait to let that green cloud sear your skin. There is no mark on you, nor will there be.

Sprinting is expensive. You inhale air, and the patch on your forearm glows red, warning about the cost. You skid into a servant's entrance just before the rain begins.

"Do you have it?" asks Vassaf, hauling you in under the marble slab roof.

You turn around to look at the alien foliage, purple and gray, veined with thick vessels of yellow. Garbage-bag flowers open up to greedily suck at the acid rain. The air around you slinks into a familiar acridity.

"Yes." You hand over the pissed-off cat, its hackles raised, ears flat back.

Vassaf grimaces as DW claws its way among his arm up to his shoulder. DW's tortie brown and black fur is puffed out, orange eyes tight with frustration. "Is it always this annoyed?"

Vassaf's arms are scarred from acid. His face sags on the left as if he has had a stroke. The sign of someone who has spent his life working in a Gheda district.

"It's a cat." You shrug. "They're always pissed off about something."

Vassaf looks outside as bubbling liquid coalesces down the street to scour it clean. "I came here because they said the streets were made of gold."

"Same here. I thought, if I could just snap a piece off, I could go home and live well." You grin.

Gold doesn't react to acid. The streets are long ribbons of it that snake through the alien vegetation.

"Idiot," Vassaf says.

The metal isn't really worth anything. Not to an alien race that can cross the stars, buy the unused planets of the solar system, and own almost every patent ever and demanded the human race work to pay off back royalties for thousands of years of unapproved use of inventions like the wheel.

The streets Lower Fourteen are paved with gold, and yes you could chip a piece off for yourself, for all the good that it would do you.

But you got a cat instead. DW might make you far richer than gold ever could. Even in the old, pre-contact days.

In an orbital, there's no reason for a cat. You're looking at a fuzzy creature that sheds. That fucks up the air filters and increases your maintenance schedule. It eats into your oxygen budget, which the Gheda monitor and charge against your income.

This is even before you need to start thinking about feeding the creature.

Old Earth, the great Down Below, is lousy with the creatures. The place where the air is free, as much as you care to breathe. But there are other prices you pay for being on the ground, though. You really can't get away from the Gheda.

Are you willing to pay for a housing royalty? The Gheda invented most of the technology found in any given structure, particularly the type of structure found in any urban area. There are entire countries that will never dig themselves out of bond debt, and the taxation and forced labor camps are brutal. Particularly in the more developed areas of the planet.

The planet groans under the alien yoke below you.

Better to look outward, toward the inky depths and invisible paths traveled by humanity's masters.

Better to try and create a fortune via the creatures that rule. Even a pittance from them is a fortune by the standards of the old world.

Which is why: cat.

"What's the cat's name?" Vassaf asks, still holding it at arm's length as you walk in the tunnels of the mansion.

"Doesn't matter," you tell the old servant.

"Come on, I'm told they all have names."

"It won't respond to it," you say. "I call it 'DW.' When it gets to where we need to go, we can tell the new owners it has any name we want."

"What's DW?"

"Dick Whittington."

"I don't understand," Vassaf says.

"It's a story from the old world. My mother named me after a city from the region, she liked their stories."

Vassaf regards DW. DW scrabbles to get away, scratching at his arms.

"Damnit, get it to calm down," Vassaf hisses.

"Until you let it go it'll keep hissing and scratching at you," you say, something learned from long experience.

When DW first arrived, smuggled up in a supply of exotic art being sold off from the Smithsonian to cover North American debt, the cat had ripped up your forearms when you pulled him from the classic nineteenth-century lunchbox he'd been stored in.

It had been pissed-off. But, you had thought at the time, had you been stuffed into a lunchbox, launched into space, spent a day in zero-gee while trapped, and then finally unboxed, you'd have been just as annoyed.

In fact, you have some vague memories of being sent to orbit as a young orphan in similar style in a pod that was not much bigger than a child huddled in a defensive crouch.

Gheda didn't care about claustrophobia or human comfort.

The warrens of this estate were buried into the skin of the wordlet that was simply called "Fourteen." The Gheda, for all that they "invented" almost everything millennia before humanity had, were hardly imaginative. Some rebel detective scholars claimed that there was evidence the Gheda had licensed many of their initial claims from other species they'd first encountered when venturing out beyond their solar system.

After that, they'd just started squatting on the IP rights like landlords. Finding new civilizations and billing them for co-inventing an invention. Didn't matter if you were separated by light years and thousands of years. The Gheda owned the rights, and you did not.

Now they owned systems and worlds and entire peoples to do with what they felt like.

On the other side of the estate, great brass-rimmed portholes looked out into space. You notice the twinkle of other great wordlets hanging in the vacuum. And to the upper right, the cloudy white atmosphere and startlingly blue oceans of Earth.

For Vassaf, it's normal. He doesn't break stride. Your breath, however, catches.

Mother Earth.

It's all over the murals in the Upper Fourteen, where people are crammed together and far from the crust of the wordlet. But many of the humans crammed into the hive that is Fourteen have never even seen the world that they once hailed from. Even the ones painting those very murals. Many are second or third-generation. Earth is a distant place, its history as much legend as fact.

After the portholes are the loading docks where massive ships sit in the bays surrounded by a scurry of automata loading cases into their rectangular bays.

"Here we are," says Vassaf.

"You understand that this is a life's work," Vassaf had told you, a year ago, leaning in over a bowl of horridge. Human porridge, with all the nutrients a worker human needs to not starve, and none of the taste.

"I understand."

If this worked, you wouldn't have to ever shovel horridge past your lips again.

Vassaf had been working on getting a small slot on one of the outgoing homeworld caravans. And his father had worked on that before him.

Rumor was that, possibly, there was a whole country working behind him. A foreign affairs department that had pulled strings after selling a major portion of a country's parks to the Gheda to get Vassaf's family installed in a wordlet manor.

"So, fuck this up, and I will not take it ... well," Vassaf had said as he leaned forward, eyes suddenly predatory.

Vassaf, the house steward to the most powerful Gheda administrator in the entire system. Who had done things you could only imagine to maintain his position, as well as his family's position.

"A lot of people depend on this."

You raised the kitten that they'd smuggled up to orbit. It hasn't been easy. It's a cat. On a wordlet. Cooped up in a tiny little cubby. That's all you have to live in, a bed recessed into the wall of a cooperative home. The bed's not even yours alone. You timeshare it with Paris, who takes the third shift in it, and he's never been thrilled with the idea of a furry, shedding creature that purrs and kneads his stomach when he's come off a shift at the algae tanks. He just wants to pass out, not shove a small Earth animal away from him every few minutes.

You take the cat out where you can, with him in a small duffel bag. There are some small common areas you can release it in. DW slinks around those, sniffing everything suspiciously.

In some cases, DW has taken off, wriggling into the most absurd places. Cats are escape artists and curious as hell. Thankfully the oxygen monitor that's twinned to yours lets you ping and track his location. To DW's annoyance.

Paris expressed disgust by the litter box at the foot of the cubicle bed. You had to pay him off with a line of credit with a bookie near the squirrel track.

The trickiest part was licensing DW to live here. You had to get him chipped so that his oxygen use was officially monitored. Get caught by one of the robotic stationeers having an unmonitored breather and you'd end it all pretty quickly. The Gheda would put you in storage, suspended animation, deemed "unproductive." The aliens did not believe in anything that didn't contribute.

But Vassaf had allies working in the AQD who hooked you up with authentication.

Sometimes, to hit your monthly quotas when income was too variable, you'd spend days lying in the bunk breathing as slowly as you can to not run up the oxygen debt. The flexible monitor burned onto your wrist would blink alarmingly and you'd wonder if this was it because if you didn't get any assigned work your debt would run up with each breath until some Gheda algorithm would tag you as a burden to the wordlet. Then you'd have seventeen hours to settle your debt or be suspended.

DW would shove his head against the crook of your arm and purr and the two of you would just lay there and conserve your energy until Paris came back to claim his time in the bed and kick you out.

You always felt that DW understood you were trying to conserve air. Why else would the cat spend almost twenty hours of the day doing nothing but sleeping?

"What are the Gheda going to use the cat for?"

You asked that last month when Vassaf met you for vodkas to celebrate the plan coming to a head.

Vassaf had drunk himself glassy-eyed and he rocked back and forth in his chair. "What do you care?"

You had feigned nonchalance then. Leaned away from him and studied the clear liquid in the bamboo cup. "Curious."

Vassaf's eyes narrowed. "They say people become close to pets. They ... *love* them."

What use was love in a world of Gheda contracts and ownership?

Where every breath was tracked? Where half-human, half-metal creatures roamed the worldlet to keep an inhuman order intact?

You shrugged.

And Vassaf had laughed. "Maybe they eat the animal. A delicacy from Earth."

Generations of hard work, bribes, humans trying to work the alien bureaucracy, all led to this moment: Vassaf puts DW in a small box.

DW approves. It's a box. Apparently, that's something a cat cannot *not* sit in.

In your experience, at least.

You think back to Vassaf laughing over vodka again. You keep doing that. You've been doing that all week.

*Damnit.* You're not going to lose it over the damn creature.

Not when you are *this* close to the end of the plan. There are humans that will take the cat on the other side of the ship's journey and they've promised a major deal for being the first to deliver this particular Earth fauna to the Gheda colony administrator that requested it.

But your heart is hammering away, and you can feel a flush in the corner of your eyes.

You will not cry about a cat in front of Vassaf. Not when it could mean your fortunes. Never having to worry about oxygen debt again. Or work.

You could get another cat afterward, right?

But it wouldn't be DW, pawing you awake or biting your ear in the morning, would it?

If this were one of the wordlet sagas, you would grab the cat and run. Hide in the fan corridors, kill and eat rats, live free, die when the stationeers find you, but die with pride.

Or you would build a heatshield, try to escape back to the Mother World. Like Memphis Autunga.

But none of that will work. You don't want to die in a duct or burn up on reentry. Besides, Vassaf would kill you personally long before any of that. And then he'd take the cat and send it off. You don't keep a job like his without a certain talent for ruthlessness.

So instead, you do the only thing you can. You rip off the oxygen strip from DW's neck. "Don't need this anymore, do you?"

He howls and rips skin from the back of your hand with his claws.

"Holy shit, it has claws," Vassaf shouts and jumps back.

You close the box. It rattles and thumps a bit for a while, then settles.

"I'll walk it over," you say.

One last moment with DW.

"Goodbye, old friend."

And you do the only thing you can do as you set the box in a container that will be loaded into the starship that dwarfs you: you ever so slightly bend the latch on the box.

Hopefully, no camera catches you. Vassaf certainly does not. You have plausible deniability.

You watch as the container is shut by two workers. A forklift grabs it and walks it over to the bay doors.

"In another life, DW."

It'll take a day or two by his frame of reference. There's some food in the box and a small dish of water. But thanks to the vagaries of space travel, years will have passed for you.

But whether anyone will find a cat when they open the container at the other side, who knows?

DW is damn good at escaping every time you lock him away. And he's even better at hiding away in crazy tiny places when he's scared. You've been to parts of Fourteen you didn't even know existed. DW will have a chance to figure things out on his own, even if alone on some far-off alien world.

If there's one creature from Earth that you're sure could handle figuring out exploring an alien world on its own, it's a cat.

## AUTHOR NOTES

Here's a deep cut. Even though I grew up in the islands, my mother was British, and one of the books I had as a kid was the illustrated tale of Dick Whittington's cat. It's a legend of the rise of Dick Whittington, a wealthy merchant who became the mayor of London in real life, but in legend, his cat helped him get there because he was able to sell the pregnant cat to people overwhelmed by rats at a feast. It was a rags to riches story, and those kinds of stories really appealed to me.

I took the setting of "A Jar of Goodwill" to tell the story about someone trying to pull off a DW story.

It's fun, I'm fond of it.

# THE VERY LAST CURATOR OF
# WHAT LITTLE REMAINS OF
# THE WESTERN WORLD

The pod around you shatters, and a brittle plastic wrap clinging to all the pieces sizzles and spits as it melts away.

"Come, come," says a tiny man with round spectacles and tightly curled hair pulled up into a topknot. "Step away from all the toxic preservatives."

You unsteadily take his hand and step over what is now hissing slime that makes you cough.

Your hand is so pale you have to stare at it.

"We've kept you out of the light, and there's no flash photography allowed," the man says proudly, seeing your stare. He helps you wrap up in a scratchy old towel.

You're in a dusty basement, poorly lit with bare light tubes in the ceiling, with hundreds of crates looming in the dimness and dust.

"Where ..." you croak, voice creaky and leathery.

The nearest crate is stamped "MONA LISA. FRAGILE!" in red, blocky letters. And then, underneath that, sigils and swirls that look like no alphabet you have ever seen.

"You're under the Feldt-Thn Museum of the Greater Western Continental Administration Zone," the man says. "We built it when there was so little left to display we could bring it all into one building. We tried to keep the big ones here, or at least, what we had of them. Plus, having just one stop helped us advertise it as a tourist destination."

He guides you to a small wooden table with three chairs. There's a kettle of hot water sitting on it along with two porcelain cups.

"I'm told this might help," he says hopefully, busying himself with pouring water. Then he presents a cherry-wood box full of teas.

You sit down and cradle the warm cup, ignoring the box of teas.

"When?" you ask.

"A couple hundred years. You've done it," the man says, picking out an orange-hibiscus tea and dropping it in the cup with a reverence and yet defiance that seems like it was a revolutionary act. "You've traveled to the future!"

He has bright purple skin and teeth that flash silver in the light.

You look back down at the box of tea. Exhibit —2467-Kb: BRITISH TEA SELECTION, LATE 22$^{nd}$.

He notes your glance and taps the box conspiratorially. "I won't tell if you won't!"

You're not sure what to do with that. Your brain is still fuzzy. All those chemicals pumped into you to … slow down metabolism, stabilize your body against degeneration.

You need to get more information about your situation. You expected to be decanted surrounded by scientists, or, at least, doctors.

Not a dusty museum basement.

"I'm afraid I didn't get your name," you say politely.

"Ah. Seville Smith-Anuah of Terra," he says. "And, of course, I know your name, I've been walking past you on exhibit for the past fifty years as I give tours."

You look down at the towel covering you.

Seville makes an apologetic sound. "Well, that's the way it always is, isn't it? The Europeans often paraded around people captured from other continents naked to show their physiology. Our current masters insisted on no modesty for your exhibit. Whether it comes from the stars or the old empires, colonialism is colonialism. They wanted to see *all* of the ancient, preserved human in the pod."

You shudder to think of thousands of people parading by the hibernation capsule in a museum staring at your nakedness on display. You wonder what the information plaque said. *"Here Lies a 21$^{st}$ Century Time Traveler, Seeking To Boldly—"*

"If it makes you feel any better," Seville interrupts your thoughts, "it was mostly *them* taking the tours. We don't really have the time or coin to do something like visit museums."

"Them?"

"*Them.*" He spreads his hands and makes wiggly, waving motions. "Our masters from beyond the stars."

"How … what …"

"Does it matter?" Seville slurps the last of his tea with a shudder of satisfaction. "They're weird creatures from the dark that slammed in from the sky, and before we knew it, everything had changed. We don't remember much about before. Most of it is just, whatever we have left in the museums. I always thought, one day, we'd decant some of you and ask a lot of questions."

He looks at you and shrugs.

"Why are you purple?" you ask, seizing on something immediate, nearby, and concrete to figure out. The enormity of everything else threatens to dizzy you.

Time to fall back on training and figure out what you can, stay present, and orient yourself. There's pen and paper on the table. You surreptitiously pocket the pen and a piece of paper that you fold up under a palm.

You never know what tools you'll need.

Seville exhales and looks at his forearm. "Chemical peels," he says. "Can't look *too* weird to the aliens, need to do what you can to adapt."

He checks a bedazzled timepiece that he pulls from a pocket.

"We need to keep you moving," he says. "We don't have a lot of time."

He picks up a crowbar nearby and uses it to smash in a nearby box. You wince as he breaks display glass inside and shoves over a mannequin.

"It was the height of eighteenth-century fashion," he murmurs. "And you have to admit, that coat is simply stunning."

It smells ancient as Seville casually tosses the cloth over to the ground by your feet.

"I can't possibly wear that," you say.

"Not much in the way of choice, really. It's that or run around in a towel, and you'll need a good coat outside. The rain and weather are not what you'll be expecting."

You stare at the gold threads and brocade. You're sure you've seen a picture of this ensemble somewhere in a history book.

"Come on, we don't have much time."

"What's going on, really?" you demand.

Seville puts the timepiece away. "It's all packed to the highest bidder and ready to be shipped out off-world," he says. "The whole fucking museum. And it's one thing to watch the paintings get packed away and readied, but another to see a person I walked past every day get boxed up. So, I'm releasing you."

"Where do I go, what do I do?" you ask. You need to know more about the world you're in.

"It was an impulse, not a plan," Seville mutters. "I considered burning it all down. Better to take it from them than to have the last of it stolen. But I didn't have the courage."

The purple man sunk in on himself a bit.

"Maybe," he continued. "Maybe I shouldn't have done it. Maybe it's a cruel thing to free you into a world where we're all under their thumb. You remember what the world before was like. Maybe you can help them remember."

He checks the time and stands up, eyes wide.

It's time.

The curator pulls you along by a purple hand. The two of you hustle up the stairs, and you blink as you enter large halls, all of them empty. Plinths and display cases lay empty all around you, and spotlights dazzle the empty air.

There's a roar in the air above the museum. A deep note in the air makes the dust dance and the earth vibrate.

"It took too long to wake you, we're cutting this rather close," Seville says. "Do hurry."

Your leaden limbs protest, but Seville's obvious fear motivates you.

At the great steps to the museum, he points towards a road leading off into what looks like a great park. There are no cities, no gleaming spires, no megastructures, just carefully manicured lawns and trees.

"Head north, and in half a day's walk, you'll start meeting folk."

"Who should I look for?" you ask, trying to discern his plan.

"How should I know?" Seville says. "I have never been off the grounds in my life. I was born in the museum, bonded to it. But I'm told I still have cousins that way."

"I need food, water—"

A shadow falls across the steps. Something massive hangs in the air far above us. It shoves clouds aside as it gently lowers itself toward the ground.

"In the archives, there was an article I read about a delegation from a part of the world, before our skies were filled like you see it now, who came to one of the old museums to ask for an artifact back. They were turned away by the museum." Seville picks up an oval-shaped chunk of wood from where it lies next to the door. He hands it reverently to you.

"What is it?"

"A shield," he shouts over the rumbling.

"Will I need it to protect myself?" Will there be ancient weapons as well? The wood bark that makes the shield, though, does not look like it could stop much.

Certainly not alien weapons.

"Eventually, like you, shouldn't an artifact be returned to where it came from?" Seville shouts at you. "Or maybe, maybe I am just trying to buy a piece of historical forgiveness. Maybe, maybe someday our overlords will see the sense in this and return everything they have taken."

Hundreds of years ago, when Captain Cook first encountered Indigenous people the first contact went wrong. His men fired on the Australians and picked up the shield you're holding.

It has been shown in Western museums ever since.

"Take it home," Seville says. "And maybe, someday, they'll bring ours back."

And then it's time to run.

Seville sits on the stairs with a bottle of wine taken from the cellars, drinking it and staring up at the massive alien starship descending to land on the grounds outside the museum.

You think that will be the last image you have of him. But the aliens catch up to you in a few hours. They look like purple, metal crickets with helmets and backpacks on. They surround you and fire plasma into the air from their fingertips.

There's nothing you can do but surrender. You make a fine sight, your eighteenth-century finery all muddied and scraped with brambles, your hair flying every which way, eyes wide with fear.

You drop the shield in on the grass and they take no notice of it as they order you toward a beetle-like shuttle that hovers above the ground nearby, waiting.

"I'm sorry," Seville says when you are returned to the museum. Because you aren't going to be staying on Earth. You're an exhibit. Property. Ruined, but still of interest to the aliens.

There are still ways to put you in a display and tour you around distant stars for strange eyes to stare at you.

At least the shield will stay behind. Maybe, with luck, it will be found by someone. You left a note on it, written on a scrap of eighteenth-century silk with the pen you stole.

"Please return to owner ..." the note starts, before giving the address.

It should have never taken becoming property yourself to make you care about its return, you think, as you are taken off into a starship to see the universe against your will.

## AUTHOR NOTES

Here I'm goofing off with titles again. Though at least it's more engaging than just a single descriptive word like "Sunset."

I've studied enough postcolonial history to grow some outrage against the past injustices of colonial empire for stealing other culture's most treasured artifacts, and spiriting them back to the seats of their power. As you've seen in some other stories, I like to explore the metaphor through the tools of science fiction. What would it look like if aliens plundered Earth's treasures?

# A GIRL AND HER ROVER

He's not a dog, but he is a rover, and that's about as close as she's going to get here on the moon while on her adventure to find a golf ball so that they all don't get sent back to Earth. And unlike a dog, Rover can spring his way around the lunar surface without needing a spacesuit, so he's far more useful.

Anne hates that Candice calls it Rover and that Candice insists on using verbal commands only to interface with the six-legged mechanical crab that they use as a mobile sled. But standing in front of Candice's imagination is like trying to beat back the tide with a sword. That's what Dad said to Anne with a wry smile.

"Come on Rover!"

Ten miles Candice has legged it in an EVA suit. Her breath has fogged the glass helmet so bad that rivulets of water pool around her neck, causing a crackle in her throat mic.

The damn things were built for tourists to go out and bounce around a bit, check out the Apollo memorials via the protected chain-link walkways, and then go back over the hill to the hotel where they could go moon buggying, dancing, or just sip mojitos.

Moon mojitos, with homegrown lunar mint!

Candice sits down on the edge of a crater to catch her breath, and Rover hippety-hops over to her side and sits down on its haunches like a dog.

"Thank you, buddy," Candice says, patting the shiny aluminum back of her constant companion.

It's getting more than just wet inside her helmet. The air quality is making her dizzy.

"Look up at that, it's a full Earth," she whispers to the rover looking up at the sky with her.

The pale blue orb always above their home runs through its various phases and only slightly wobbles about its steady place in the sky.

Candice never, ever wants to go back there.

Besides, she's waiting to see something more beautiful than a blue Earth from here.

Candice has heard the whispered discussions between her father and Anne by standing on her bunk and pushing her ears to the air duct's grill.

Wrong to eavesdrop. Sometimes she hears things she doesn't want to.

The parks department is going to shut down the Apollo 14 exhibit. They'll keep a minimal security presence to prevent anyone from traipsing around and destroying the footprints that Alan Shepard and Ed Mitchell left behind on their two EVAs all the way back on February 5th, 1971, and then on the 6th.

But the awful truth is, this is the Apollo 14 landing site and not the Apollo 11 site. Number one. Apollo 11 is the *first* place humanity set foot on the moon. It's way shinier.

When Dad gives the tour for Apollo 14, he makes sure to tell the tourists all about the difficulties the astronauts had on the way down to the lunar surface.

"There was a faulty switch, a piece of floating solder, that kept causing a connection in the abort switch. The two astronauts had to reprogram the lander by hand using instructions from Mission Control and finished just in time for the landing to proceed."

He would also add in that Alan Shepard had to keep rebooting the radar until they were just 18,000 feet high, but managed to land closer to their intended target than anyone else had.

That's a point of pride for those of us stationed at the Apollo 14 park.

But it's Apollo 11 that landed first. Apollo 12 the second. Apollo 13 would be forever remembered for its epic save: NASA and its trapped crew rescuing themselves from the jaws of near defeat.

Apollo 14 was number three.

Apollo 14 did what 13 was supposed to do.

So, the tourists all flocked to number one.

Understandable.

For a while, there'd been an initial surge of people making the entire pilgrimage. People fascinated by all things lunar. They'd make the trek from lunar east to west, starting with 11 as they visited all the sites of the old crewed missions. They'd end the tour with visits to the first Chinese landers or the first private ones.

But these days, most people stopped off at Apollo 11 on the way to the real lunar activities.

So, because of that, there are budget cuts, and they're cutting all the ranger jobs. A lucky few are being reassigned to 11. Everyone else? There are plenty of jobs in the rewilding zones. If Dad wants it, there's a place for the family somewhere back on Earth.

No park jobs on the moon anymore outside Apollo 11.

Listening to Dad and Anne try to figure out what to do, Candice had thought she could see the end of her life ahead of her.

Ironic, she thinks.

"So much for complex plans," Candice whispers in the thin air of her helmet to the robot next to her. Her voice sounds tinny.

Initially designed to carry loads over rough terrain for military forces on Earth, the rover's been repurposed to carry extra air, rock samples, or ice here on the lunar surface. Six legs, and a robotic mind that lets it listen to basic instructions to follow someone around faithfully.

The doglike machine that Candice takes on all her adventures has a puppy patch that she spliced into its code a year ago. It can beg, roll over, fetch, and barks in synthesized torrents of static.

When it's confused about her orders, it cocks its central processing "head" to the side and stares at her with silvered camera lenses.

She loves Rover as much as you could love anything not fuzzy.

The crater she's sitting on the side of is a mile away from Apollo 14's park. A mile.

Just a mere mile.

On Earth, that would be nothing. A walk. A run. Some skipping.

Here?

Candice looks to her wrist to check the air levels and flow again. "It's low, Rover. So low."

She's sitting still to conserve her air. Because there's a glide path, some math that she's run in the back of her head. Hop, hop, hop on the way back and come up a quarter of a mile short. She'd die, gasping, just out of reach of safety.

"My own dumb fault," Candice mutters.

There's a set of best practices to surviving on the moon. Things that have been drilled into Candice since she could first walk. Even before she could talk, she'd been shown safety rules.

The new rebreathers made paying such close attention to the air levels less of a do-or-die thing. As long as you had a good tank on your back the loss rate on the recycle could keep you going for days.

So, Candice left without the usual strapping of the extra "just in case" air bottles to Rover. Left without telling anyone where she was going.

That latter one, even on old Mother Earth, would have been a park ranger no-no.

"The moon is a harsh mistress," Ancient Joe kept telling her before she would cycle out of an airlock. The eighty-year-old mechanic with his bushy white beard and Apollo tattoos never tired of saying it.

"Personifying the moon doesn't make it any less dangerous," Candice tells Rover, and it wiggles itself closer to her.

The only creature that caused the problem here is Candice. She'd come up with a plan to keep them all on the moon.

The plan is a golf ball.

Back in 1971 Alan Shepard attached the bottom of a golf club to a lunar excavation tool and hit two golf balls. The second one flew "miles" according to Shepard.

The Apollo 14 park and historical preservation area did not extend for miles.

"If you're out taking a morning jog, make sure you keep your eye open for it!" Candice's dad always joked when taking tourists out on tour. "Because if you find it, it doesn't belong to the park! You'll have your very own, historically significant, souvenir."

A souvenir worth a lot of money to collectors.

Candice began her search weeks ago, heading out into the gray hills with Rover to crisscross marked out search grids loaded up into Rover's navigation systems. Day in and day out, she has been walking off little squares looking for a tiny, dimpled golf ball.

It got boring pretty quick.

But Rover kept her company, gamboling about while keeping his "nose" to the surface as he covered ground searching neighboring sectors for her.

There've been some treasure hunters before that covered the ground. Drones that floated about over the moon's surface.

Candice can go crawling about in craters with Rover that the prior drones just floated over. The young girl and walking robot check out the nooks and crannies that previous hunters missed.

Her father and Anne had started boxing up their lunar dorm's personal possessions. Candice's entire life, all labeled and nestled carefully between bubble wrap and inflated pillows.

"There's so much you don't know about Earth," her father once told her. "So much for you to see. Mountains to climb, vast lakes to cross. Trees. It's going to be exciting."

That sadness in his voice broke Candice's heart.

Alan Shepard's golf ball flew miles, hit a rock, ricocheted this way and that inside of the crater, then buried itself under a small ledge in the dust.

Rover found it, sent her the picture with a question mark of static, and Candice leaped down and slid down the scree to the bottom of the crater.

She'd lost her footing, tumbled, bounced, smacked off the side of a rock, and ended up sprawled a few feet away from Rover.

Fear of messing up felt like a bucket of ice water dumped over her. But as Candice checked her suit integrity, she found nothing ripped or leaking air.

It wasn't until she picked up the golf ball, carefully making sure to record the moment with Rover standing at an angle that made it clear what was happening so that provenance could be authenticated with location metadata stamped to the video file, that she realized she'd broken the rebreather.

From that moment on, her time started ticking down.

Rover is screaming into the electromagnetic void now that they have a direct line of sight with the resort buildings. Candice lies down on the ground, still staring up at Earth.

She slowly moves her legs and arms back and forth.

Lunar angel.

Three years ago, Dad took her to the mother planet. A beastly journey, packed into a ship like supplies and living for three days in her spacesuit.

Then the terrifying shake and burn through the atmosphere. She'd been lying inside a fireball, screaming as deceleration pinned her against the seat and crushed her chest so hard she stopped breathing and could only hear the panicked thump of her heart.

It should have stopped, but it never did. For the rest of her time walking about on Earth, it felt like something kept pushing her down toward the ground.

Candice looks balefully up at the pale blue orb above her.

Best if it stays right up there, and she stays right here.

On Earth, they measure life in years. Right now, Candice is measuring it in seconds.

It takes 300 seconds to pull on the EVA suit for a seasoned ranger like her father. Candice can do it in 285.

Time to cycle through the lock?

If Dad is panicked, he'll blow the air out instead of cycling out and saving it. That's 30 seconds.

Then it's time to skip as fast as he can toward her. One, two, three, one, two, three ...

A quarter of a mile in 600 seconds, maybe as much as 700, using that loping lunar gait. It's feasible.

Twenty seconds to hook up a buddy hose to Candice's suit.

Nine hundred-fifty seconds in all.

Candice has run as fast as she can back toward safety with Rover struggling to keep up once she realized all she has was the air in her suit once the scrubber was broken from her fall. But when she saw 400 seconds left, looking at the speed she'd been consuming air, she slowed.

Slowed and reduced her airflow, ratcheting it down so far she knows she'll pass out. The hope is that there'll be just enough to keep her brain alive, without damage.

She knows the plan is working, too, as her head's spinning. She's spoken to Rover using residual oxygen just fizzing around in her blood. She's thinking about her predicament using only momentum. But her thoughts are fuzzy, and loopy, and confused.

The 550-second gap, it's something as vast as the Grand Canyon, that her father took her to go see when they went to Earth.

The air in her suit is like the air at the top of Mount Everest.

Or maybe higher.

Candice twists her head away from Earth, watching the gray horizon. She can see the antennas and warning lights poking up over the ridge.

And there it is! A puff of air. An airlock full venting.

Candice no longer feels like the loneliest little girl on the moon. Someone has blown out the airlock using the emergency vent. It can only mean that Rover's emergency was noticed.

Help is 600-720 seconds away.

That puts a smile on a face, Candice thinks.

She's lying on her side, facing the puff of air slowly dissipating into nothingness. The most beautiful sight on the moon.

Candice holds the small, dusty white golf ball up in the air so that it's the same size as the blue Earth. There's a market for memorabilia throughout the solar system. Sotheby's would put this up for an auction, and no one would have to return to Earth, their tails tucked between their legs.

Even if she doesn't make it, even if she dies here in the dust, Candice thinks they'll find the golf ball in her hand and understand.

Six hundred seconds.

It is an eternity.

It is a blink of an eye.

To both the person bounding out across the lunar waste desperately toward her and the unconscious mind on the back of the Rover that has picked her up and is trundling her across the moon toward safety.

## AUTHOR NOTES

This last story, the final of the collection, examines the moment when the amazing becomes mundane. I've been lucky enough, in my life, to travel a great deal. Flying above the clouds to other countries is a technological marvel. The feat that is a plane should stun us all with every minute, and yet, it's an inconvenience to get shoved into a tiny metal tube, elbow to elbow, and eat mediocre food while wondering if my luggage would make it with me.

Space travel will become mundane. The treasured locations that are the frontiers of our abilities will become places somewhat rote and familiar. I don't think that's sad, though. The beauty of such places isn't lost. The accomplishments will still stand.

But our great heights will become tomorrow's parks, and memorials, and the great vistas that we yearn for in our science fiction will be the everyday sights out of someone's back window. That's what we're working so hard toward as we dream of those distant places, that we'll get there and embrace the everyday-ness of it all.

Because there will be new frontiers and adventures that those who come after will dream of.

Or at least, I can only hope so.

In fact, I have to hope so, because it's that same hope that reading science fiction gave me as a young reader.

# ACKNOWLEDGMENTS

Huge thanks, always, to Emily, Calliope, and Thalia, my family, for helping encourage my creative adventures. Thanks also to my agent, Hannah Bowman, for pulling yet another awesome project together when we realized I had so much uncollected short fiction scattered around various magazines, anthologies, and my Patreon.

My thanks also to editors Jonathan Strahan (who commissioned "The Mighty Slinger" from me and Karen Lord, as well as "By the Warmth of Her Calculus"), Nisi Shawl (who took "The Galactic Tourist Industrial Complex" for *New Suns*), John Joseph Adams (who commissioned "Zen and the Art of Starship Maintenance" for *Cosmic Powers*), Eric T. Reynolds ("Io, Robot" in *Visual Journeys*) and the late Gardner Dozois (who commissioned "Pale Blue Memories" for the anthology *Old Venus*). Each invitation to write a story for an anthology is deeply appreciated. My thanks also to Neil Clarke at *Clarkesworld* for taking my story "A Jar of Goodwill," a story that has remained high on the list of reader favorites since its first appearance in that magazine.

I also owe the supporters of my Patreon the biggest thanks. Their support has given me the space to write a lot of new short stories over the last few years, including many of the stories in this collection. Without them, this book just wouldn't even exist.

I'm never sure what tools or venues will bubble up into creation or disappear, but the last few years have leaned on rewarding me for writing more short fiction. Thank you, however you find, support, or buy my stories!

# ABOUT THE AUTHOR

Tobias S. Buckell is a New York Times best-selling author and World Fantasy Award winner born in the Caribbean. He grew up in Grenada and spent time in the British and US Virgin Islands, which influence much of his work.

His novels and almost one-hundred stories have been translated into twenty different languages. His work has been nominated for awards like the Hugo, Nebula, World Fantasy, and the Astounding Award for Best New Science Fiction Author.

He currently lives in Bluffton, Ohio with his wife and two daughters where he teaches Creative Writing at Bluffton University. He is also an instructor at the Stonecoast MFA in Creative Writing program.

Find him online at www.TobiasBuckell.com.

# ALSO BY TOBIAS S. BUCKELL

**NOVELS**

*The Stranger in the Citadel*

*The Tangled Lands* (w/ Paolo Bacigalupi)

*The Trove*

*Hurricane Fever*

*The Apocalypse Ocean*

*Arctic Rising*

*Sly Mongoose*

*Ragamuffin*

*Crystal Rain*

**NOVELS BASED ON THE *HALO* VIDEO GAMES**

*Halo: Envoy*

*Halo: The Cole Protocol*

**COLLECTIONS**

*Shoggoths in Traffic and Other Stories*

*Xenowealth: A Collection*

*Mitigated Futures*

*Nascence*

*Tides From The New Worlds*

**NONFICTION**

*It's All Just a Draft*

# AVAILABLE NOW

KAMERON HURLEY, AN AWARD-WINNING AUTHOR AND EXPERT IN THE FUTURE OF WAR AND RESISTANCE MOVEMENTS, HAS CREATED EIGHTEEN EXHILARATING TALES GIVING GLIMPSES INTO THE WARFARE OF TOMORROW.

ISBN 9781955765008                    APEXBOOKCOMPANY.COM